SO CLOSE TO FREEDOM ...

Wardell's chest ached as if he'd been shot and his legs felt as if fifty-pound weights had been strapped to his ankles. But he forced his mind off the pain.

Up ahead, on either side of the track, he could see lights. That must be the British zone. The sight gave him strength.

Then a soldier stepped out of nowhere and pointed a weapon at him and barked a command in Russian.

Wardell was moving fast and, with safety so near, he never considered stopping. To the soldier's surprise, Wardell barreled into him, sending him flying with the entire force of his two-hundred-forty pounds. The impact knocked Wardell off balance and he stumbled three steps before falling.

As he was scrambling back to his feet, the weight of a body fell on him, knocking him into the gravel. An arm locked around his neck, choking him—trying to stop his bid for freedom. . . .

MORE THRILLING READING!

BY IRA CORN, JR.

ZEBRA BOOKS
KENSINGTON PUBLISHING CORP.

ZEBRA BOOKS

are published by

Kensington Publishing Corp.
475 Park Avenue South
New York, N.Y. 10016

First printing: May, 1984

Printed in the United States of America

ACKNOWLEDGEMENT

The author wishes to thank Thomas Biracree
for his help in organizing and editing the manuscript.

I

HIROSHIMA

PROLOGUE

August 6, 1945 — The young lieutenant colonel crossed to the bar without saying a word, poured himself two fingers of bourbon, and downed it in a gulp. He poured himself another and turned to face the man sitting in an overstuffed chair.

The man saw the big smile on the lieutenant colonel's face and asked, "Hiroshima?"

The officer nodded. "I just took the dispatch in to General Groves."

"A success?"

"Read the copy yourself," the lieutenant colonel said, crossing to hand him a sheet of paper torn from a teletype.

The man scanned the military dispatch:

... FIRST THERE WAS A BALL OF FIRE CHANGING IN A FEW SECONDS TO PURPLE CLOUDS AND FLAMES BOILING AND SWIRLING UPWARD. FLASH OBSERVED JUST AFTER AIRPLANE ROLLED OUT OF TURN. ALL AGREED LIGHT WAS INTENSELY BRIGHT ...

ENTIRE CITY EXCEPT OUTERMOST ENDS OF DOCK AREAS WAS COVERED WITH A DARK GRAY DUST LAYER WHICH JOINED THE CLOUD COLUMN. IT WAS EXTREMELY TURBULENT WITH FLASHES OF FIRE VISIBLE IN THE DUST. ESTIMATED DIAMETER OF THIS DUST LAYER IS AT LEAST THREE MILES. ONE OBSERVER STATED IT LOOKED AS THOUGH WHOLE TOWN WAS BEING TORN APART WITH COLUMNS OF DUST RISING OUT OF VALLEYS APPROACHING TOWN . . . ITS EFFECTS MAY BE ATTRIBUTED BY THE JAPANESE TO A HUGE METEOR . . .

The man put the dispatch down on the desk. "Did Groves call General Marshall?"

"He's not going to wake him until he gets the more detailed report," the lieutenant colonel replied. He handed the man a glass. "Besides, we deserve the time to celebrate before all the commotion starts." He raised his glass. "To the Manhattan Project. To the power of the sun unleashed on earth."

The man raised his glass in response, touched it to his lips, and then said, "An awesome power it is that you've harnessed. From that report tens of thousands of people must have died from the blast."

The officer looked at him solemnly. "That explosion will finally end this war and save hundreds of thousands of lives. Maybe this awful weapon will end all wars. That end alone justifies the means."

"That will happen only if no other country has the atomic bomb," the other man said.

"There's a lot of people in Washington who want us to share the secret with other countries," the lieutenant colonel commented. "There'll be a lot of pressure on Truman."

"What do you think we should do?"

"You know what I think," the officer said, "or you wouldn't be here."

The man studied him for a moment, then stated, "I think it won't happen. It's my job to see that it doesn't happen."

"How are you going to insure that?"

The other man smiled grimly. "I'm not sure you want to know the details. But we will do anything we have to." He paused to take a sip of bourbon before adding, "As you said, the end justifies the means. Any means."

ONE

The anguish on the face of the elderly Japanese doctor was excruciating to watch. Senator David G. Wardell fixed his eyes instead on the inscrutable face of the young translator. But the words coming out of her mouth were still wrenching.

"Dr. Kykuru says that two nights after the blast he was making his way through the woods to get water. He heard voices in the underbrush and went to investigate."

The translator listened to the doctor's rapid Japanese, then continued, "When he got through the bushes, he saw there were about twenty men, and they were totally burned. Their eye sockets were hollow, the fluid from their melted eyes had run down their cheeks. Their mouths were like swollen, pus-covered wounds, which they could not open wide enough to admit the spout of a teapot."

As the doctor spoke again, Wardell heard a voice beside him say, "Oh, my God." He looked over to see Laura Jameson. Her face was parchment white and

12

despite the oppressive warmth of the afternoon she was shivering.

The translator spoke: "The men were unbearably thirsty. So Dr. Kykuru got a large piece of grass and drew out the stem so as to make a straw and gave them all water to drink. They were grateful but they all cried out for a doctor. I did not tell them I was a doctor. There was nothing I could do. They would die as so many others were dying. The beautiful pine woods, the rock gardens, the ponds were full of dead and dying. And there was nothing I could do."

The Japanese doctor stood, tears streaming down his face. As he stood in the oppressive silence of the Army briefing tent, Wardell reflected, so this is the reality of the atomic bomb. The facts had been given them before they left Washington. The first atomic bomb had been dropped forty-five days before. The B-29 Superfortress "Enola Gay," carrying a cargo nicknamed "Little Boy," had lifted off from Tinian Air Force Base in the Mariana Islands at 0245 hours on the morning of August 6, 1945. The primary target, Hiroshima, had been reported clear for attack, by weather planes, as the Enola Gay approached the coast of Japan. At 0915 hours, from an altitude of 31,600 feet and a ground speed of 328 miles per hour, the cylindrical bomb—129 inches long, 31.5 inches in diameter, and weighing 9,700 pounds, of which 137.3 were uranium 235—was dropped on Hiroshima. The bomb fell to a height of 800 feet, at which point a powder charge sent half the uranium mass through a hollow tube to impact with the other half. Fission commenced.

According to the Japanese authorities, 75,000 to

80,000 people were immediately incinerated. From what Wardell had seen since his arrival in Japan, they were the lucky ones.

The doctor had gotten himself together. Wardell moved forward and said, "On behalf of my colleagues, I want to thank you very much for talking with us. Your vivid description will greatly aid our report to the Congress and the American people."

The doctor bowed, and Wardell bowed in return. The doctor was helped off by the translator.

Wardell turned to the Army officer leading their tour. "Colonel, where next?"

"Out to the bus, Senator. For a tour of the center of Hiroshima."

"Lead the way," Wardell said.

He waited until the others filed out of the tent. There were four other senators and five representatives who made up the newly formed Joint Committee on Atomic War Damage. This committee had been formed to report to the Congress on the military and civilian impact of the atomic bomb. Wardell, who as Chairman of the Senate Armed Services Committee had been one of the handful of people in Washington who'd been briefed on the progress of the Manhattan Project—the development of the bomb—had volunteered to serve as chairman of the new committee.

As Wardell moved toward the door of the large tent, he stopped to talk to one of the senior military officers accompanying the committee. When General Thompson moved off, Wardell noticed Laura Jameson still sitting off to the side.

Wardell went over to her. "Laura, are you all right?" he asked.

She looked up at him, her face still white and grim. She nodded.

"The bus is waiting," Wardell said.

She got to her feet and they walked in silence out into the hot early September sunshine. Wardell waited while she climbed up the steps of the bus in front of him; and as he scanned her tall, slender, graceful form the thought struck him, that's one hell of a beautiful woman.

Wardell had known that before this trip, of course. Laura Jameson was not an infrequent subject of conversation among the male members of Congress. The "Ice Goddess" she was called by a friend of Wardell's, one of the many who'd tried to get her into bed. In many ways, the name fit. Jameson, whose brutally long work days were a legend on the Hill, had nothing but disdain for the Washington social scene. In committee hearings and in debates on the floor of the House, her manner was cool, blunt, even severe.

But there were few who didn't have a grudging respect for the congresswoman from Iowa. After a brilliant career as a young lawyer, she'd been elected to Congress on her first try in 1940. Her advocacy of such social issues as women's rights and civil rights didn't attract many enthusiastic supporters, but her impassioned and impressively researched reports and speeches had produced significant amendments to several important pieces of legislation.

Since the Joint Committee sent to Japan was supposed to represent the spectrum of Congressional opinion, Laura had been a logical choice, but Wardell admitted to himself that in selecting her his motive had been tinged by personal curiosity about the woman.

15

Wardell slipped into the seat beside her. The bus pulled off. Laura Jameson remained silent, staring out the window at the leveled plain of desolation that had been a great city less than two months before.

No one could be unmoved by the sight. Wardell's mind was carried back to the First World War and the trenches beside the Marne. For a brief moment, he could vividly see his men being crucified on barbed wire, floundering in the mud as they were sliced to bloody ribbons by German machine guns, screaming and clawing at their throats and eyes as the mustard gas enveloped them.

That, too, was a scene of total desolation. The difference was that hundreds of thousands of men and hundreds of thousands of artillery shells had caused the destruction. In Hiroshima a single 9,700-pound bomb had been dropped.

Wardell heard a loud exhalation beside him. Laura Jameson had turned away from the window.

"What do you think of this?" Wardell asked.

Her voice was harsh. "I think it was criminal. Brutal, inhuman murder."

"War is a series of brutal, inhuman acts," Wardell replied calmly. "But those acts can't be called criminal. Hiroshima and Nagasaki were terrible tragedies, but those bombings saved hundreds of thousands of lives—most of them Japanese."

"I've heard that justification for this . . . this slaughter a hundred times," she said. "I still don't know why we couldn't have dropped a demonstration bomb first and blown up an uninhabited island—instead of killing women and children."

"I can tell you why," Wardell said. "I was party to the

discussions. The Japanese had adopted a policy of national suicide: "We shall fight on if one hundred million perish" was the slogan. We only had two nuclear weapons available. No one thought a demonstration would work. Even the first bomb on Hiroshima didn't bring about surrender. If we'd had to wait ten to twelve weeks for another bomb to be built to drop on Nagasaki, our normal nightly bombing raids would have killed an additional six hundred thousand Japanese, not to mention the cost to us of Japanese attacks."

"The rational explanation, succinctly put," Laura Jameson said coolly. "I have to grant that in the short run the decision probably saved lives. But that ignores the true enormity of the decision to unleash this horrible new weapon upon the world. Was ending the war sooner, saving those hundreds of thousands of lives, worth putting the future of humanity at risk? Did you and the others who went ahead with this practical, logical decision to end the war talk about that?"

Wardell's lips were tight and colorless. "We did," he said tersely. Then he looked away.

They rode in tense silence for a few moments. Wardell was relieved when the bus halted. He was the first off.

In front of him was the gutted ruin of the Industry Promotion Hall. Five stories of misshapen girders had once supported a majestic dome whose heavy, ornate façade, more Victorian than Japanese, had once seemed familiar to the Western eye. This ruin, christened the "atomic dome," had become the symbol of the Hiroshima blast, and had been photographed thousands of times by the world press. Of course, there

17

was little else to photograph.

The committee members gathered around the lieutenant colonel, a scientific officer conducting the briefing.

"We're near ground zero," the officer began. "When the bomb detonated, the temperature climbed to five thousand degrees centigrade. The heat was so intense that it left buildings imprinted with the shadows of disintegrated bodies, and bodies imprinted with the pattern of clothing. The concussion was so great that stone columns at the entrance to a clinic near here were driven straight into the ground. Eighty thousand people were killed and sixty thousand buildings were destroyed, most of them within the first few seconds. Injuries and radiation sickness have claimed an equal amount of lives since then."

"What about us?" a gruff voice barked. The speaker was Tom Harrison, a heavy-jowled, bald senator from Ohio. "Is our hair going to fall out?"

"No, sir," the colonel replied. "A week ago we measured the radiation on this very spot. The level was only three and nine-tenths times the normal 'leak' from the earth. That's about a thousand times below the danger level."

"Then the Japanese can move back in?" Harrison asked.

"Yes, Senator."

"Good," Harrison commented. "Things will be back to normal before no time."

"As if nothing happened," Laura Jameson said sarcastically. "We can go back to Washington and forget about it."

"Now, wait a second, young lady," Harrison said

angrily. "Where do you get off . . ."

Wardell put his hand on Harrison's arm. "Tom, this is not the place for an argument. We'll have plenty of time behind closed doors in Washington to air our differences. Not in public."

Harrison's face was red. He glared at Laura Jameson for a moment, then said to Wardell, "All right, David. But I won't forget this."

Wardell crossed over to Laura Jameson. "That caution goes for you, too."

She looked up at him, dark eyes blazing. "Congressional courtesy even among the ruins," she said. Then she added, "Don't worry, Senator. Girls from Iowa are taught how to behave."

The lieutenant colonel cleared his throat to gain the attention of the group. "If you could follow me inside the dome," he said, "we've set up a display of the plans for rebuilding the city. They were formulated by the civilian government in cooperation with General MacArthur's military occupation government."

The group moved on, picking their way carefully over the loose rubble that still covered the area. Laura Jameson's foot slipped on a blob of fused roof tiles. She stumbled and would have fallen if an Army Air Force major hadn't stepped forward to grab her around the waist.

She turned to see a pair of friendly blue eyes wrinkled slightly at the corners. The face was broad and handsome, with an aggressive jaw and white teeth showing in a broad smile.

"Thank you," she said.

"Major Bennett at your service, ma'am," the man said.

Laura smiled at him for a moment. Then she remembered that it was an Air Force major who had dropped the bomb on Hiroshima. Her smile vanished and she pulled her arm away.

Bennett looked over at Wardell and shrugged. The Senator couldn't help smiling.

At that moment, an insane animal shriek came from the interior of the ruined exhibition hall. Wardell whirled around and saw a man in one of the openings, a small man wearing the tattered uniform of a Japanese soldier. His face was a twisted mask of hatred; his mouth was wide open, a mad scream of torment pouring out. He wore a rising-sun headband and, at his throat, a snow-white scarf, the two emblems reserved for the elite Kamikaze pilots of the Japanese Air Force. Behind the man's shoulder the long hilt of a samurai sword was visible, and in his hands he gripped an automatic weapon.

The automatic weapon began to spit fire as the soldier dashed toward them. Bullets tore through the air amidst the terrified screams of the committee. The Americans tried to scatter, but several were cut down.

Wardell caught a glimpse of Laura Jameson, staring, paralyzed, at the attacker. Moving instinctively, he hurled himself at her, knocking her roughly to the rubble-covered ground. Hearing a muffled cry beneath him and fearing she was hit, he moved to cover her more closely. He could see only the back of her head, which was unbloodied but covered by dust.

Savage bursts continued to fly over them. Wardell felt another body fall across his legs. Wincing with pain, Wardell twisted to take a look.

But his eye first caught the assassin charging directly

at him. With both hands the Japanese grasped the long sword, which he held raised over his head as he ran.

Wardell tried desperately to get to his feet. The dead weight on his legs slowed him, and he turned to push the man off. The assassin was now scarcely ten yards away. Wardell slipped on the rubble once, then again. Knowing time was too short to save himself, he rolled back on top of Laura Jameson.

The upraised sword started its descent. Then a bullet slammed into the Japanese one inch left of the center of his chest. The small man staggered back, still holding the sword. A second bullet hit him in the forehead and he toppled backward, the long sword hitting the rubble with an audible clank.

For a moment Wardell couldn't move. When he got to his knees he glanced over to see the Air Force major rise from his knees, the automatic pistol that had cut down the assassin still poised and ready.

Then Wardell looked around him. Anguished moans of pain replaced the clatter of gunfire—the sounds of more dead and dying amidst the rubble of Hiroshima.

TWO

A chorus of voices filled the small hotel dining room, the site of the press conference. Senator Wardell stepped to the microphone and said firmly, "Gentlemen, please. No questions until Captain Latella finishes his briefing."

Wardell stood until the noise subsided. Then he stepped back to let the Army information officer continue.

"Let me repeat," Latella said. "The assailant was carrying a Japanese Navy paybook that identified him as Ugaki Matsuo. Japanese military records show that he was a fighter pilot stationed in Kyushu. Matsuo's parents had taken his wife and child to Hiroshima to stay with relatives after the fire bombings of Tokyo began. When news of the destruction of Hiroshima reached Matsuo, he deserted. Civilian authorities don't know yet what happened to Matsuo's family, but we can assume they were probably killed. We should know more by tomorrow morning."

"Was this attack part of a plot?" a correspondent shouted.

"There is absolutely no evidence to that effect," the Army captain said. "The investigation will continue, of course. There will be another briefing here at 0800 hours tomorrow."

A flurry of hands waved. Latella pointed to a man in the front row. "Can you give us more details about the condition of General Thompson and Congressman Potter?"

"The field hospital staff will brief the press at 0700 hours tomorrow. All I have is the condition report I gave you earlier. Both General Thompson and Congressman Potter are in critical condition. Three security people suffered less serious injuries, and a Japanese civilian, who was scavenging some distance from the site, received a superficial wound. The complete medical report will be given to you tomorrow, along with the autopsy report on Senator Harrison."

The Army information officer answered a dozen questions about the details of the attack. Then a correspondent asked, "Does the Army plan an investigation of the failure of the security procedures?"

"Let me answer that," Wardell said, coming forward to the microphone. "I was fully briefed on security before our visit. I considered it adequate at the time, and I still do. The area was swept by military police before our arrival. We were accompanied by six security personnel. Their leader, Major Grant Bennett, killed our attacker. I'm not saying the attack could not have been prevented, and I'm sure the Army will review the entire incident with great care. But history has shown us many times that it is impossible to eliminate the possibility of a successful attack by a crazed assassin willing to forfeit his own life."

"How do you know he was crazed, Senator? He was killed before he could be questioned?"

Wardell looked steadily at his questioner. "I saw his eyes," he said firmly.

A rush of voices broke out again. Wardell recognized a man who asked if the committee's visit would be cut short.

"No," Wardell said. "Though obviously we're stunned and shocked. We'll also miss the tremendous contribution Tom Harrison and Ned Potter would have provided. But the issue of atomic weapons is far too important to the American people, and to the rest of the world, to let our grief interfere with our work. I've spoken by telephone to Tom Harrison's widow, and she told me Tom would want us to carry on. I agree, and so do the rest of the committee. At a meeting tomorrow, we'll choose one member to escort Senator Harrison's body back to the States, and we'll continue on to Nagasaki."

"Do you think this incident will affect the committee's report, Senator?"

"Our charge is to investigate the consequences of the use of atomic weapons. I'm sure the committee will continue to concentrate on that broader issue."

"How does the committee feel to date? Will you recommend that the atomic bomb never be used again?"

"I'm in no position to speak for the committee, even if this were not a totally inappropriate time and place."

More voices were raised. "One last question,"

Wardell said, pointing to the rear of the room.

"Do you think the smoke of Hiroshima will ever settle?"

Wardell's facial expression remained somber. "No," he said. "At least I pray that it won't—not while there are men of conscience in the world."

Three hours later, Wardell descended the main staircase from his suite. The hotel was now guarded like a fortress; military police were stationed at every door. The lobby was deserted, except for a lone Japanese behind the desk.

To Wardell's relief, the dining room was also empty. He was totally drained mentally and physically. After the attack, he'd spent nearly three hours on the telephone—with General MacArthur, with officials in Washington, with the wives of the casualties, and even, briefly, with President Truman. Then he had to spend additional hours accepting formal apologies from Japanese authorities appalled at the insult to their guests. At one point, the senior district police commander had to be forcibly restrained from committing *seppuku*, ritual suicide, to preserve his honor and atone for his inefficiency.

After the Japanese had been dealt with, there was the grueling press conference. Finally, Wardell had retreated to his room for a nap.

But he couldn't sleep. The horrors of what he'd seen on this day kept him wide awake. After staring at the ceiling for over an hour, he'd showered, dressed, and decided to get something to eat.

When the Japanese waitress entered the room to

25

take his order, he found he wasn't hungry yet. He ordered a double bourbon on the rocks.

Whiskey had never tasted better. He drank half the glass in two belts, then took a packet of cigarettes and a silver lighter from his pocket. He shook a cigarette loose from the packet, lit it, and turned the bourbon glass slowly on the table top, staring at the surface of the amber liquid. He finished the cigarette, the bourbon, then ordered another drink.

He was studying the menu when the dining-room door opened. He turned to see Laura Jameson crossing the room toward him. He rose as she approached.

"Am I too early for dinner?" she asked.

He shook his head. "I suppose the others aren't hungry."

"Neither am I. But I couldn't stay in the room alone any longer. I'm glad someone else is here."

He held the chair while she seated herself. The waitress arrived with Wardell's drink.

"What's that?" she asked.

"Bourbon."

"Do you think I could get a Scotch?"

Wardell turned to the waitress. "A Scotch, please." The waitress nodded and moved away.

"You speak Japanese well," Laura said with a smile.

"I try," Wardell said. He looked at her a moment, his eyes on the double strand of pearls that drew attention to her long, graceful neck. Then he asked, "How are you?"

"Better," she said. "They gave me a sedative at the field hospital, and for once I took it. Five hours of oblivion helped. I could still hear the screams of that . . . that man . . . and the others who were shot." She paused for a moment, then looked at Wardell. "I want to thank you for saving my life. It was very gallant."

"Instinct," Wardell said. "But I can't take credit for your life. If it wasn't for Bennett's quick reaction, the man would have killed both of us."

"Bennett. Yes, that major. I was rude to him, too. I'm afraid I'll have to apologize to him as well as to you."

"No apologies needed here," David said. "You have a right to your opinion. That's why I wanted you on the committee. This issue is so important it has to be dealt with by people of strong personal convictions, not by politicians following a party line."

Laura looked at him. "Wardell, the great mediator," she said, a touch of admiration in her voice. "The Senate's voice of reason. The one man in Washington without enemies."

Wardell smiled a touch uncomfortably. "I wish that were true. Sometimes it's easier to make enemies making sure everyone gets a say. The ideologues don't like that, and they don't like me. But I don't care."

"You sound passionate on the subject."

"That's why I got into politics in the first place," Wardell replied.

"Really?" Laura said. "How was that?"

"Long story."

"I'd love to hear it," she said. "I mean it."

He hesitated a moment, then said, "Okay. I'll make it brief." He lit another cigarette before beginning. "It was in the summer of 1932. I was in Little Rock on business. Huey Long had come to town to campaign for the widow of Senator Caraway. She'd been appointed to serve out the rest of his term and she was seeking the nomination for a term of her own. Anyway,

Long had always fascinated me, and I decided to go to a rally at which he was speaking."

Wardell paused to take a sip of bourbon. He finished it, motioned for another, then continued. "There were eight thousand people there—I couldn't believe the crowd. The public address system wasn't working right, so you couldn't hear the introductory speakers. They got it repaired by the time Hattie Caraway made a ten-minute speech. She was so dull I almost left.

"Then Long came to the microphone, and the atmosphere immediately became electric. First of all, his physical appearance was impressive. The evening was very hot and humid, but Huey was decked out in a long white coat, white trousers, and a dazzling white shirt. He had on a red polka-dot tie and a bright pink handkerchief was stuffed in his coat pocket. His expression was stern backwoods Baptist, and he clutched a Bible in his hand."

Wardell paused for a moment, picturing the situation in his mind, before going on. "Once he opened his mouth, he had the audience in the palm of his hand. He never stopped moving, gesticulating, brandishing the Bible in his left hand for emphasis. I was caught up in the emotion like the rest of the crowd. Then, suddenly, a photographer began shooting flash bulbs. That infuriated the Kingfish. He cursed the photographer from the podium and demanded the police remove him, which they did.

"Then Long resumed the speech, but the incident broke the spell for me. I began to concentrate on what the man was saying. I was appalled. Every cliché in the book, cloaked in the mantle of religion. 'The Lord says the country has to redistribute its wealth every fifty years.' 'The Lord demands vengeance on the vultures of Wall Street.' 'I didn't go to war because the Lord directed me not to mislead our boys.'"

Wardell shook his head, "I'll tell you, Laura, it scared the hell out of me. That such an obvious demagogue could move a crowd like that. I was reminded of Mussolini, strutting and posturing, and the young Hitler, who was about to take power in Germany. I was so shaken I had to leave.

"And the effect deepened as time passed. I was in the mood to do something. My business was practically running itself. My wife and son had been killed in an automobile accident a year and a half before. I was restless, and the idea of going into politics to fight men like Long had great appeal. Two years later I was elected to the Senate."

Laura Jameson looked at him appraisingly for a few moments. Then she said, "That's fascinating. I never knew that secretly you were one of our little band of crusaders in Washington."

"You consider yourself a crusader?" Wardell asked. "Is that why you got into politics?"

"My story's simple," she said. "Practicing law was too frustrating. I realized that change would come only if the laws themselves were rewritten. I was very fortunate that enough people in my district agreed with me."

"Any personal reasons?" Wardell asked.

"My life is my work," she said.

"I see," he said.

She looked at him and smiled slightly. "I know what you're thinking. The 'Iron Maiden.' I admit I've cultivated the reputation. It saves me a lot of time warding off the most predatory of my colleagues—and you know how many of them there are in Washington. I'm not really as forbidding as I seem."

"I never thought you were," Wardell said. "I've always considered you a very beautiful woman."

Laura smiled again. "My, Senator. Some people might consider that a proposition."

Wardell's eyes met hers. To his surprise, a strong current of desire rippled through him. "In some circumstances, that might be a proposition," he said.

Laura held the gaze. "But not these?"

Wardell didn't reply right away. Then the waitress appeared, breaking the tension.

Wardell smiled awkwardly. "How about some food?" he asked. When she hesitated, he added, "You should try to eat. We have a very arduous schedule ahead."

"Okay," she said.

They ordered fish, which had been flown in frozen from the States but which was stir-fried in the Japanese style. They talked little until they'd finished and coffee was served.

They talked of innocuous committee matters, but Wardell could feel the sexual tension building again. He was reminded again of the strange link between violence and sex. In the trenches during the First World War, between the savage attacks and the awful shelling, conversation and thoughts turned obsessively to women. Wardell didn't understand it, but it was very real.

Wardell took a sip of coffee, then looked across the table again. A stray lock of hair had fallen down over Laura's forehead, and he had the urge to reach across the table to tuck it behind her ear.

After a moment's hesitation, he did. She took his hand in hers. They stood.

"Nightcap?" Wardell asked.

She nodded.

Then the door to the dining room opened. Wardell released Laura's hand as Major Bennett strode toward them. His face was grim.

Bennett nodded toward Laura and said, "Sorry to disturb you, Senator. But I have to talk with you privately."

"It's late, Major. Couldn't it wait until morning?"

"I'm afraid not, sir. I have orders from Washington to brief you immediately."

Wardell grimaced. "All right," he said. He turned. "Laura . . ."

She smiled. "I understand. I'll see you in the morning, Senator." She paused, then added, "Thanks for the company. I needed it."

Wardell said, "That goes for me, too."

"Good night, Major," the congresswoman said. Then she walked toward the door.

Wardell waited until the door had closed behind her. Then he said to Bennett, "Well?"

"Not here," Bennett said. "Let's take a walk out in the garden."

They walked in silence through the lobby, then through double doors flanked by two MP's. They saluted Bennett as the doors opened.

The small Oriental garden was dimly lit by three colored lanterns. Bennett led the way to the far corner, away from the hotel. He stopped by a narrow bench near a small pool with orchids floating in the water.

"Now," Wardell said. "Can you tell me what this is all about?"

"General Thompson died on the operating table about an hour ago," Bennett said.

"I'm sorry to hear that," Wardell said. Then he added, "You didn't have to bring me out here to tell me that."

"No, I didn't," Bennett said as he offered a cigarette to the senator. Wardell took one, which Bennett lit. Then Bennett said, "I did need the privacy to tell you other things. The first of which is that my name is not Grant Bennett and I'm not an Army major."

Wardell's eyes narrowed. "That's a rather dramatic statement. Just who are you?"

"My real name is Sage, but I haven't used that in a long time. I spent most of the war as Jason Tulley, an attaché in the U.S. embassy in Moscow."

"Why should I believe that?" Wardell asked. "And why is that important?"

"It's not important who I am," Bennett replied. "What I'll tell you is. But if you want to verify my identity, call General Dolan in Washington."

"Mack Dolan?" Wardell said in surprise.

"Yes, sir."

General Dolan was chief of military intelligence in the Pentagon, and an old friend of Wardell's from World War I. If this Bennett, or whoever he was, was lying, he'd picked the wrong man as a reference. Wardell was tempted to call Dolan, but he decided to hear Bennett out first.

"I'll call Mack later," Wardell said. "Finish your story. I'm still not sure why I'm out here."

"I've been instructed to tell you the real facts about

the attack this morning."

"Such as?"

"The assassin's name was not Ugaki Matsuo. The real Matsuo was a pilot who did desert, but a week before the bomb fell. He evidently wasn't too enthusiastic when his turn came to give his life for the emperor in a *kamikaze* attack. Unfortunately for him, heading to Hiroshima to see his family obviously produced the same effect. His family lived very near ground zero, and he was probably killed instantly."

"How do you know this?"

"Let me go on. Also, contrary to the briefing, the attack was a well-planned conspiracy. Two district policemen allowed the killer access to the sealed off area. We tried to talk to them but both committed suicide. Fortunately, we discovered they were secret members of the Japanese Communist party. We raided their headquarters and persuaded a couple of people to talk."

The story riveted Wardell. "Go on," he said tersely.

Bennett continued. "The attacker's real name was Naioki Kamiko. He was an army captain who had been captured by the Russians in Manchuria in 1936. Supposedly, he managed to escape from a prisoner of war camp two years later. We believe that he spent the two years being trained as an agent by the Russians. In any case, he was repatriated to Japan and became an active member of a Communist cell."

"How did this man get Matsuo's paybook, if Matsuo was killed?" Wardell asked.

"The paybook was a forgery. That's the first clue that sparked the rest of our investigation."

"The investigation seems to have been conducted

33

with record speed," Wardell said.

"We were expecting trouble. That's why I was assigned to head the security."

"If this man was a communist, as you say," Wardell said, "I don't understand what he was trying to accomplish."

Bennett looked Wardell in the eye and said, "He was trying to kill you. On orders from Moscow."

Wardell's mouth dropped open in surprise. Then he stiffened. "That's preposterous," he snapped. "Why would the Russians want me dead at all, much less badly enough to stage this elaborate attack?"

"Because you're a powerful political leader who's also a totally rational man."

"That's a reason for assassination?"

"It is in these times," Bennett said. "Let me explain something. During my four years as an agent in Moscow, I discovered irrefutable proof that Stalin has absolutely no intention of stopping at the borders agreed upon at Yalta. His goal is the entire continent of Europe—for starters. And with the European countries ravaged by war and in political turmoil, he could achieve that goal . . . except for one thing."

"The bomb," Wardell said.

"Exactly. But at precisely the time we should be using our advantage to curb Russia, there're a lot of people who were so appalled by Hiroshima that they want us to destroy our bombs. More want us to share the secret with other countries including the Soviet Union. That would be playing into Stalin's hands. The Russians will have the bomb in three or four years as it is."

"I've been told it will be more like fifteen to twenty

years," Wardell said.

"You've been told wrong. I have more information for you. Last Sunday, Canadian Prime Minister Mackenzie King flew to Washington to see President Truman. The reason was information provided by a Russian defector, the principal cipher clerk in the Soviet embassy in Toronto. The clerk brought with him documents that revealed a massive espionage ring, including informers high in both the American and Canadian atomic research facilities, has been providing the Russians with atomic bomb secrets for years."

Again, Wardell was stunned. He took a moment to collect his thoughts. Then he asked, "I assume this can be verified also?"

"You can verify it with General Dolan or, I assume, the White House."

"If this is true, it complicates our foreign policy and military planning immensely," Wardell said.

"That's why you've been told," Bennett said. "It may affect the report of your committee. And you're the only member of the committee whose security clearance is high enough to be told."

Wardell sighed. The burden of the knowledge at the end of the arduous day reminded him of his exhaustion. He was too tired to analyze what the information meant.

"I'll want to talk with the general at length when we return to Washington," Wardell said. "Is there anything else I should know now?"

"No more information. Just cautions. We've taken increased security precautions for the rest of your stay in Japan. Then you had planned to go on to Hong

Kong. We think that would be far too dangerous, considering the circumstances."

Wardell stiffened at the mention of Hong Kong. "That's a personal trip. I intend to make it."

"But we can't provide—"

"I don't need security. It's a private trip for a private reason," Wardell said. He stood and faced the man in the major's uniform. "I assume that most of what you say will be verified. But I can't believe that the Russians have assassination teams following a U.S. Senator around the world. I will take the precaution of making my trip private—I'll cancel my courtesy calls on the local administrators. I do, however, intend to go."

Bennett shrugged. "That's up to you, Senator. We can only do what we can."

Wardell looked at him for a moment, then his features softened. "I do appreciate your providing the information . . . and saving my life this afternoon. I'll be sure to tell Mack Dolan how competently you performed."

"I don't need kudos, Senator. I have a job to do. So do you, and we want you alive to do it."

THREE

For security reasons, the remainder of the committee's trip was compressed into seven days. The pace was grueling for Wardell, the two other senators, and the three remaining members of the House of Representatives. After touring the blast site at Nagasaki, the committee often split up to conduct exhaustive interviews with victims, doctors, civilian authorities, military men, Japanese scientists, and engineers.

Despite the importance of his job, Wardell increasingly found his mind wandering away from the site of the tour he was on or from the interview he was conducting. Two themes played in his thoughts. The first involved the strange talk with Bennett in the garden and his subsequent phone call to General Dolan in Washington.

The phone call had been quite short. Mack Dolan cautioned him immediately that the line was not secure and that he could not answer Wardell's questions. He did say that Wardell could trust their "mutual friend," and they'd have a long conversation about their friend when David was back in Washington. Finally, he told Wardell that for his own protection he should return to the States immediately after the conclusion of the committee's work.

Wardell once again said firmly that he was going through with his plans. When he hung up, however, he felt doubt for the first time. Mack Dolan was a blunt, hard-driving, totally pragmatic military man. The obvious concern in Dolan's voice disturbed Wardell far more than the meeting with Bennett, which at times had seemed like a scene from a bad spy novel.

Wardell had to accept as real the possibility that someone wanted to kill him. Of course, he'd faced that before in the First World War. But then it had been impersonal, a condition of conflict. After the war, when he'd been building the trucking company that had provided him with his fortune, there had been threats on his life. But again, Arizona at that time was still the frontier, and Wardell had accepted the danger in return for the great opportunities the Southwest offered.

His mind could not accept, however, the idea that some person—or some foreign power—could want to kill a man just because he was a rational, careful decision maker. War over territory or war over money, he understood. But not wars over ideas, which were the province of reasonable, intelligent men. That, indeed, would be a dangerous return to the Middle Ages, a terrible time for mankind.

Then the thought struck Wardell, as he was making a heart-wrenching walk through the children's ward of a hospital outside of Nagasaki, that the atomic bomb had brought a new era to the world. Scientists had told him that the bombs dropped on Japan were fire-crackers compared to the weapons that would soon be developed, weapons with a hundred or a thousand times the explosive power. Those weapons in the hands of anyone other than rational, careful, humane leaders could bring about the destruction of civilization.

Were the current leaders in Washington such men? Wardell had thought so, but a great deal of the recent postwar rhetoric disturbed him greatly. Suddenly, he knew why Dolan had sent a man to talk to him. He had a job to do now that was even more important than heading the Armed Services Committee during the war. Wardell wouldn't—couldn't—change his plans to go to Hong Kong. He determined, however, to take every precaution possible.

With that in mind, he changed from a commercial airline to a military flight. The change gave him an extra night in Japan. He spent the late afternoon and early evening hours in his hotel room in Tokyo, going over the documents in a thick packet he'd received from his office in Washington.

A little after seven there was a knock at his door. The sound startled Wardell. He got to his feet and called out, "Who is it?"

"Buy a lady a drink?" came the reply.

He crossed to the door in two long steps.

"Laura," he said with pleasure when he opened it. "I thought you left with the others this afternoon."

"I've got to stay for a couple of days to make some commercial contacts for constituents. I saw that you hadn't checked out so . . ." Her voice trailed off as she looked up at him. She smiled and asked, "Do I have to stand out here in the hall or . . ."

"Come in," he said.

As she moved by him into the sitting room of the suite, he inhaled the subtle musk of her perfume. Once again, he felt a strong surge of desire go through him, the same sensation that had seized him so powerfully at dinner on the night of the attack.

He'd thought a lot about that night since. It had been a long time since he'd really been stirred by a woman, or at least a woman he could care about. A tall, handsome, distinguished man, Wardell attracted more than his share of the available females who flocked around the powerful men in the nation's capital. Celibacy had no attraction for him, and he'd had a series of affairs, though far less frequently during the war years.

None had meant anything to him, however. The women in Washington had seemed so insubstantial, so fragile, more like cut flowers purchased for a bouquet than hardy perennials that would weather the storms of life.

Of course, Wardell knew, he'd been spoiled by Amanda. From the moment he'd met her at the University he'd been drawn to her like a powerful magnet. A tough, determined man himself, Wardell had never known anyone who approached life with the passionate intensity of his wife. She was not a classically beautiful woman, but the fire that burned within her made her extremely desirable. She was also intelligent and sympathetic, with a sense of humor that would bubble up joyously to the surface at the most unexpected times.

Wardell had proposed three months before he'd been sent to Europe in World War I. When he'd

40

returned, they'd married and had a son, and together had built from scratch the enormously successful business that had made him one of the wealthiest men in the state of Arizona.

Then came that day in 1931. Characteristically, Amanda headed home from a neighboring ranch despite the fierce storm outside. Ten miles later a flood washed her car off the road, killing her and ten-year-old Charlie.

For Wardell, it was at first as if the sun had set, never to rise again. The pain was constant and overwhelming. But as time passed Wardell realized that spending his life obsessed by death would be the worst possible way to mourn a woman who loved life as much as Amanda. Gradually, he picked up the pieces, pouring himself into politics. The only lingering effect, other than the still painful memories of so many happy days, was that all other women paled before the image of his wife.

All, that is, until he'd met Laura. Her background, her looks, were totally different. But she too had that fire and intelligence Wardell found so compelling.

Rationally, the difficulties of a relationship between two members of Congress were many—time demands, the constant public spotlight, the drain of campaigning and constituent service. And for Wardell there was the complication of the atomic bomb issue and the secret intelligence to which he was privy. But reason didn't always triumph over emotion, and tonight Wardell was delighted to see Laura.

He poured her a drink, and they moved to the couch.

Laura took a sip of her Scotch, then nodded toward the stack of papers. "Work?" she asked.

"Reports from Washington," he said. "The flow of paperwork is incredible. It'll take me months to catch up when I get back."

"You flying back tomorrow?" Laura asked.

"I'm going to Hong Kong," he said.

"Senate business?"

He stiffened slightly. "No."

There was a moment of awkwardness. Then Wardell said, "I hope you'll have dinner with me tonight."

She said, "That's the reason I came by." She paused, looking into his eyes. "At least, part of the reason."

Wardell set his drink on the laquered coffee table. He moved over next to Laura, put his arm around her, and drew her head toward his.

Their lips touched, tentatively at first. Wardell felt her lips part and their tongues met. He could feel her tremble, and the thrust of her breasts against his chest stirred him deeply.

Then she pulled away. Her dark eyes were shining. "Thank you," she said.

"For what?"

"For making me feel like a woman."

He smiled. "Any time."

They kissed again, this time longer and more gently. When they broke Laura said, "Dinner?"

Disappointment must have flashed across his face, for she added with a grin, "Don't rush, Wardell. Remember, I'm a member of Congress. I'm used to being lobbied."

"So am I," Wardell said.

"I'll bet you are. I've heard stories."

"None of them are true."

"Then tell me your version," she said.

"Later," he said, getting to his feet. "Give me a minute to change. Downstairs all right for dinner?"

"Fine," she replied.

A half-hour later they were finishing a delicious cold soup. The waitress cleared the dishes. Wardell lit a cigarette for Laura, then one of his own.

Laura leaned back. "After the schedule we've been on, relaxing at dinner seems luxurious."

"You should take a vacation before heading back," Wardell said.

"This was my vacation, or, rather, all the time I could spare from my work."

"You drive yourself too hard," he said.

She raised her eyebrows. "I think that's the pot calling the kettle black. I saw that stack of papers."

He grimaced. "I guess you're right."

"What is happening in Washington?" she asked.

"Endless debates, what else?" he replied. "On nuclear weapons, for one thing. Truman is yet to declare a position. I just received the summary of a pretty acrimonious cabinet meeting. The rift gets wider instead of narrower."

"Between?"

"People like Henry Wallace who want us to share the secret fully with every nation, including the Russians. And those like Vandenburg and Taft, on the other hand, who want us to do everything possible to increase our nuclear advantage."

Laura's face was suddenly grim. "How can they think of such a thing? They may not have been here in person, but they've seen the pictures, heard the stories.

43

After what we've experienced, I'm more convinced than ever that the bomb dropped on Nagasaki must be the last dropped by mankind. Nothing is worth that terrible price."

"Nothing?" Wardell asked. "Isn't that a little extreme?"

"What do you mean?"

"I mean, that assumes the good will of the leaders of the rest of the nations of the world. And if we've learned any lesson out of this last horrible conflict, it's that we have to be less accepting of the good will of madmen like Hitler and Tojo. The way to insure that the bomb isn't dropped again is to make the price for dictators far too high for even their twisted minds to accept."

"And who do you think these dangerous men are?"

"Stalin, for one."

"My lord," Laura said sarcastically. "I didn't know I was having dinner with General Patton. We should probably get up and check to see that there are no communists hiding behind the drapes."

Wardell's lips tightened. Then he said, "Laura, I'm not a blind anticommunist fanatic. But I'm also a realist. I know for a fact that our erstwhile wartime ally has very dangerous postwar plans."

"And what are these facts?"

Wardell thought for a moment. Then he said, "I'm afraid the information is classified. But I can assure you that—"

"You can assure me what?" Laura interrupted. There was anger in her voice and fire in her eyes. "You can assure me there will be another war? I should have known, Wardell. Chairman of the Senate Armed

44

Services Committee. You're steeped in that same military attitude that's kept mankind in conflict for thousands of years."

"What attitude is that?" Wardell demanded.

"The aggression of the male of our beleaguered species," she replied. "No wars, no uniforms, no medals, no chance to strut. Peace just isn't satisfying, is it? In peacetime, with no enemy real or imagined at the gates, there's too much chance women can achieve some sort of equality with men. Whenever that threatens to happen, it's time to start another war so he-men can go out with their guns and tanks and planes and kill a few hundred thousand more people. It happened in the early part of this century, after the success of the woman's suffrage movement. And again after the gains women made in the labor movement in the thirties."

Wardell sighed in frustration. "I can't believe it. You're trying to foist on me the crackpot idea that this last war had nothing to do with Hitler's madness or Japan's territorial ambitions, but that it was an international plot to keep women subjugated. That's so simplistic it makes General Patton seem like Socrates."

Laura rose, her face red, her eyes flashing. "You don't understand, do you? I thought you were different, Wardell. I thought you were the type of man who'd have a true emotional response to what we've seen. But I was wrong. I'm glad I found out now rather than later tonight in your bed."

She turned and stormed out of the dining room. Wardell, stunned and hurt, watched her leave.

FOUR

Just before dawn, the C-54 transport plane came in low over Victoria Harbor. Wardell picked out the single runway of the Kai Tak airport, built out into Kowloon Bay, and the marine terminal beside it. South, over the harbor, a peak rose in the distance, dominating the island part of Hong Kong. Below, the harbor narrowed to a strait that seemed the hub of the city. Water traffic was already heavy, and many small craft were docked in tight clusters where the coast retreated into small coves and anchorages, floating villages that lined the shore. The city of Hong Kong seemed to hang above the water, its buildings clinging to the hills.

The big plane banked left, leveled, then set its bulk down on the runway. Wardell turned away from the window, yawning and stretching.

He felt exhausted and stiff. Last night, after Laura's sudden, bewildering explosion at dinner, Wardell had decided he'd had enough of Japan. He hurriedly packed and rushed to the airport, barely making the last transport.

He'd hoped to sleep on the flight. But his mind wouldn't turn off, flashing images of Laura, of Hiroshima, of Nagasaki, of the attacker who had nearly taken his life. The experience made him feel uneasy, almost haunted.

The transport taxied to a halt at the terminal. Wardell was quickly cleared by the military administrative officers. He gathered his luggage and then found an ancient taxicab that drove him down along the water on the Chatham Road to the Peninsula Hotel at the bottom of Nathan Road.

After Wardell paid the driver, he paused to stare at the distant shoreline, which seemed much closer than he knew it to be, and the high-sterned sailing junks, their sails spread like webbed reptilian feet. The sight stirred deep emotional memories. Suddenly, Japan felt far away, and Wardell's mind focused on the disturbing task in front of him.

A porter came up to take his bags. Wardell followed him past the two stone Oriental lions flanking the wide stairway to the ornate entrance of the hotel. The spacious lobby at the top was shaded and dim, part of the quiet grandeur of another age. All sound was muted, lost in the heights of the vaulted ceiling. Beyond the entrance hall, he could see the light filtering through from a courtyard, diffused and greenly cool.

Wardell registered as David Burke, then was escorted to his room. A ceiling fan turned slowly, ruffling the humid air. Wardell unpacked his bag, then lay on the bed. The heat and the low hum of the fan were like a sedative. He fell sound asleep.

*   *   *

The woman sat in the shade of a broad umbrella in a corner of the large veranda. The gin rickey on the table in front of her went untouched as she nervously played with a lock of her long blond hair.

She patted the lock back into place as she saw him, threading his way between the tables. She took a quick sip of the drink, then looked up as he approached.

"He's here," the man said. He sat opposite the woman and signaled for the waiter. He ordered a beer.

"I'm nervous," she said.

"Of course you are, sweet," the man said. "But he's just another man. You know how to handle a man."

She frowned. "If he's just another man, why are you making me go through all this?"

The man's features hardened. He reached over, took the woman's hand, and squeezed. "Listen, my lovely. There were many more unpleasant ways to go through this last little war than living in that nice hotel suite and sitting here on this veranda drinking champagne. You made your bloody choice and now you're going to pay the bloody price. That's the bargain. Understand?"

She nodded.

He released her hand.

They sat in silence as the Chinese waiter delivered the beer. Then she said, "I don't understand. What are you going to do to him?"

He didn't answer for a moment. Then he smiled and said, "We're not going to do anything, sweet. It's what you're going to do to him."

Wardell felt as if he'd been drugged. He awoke after dark, ordered a meal from room service, touched little of it, then went back to sleep.

The next morning he felt refreshed. He dressed quickly and, after having breakfast on the terrace, went out onto Salisbury Road.

It was a hot, brilliant day and a flock of rickshaw boys in ragged blue vests and shorts zoomed toward him. They were shouting excitedly, their long red barrows crashing and bouncing behind them. For a moment Wardell hesitated. He hadn't been to Hong Kong in so many years that he once again found unsettling the idea of one man being a beast of burden for another. Then he saw the grinning, eager face of the wizened man who'd won the race, and reflected that the man would go hungry if his barrow went unoccupied.

Wardell climbed into the rickshaw. "The American Cemetery," he said. He began to give directions, but the Chinese man was already moving off at a fast trot.

Wardell leaned back, looking at the surging impoverished populace of the war-torn city. On his last visit, in 1939, he'd seen a very different Hong Kong—a city that had become a refuge for those affluent Chinese and Europeans who had escaped the Japanese invasion of the mainland and the fighting that had been tearing China apart since 1932. The mood was one of eleventh-hour hysteria, as these rich men and the beautiful women they brought with them lived a life of frantic gaiety in the crowded luxury hotels. While the parties went on, the city neglected its defenses, in Wardell's opinion at the time sealing its doom should the Japanese decide to invade. They did.

The rickshaw arrived at the cemetery. Wardell asked the driver to wait. He walked through the silent rows of stones and markers to the chapel, where he found the verger. Receiving directions, he moved deeper into the grounds, climbing up several stepped terraces. Sunlight penetrated the overhanging trees and reflected from myriad gray stone markers and sculptured monuments that bore epitaphs carved in Cyrillic letters, in English, and in French.

He stopped at a section of neatly ordered wooden markers, simple crosses with names and dates engraved and blackened to stand out against the white of the wood. He searched for five minutes before he found the marker he wanted:

CHARLES B. WARDELL

BORN OCT 10 1898   DIED DEC 23 1941

Charley, Wardell thought. He closed his eyes and saw the stony hills of Arizona where he and his brother had been raised. They were hunting jackrabbits and every jackrabbit was an Apache. He was Davy Crockett and Charley was just Charley, mad as hell because their old man had not seen fit to name him after a frontier hero, too.

Wardell and his brother had fought like wildcats while growing up, then had fought shoulder to shoulder on the college campus in Phoenix when taunted as "saddle bums." Their mother had died the year after Charley was born, and that brought them closer together, the two brothers and the old man. They owed their father everything.

The old man had died in a senseless riding accident during their freshman year in college. The two brothers had shed their first real tears together at the funeral, vowing to make something of themselves in the old man's memory.

They had. They worked seven long days a week building the trucking business, even though Charley had hated every minute of it. He'd had a fierce desire to travel, and as soon as there was enough money he was off to the Orient. By the late thirties the profits from the import-export business Charley had developed exceeded the profits of the trucking operation.

Despite the distance, Wardell had felt closer to Charley than to anyone else. Every year until 1940 he'd managed to arrange a trip to Hong Kong, where Charley had established permanent residence, or to Hawaii, where they'd vacation on the beach. In 1940, with war on the horizon, Wardell had been unable to leave Washington. He'd pleaded, in numerous cables and letters, for his brother to return to the safety of the States. Charley assured him he would leave when the time came.

That time should have been after the attack on Pearl Harbor. Wardell used his considerable influence to insure that Charley would have no trouble getting a seat on one of the U.S. planes evacuating embassy personnel. The last plane left on December 22, the day before the Japanese overran the colony. Charley wasn't on it. Later, word reached Washington of his death.

Wardell had come to Hong Kong for two reasons. One was to bring Charley's body home, to rest in the family plot next to those of his mother, his father, his wife, and his son. The second reason was to find out why Charley hadn't left, why he had thrown his life away.

Wardell wasn't a superstitious man. But the feeling

51

that he was afflicted by some strange curse was hard to shake. His father died before his time, his wife and son the same, then Charley. Why?

Wardell continued to stand in the brilliant sunshine, staring at the wooden cross. Finally, he sighed and turned away. The bleak grave marker couldn't tell him anything. He had to find someone who could.

He made his way back down the terraces to the chapel. In a small, cluttered office at the rear he found the director of the cemetery, a lanky, gray-haired Australian. Wardell introduced himself and told him what he wanted.

"No problem if the bloody paperwork's in order," the director said.

"The American embassy cleared it for me in advance. A messenger will bring it over when you need it."

The Australian's thick eyebrows rose. "VIP, huh. Makes it easier."

Wardell frowned. "The paperwork. Not the death." He paused for a moment, then asked, "Were you here when he was buried?"

"Must have been," the man said. "Don't remember it, there were so many bloody bodies. I was lucky to escape internment—Nips have a thing about the dead, left me pretty much alone. Bloody hard to eat, though, especially toward the end."

The man shook his head, stuck a pipe in his mouth, and lit it. Then he looked up at Wardell and said, "I suppose you'll want the flowers stopped?"

"The what?"

The Australian had a puzzled expression on his face. Then he said, "Bloody stupid of me. No way you could have arranged for it in the States."

"Arranged for what?"

"The wreaths. Once a month, on the twenty-third, a big floral wreath is delivered for your brother's grave. Been arriving since a few months after the occupation. You didn't see last month's, because in this climate the thing starts rotting in a week. We toss it out."

A ripple of excitement went through Wardell. "Who sends the wreaths?"

The Australian shrugged. "Never asked. Bloke who makes them up could tell you. I'll give you his address."

The man wrote on the back of an envelope, handed it to Wardell, and said, "As soon as the coffin and the paperwork get here, I'll have the boys disinter the body. Ship it to the airport so it will be all ready to go." The man bent to open the bottom drawer of his desk. He pulled out a bottle of whiskey, and started to say, "How about a . . ."

Wardell had already left.

It was midafternoon when Wardell reached the waterfront, paid the rickshaw driver and boarded the Star Ferry. He stood at the rail, slowly watching the frothing waters of the harbor recede as the craft chugged toward the mainland part of the colony.

The day had been intensely frustrating. The ancient Chinese woman who delivered the wreaths told Wardell she had no idea who ordered them. A servant arrived each month with the money; it would be two weeks before the servant came again.

Then Wardell had gone to the embassy. Only one of the handful on the staff who'd been in Hong Kong before the invasion remembered Charley. But he'd

53

known Wardell's brother only casually, and could provide the names of few people for the senator to contact. So many people had died in internment, others had fled.

Wardell did get the name of a club his brother patronized, but that wouldn't open until evening. With time to kill, Wardell decided to make another pilgrimage, one that he and Charley had always made on the first day of Wardell's visits.

The ferry reached the mainland, and Wardell took a cable car that whisked him up to the observation point at the top of the peak. He moved away from the other passengers until he stood by himself, looking out over the finest panoramic view in all of Asia. The glittering blue of the bay was nipped in the middle by great white blocks of skyscrapers that created concrete canyons and glittering towers which soared into the skyline. Behind the mainland city, he could count the hills of the Nine Dragons; they formed a purple barrier to China.

It had been over those purple hills that the Japanese who had killed his brother had poured. A wave of loneliness that had been growing more and more intense since he had sat, stunned, watching Laura Jameson walk briskly out of the dining room in Tokyo, overwhelmed him.

Wardell was a strong man; he knew his life still had meaning, that he had work he should and would do. But no national or international problem, no matter how vital, could fill up his personal void. Wardell was totally alone.

For the first time since the death of his wife, Wardell felt his eyes moisten, his grief for his brother finally coming to the surface. He stood for a long time, gazing unseeingly outward.

Then, later, he said to himself, "Enough." He had to get his feelings under control.

He turned and followed a narrow path that led behind the shoulder of the rising hill to his left. He walked slowly, pausing as each fresh panorama came into sight: the green wooded slopes leading down to the bay on the far side of the island; the sea and sky merging into a white haze that was like a soft wool blanket covering the outlying islands; in the far distance, two tiny junks under full sail, black outlines floating motionless against the clouds.

He reached the summit after a final steep climb. He stood breathing in the crisp, clear air, and gazing out over the warships and freighters sailing between scattered islands which formed dark patches against the silver-blue sea.

He didn't know how long he'd been standing there when he heard a woman's voice say, "David?"

He whirled.

For a moment he thought she must be a vision. Her long blond hair framed a face of almost ethereal beauty—delicate nose, china blue eyes, flawless skin. A diamond choker highlighted her long elegant neck. She was tall, slender, and when she took two steps toward him, he was struck by the athletic grace with which she moved.

She spoke again. "Yes, it is you. You look so much like him. I'd know you anywhere."

"Like who?" Wardell asked. "Who are you?"

"My name is Susan. I am . . . I was, your brother's wife."

Wardell was stunned, his mouth dropping open. "What . . . what are you doing here. How did you—"

"Madame Wong at the flower shop told me a man was asking about Charles. The war made us all so . . . so careful. One of her people followed you to the embassy, and that's where I picked you up."

She paused for a moment, looking down at her hands. When she looked up at him again there were tears in her eyes. "I was hoping so much that it would be you. You have no idea how lonely I've been."

Before he could say anything she'd stepped forward and put her arms around him. Instinctively he held her close. He could feel her shaking as she cried. He stroked her hair soothingly as her head rested against his shoulder.

While he did so, his mind raced. Charley married? How could that have been? He'd talked to his brother just a few days before the invasion—just a few days before his death.

The woman's sobbing subsided. She pulled away, turned, and took a few steps toward the drop on the harbor side of the summit. Wardell waited while she took a handkerchief from a pocket and dabbed at her eyes.

She spoke without looking at him. "I'm sorry," she said. "I didn't mean it to be this way. Not here."

She turned back toward him. The color in her cheeks made her even more beautiful.

"I didn't have to follow you," she said. "I knew you'd come here. This was Charley's favorite spot, too."

"I really don't understand," Wardell said. "Charley never said anything to me about you. Not even the last time we spoke."

"You mean the last time you spoke before the date on the grave marker," she said. "One of the many things I have to tell you is that you have to cancel that exhumation order. The grave in the American cemetery is empty."

A jolt went through Wardell. "What? Charley's alive?"

She shook her head sadly. "If only he were. He was killed a little over a year ago."

She saw the puzzled look on David's face. She said, "Let's sit down. I'll tell you the story."

They moved to a bench in the shade of a tree. She took his hand.

The warmth of her skin startled Wardell. He was suddenly conscious of her as a woman, an extraordinarily sensual woman. He struggled to concentrate on her words.

"My name is Susan Gordon," she said. "I—"

"Susan Gordon," he repeated. "For some reason I think I should know that name."

"I'm an actress," she said.

"Of course," he said. "I should have recognized you."

"I've changed," she said. "It's been a long time between films. But perhaps I've done my best acting since I left Hollywood."

"What do you mean?" Wardell asked.

She told the story from the beginning. She'd met Charley in Honolulu, where he'd gone for a short business trip. As soon as the shooting for her film had been completed, she'd followed him to Hong Kong. Then came the attack on Pearl Harbor.

"We intended to leave, of course," Susan said. "But Charley was determined that all of his employees would get away, also. Three days before the invasion, he drove a group down to Aberdeen on the south coast, where a boat was to meet them. On the way back, his jeep was strafed by a Japanese fighter. It was a miracle he survived. But he was badly wounded, so badly he couldn't travel."

She paused to take a few deep breaths, the memory obviously disturbing her. "Some Chinese friends took Charley in. There was great danger—the city was filled with Japanese agents, and your brother's antagonism to Japan's expansion was well known. They would have made sure that his internment would have been fatal."

"That's why the ruse of his death?" Wardell asked.

"Yes," she said. "There was such confusion that it wasn't difficult. The sending of the wreaths every month was a part of the plan."

"I see," he said. He thought for a moment, then asked, "What about you? Did you hide with him?"

"No," she said. She bit her lower lip and lowered her eyes as she continued, "There was so much more that I could do if I were free to move around. I . . . I found a protector. A Japanese general. A kind man, actually. An intellectual. We used to read Shakespeare's plays together. The English monarchy fascinated him."

She was silent for a moment.

Wardell squeezed her hand. "I understand," he said.

She dabbed at her eyes again. Then she said, "My friend was not a demanding man. I was able to visit your brother three or four times a week. It was nearly a year before he got his strength back. I almost wish that he hadn't."

"Why?" Wardell asked.

"I pleaded with him not to be impatient, to stay in hiding where it would be safe. But he wouldn't listen. Despite the danger, there was an underground resistance group organized primarily by the Chinese. At first they limited themselves to gathering intelligence. Then, later, they began conducting sabotage activities. Charley joined them."

"That sounds like my brother," Wardell said. "He was never a man to sit on the sidelines."

"He was so restless," Susan continued. "Finally, maybe inevitably, something went wrong. Four men, including Charley, were pulling a cart of explosives down to the harbor to blow up a cargo ship. They were stopped by a Japanese patrol. Shooting broke out, then the explosives detonated."

Tears were streaming down her cheeks again. Wardell reached out and brushed them away with his free hand. Then he asked, "What about Charley's body?"

"There were no remains. The Japanese were killed, too. The only way I found out what happened was through my friend."

She put her head on his shoulder again. He held her close for a long time. Finally, she raised her head and said, "I'm sorry. It's been long enough for me to recover."

"You have nothing to be sorry for," he said. "I can't tell you how much it means to me, finding out what happened to my brother. That's why I came to Hong Kong."

"There's so much more to tell you," she said. "But . . ."

"Don't feel you have to get everything out now,"

Wardell said. He got to his feet. "It's time we went back. You can get some rest this afternoon. We'll have dinner and talk. Okay?"

She looked at him, and for the first time a faint smile appeared on her face. "I think that's a wonderful idea, David. I haven't had anything to look forward to for a very long time."

FIVE

General Mack Dolan was the first man out of the plane. He was a bulldog of a man—thick barrel chest, jutting jaw, thick black eyebrows, broad forehead. Despite his pugnacious appearance, he was a man of considerable intelligence. John Sage had heard rumors that Dolan was on the short list of candidates to be the next Army chief of staff.

Sage had arrived in Hawaii from Japan only two hours previously. "Bennett" disappeared when he shed the Army major's uniform on the flight. He was now in civilian clothes, as was the other man in the Quonset hut.

Sage turned away from the window. "He's here," he said to his tall, muscular companion.

"Does it look like good news," the man asked.

Sage shrugged. "With Dolan it's impossible to tell."

The door opened. General Dolan walked in, followed by two aides. He crossed and shook Sage's hand.

"Good job in Japan," Dolan said. "Wardell's death would have been catastrophic."

Sage looked at him. "Bad news from Washington?"

"Let's sit down," Dolan said. He took the chair at the head of the table.

When the others were seated, he asked Sage, "You've cleared the area?"

"We can talk," Sage said.

"Good," Dolan said. "Now, brief me on Japan."

Sage reviewed the attack on the Congressional party, the discovery of the conspiracy, and his conversation with Senator Wardell.

"What was Wardell's reaction?" Dolan asked.

"He listened. But he was noncommittal."

"That's Wardell. He's a very careful man. That's precisely why he's important to us. People listen to him, including the president."

"We've got no other political support?" Sage asked.

"The voters want peace, so the politicians want peace. The Russians could walk into Paris, and we'd hand them the key to the Eiffel tower, smiling all the time." Dolan shook his head in disgust. "Ike made the biggest mistake of the war when he stopped Patton from marching all the way to Moscow. But he's become a damn politician, too."

Sage looked at the general. "Does Eisenhower know about Scalpel?"

"No," Dolan said. "Only a half-dozen senior officers outside of this room know the whole plan. Of course, I've sounded out Admiral Leahy, Marshall, and a few others about the general concept. Every realistic military man I've talked to is worried to death about the Russians. But they all say the chances of getting politicians to authorize any military action are negligible; those of getting approval for a raid to wipe out the

Russians' atomic bomb research center are worse."

"And the Scalpel force?"

"Still in place," Dolan said. He turned to the major sitting next to him. "Jerry, what are those figures?"

"A thousand Russian Army uniforms and enough small arms and equipment for seven to eight hundred men. Eleven Russian transport planes, twenty-four fighters, and three reconnaissance craft. All the aircraft have been serviced and armed."

Dolan looked back at Sage. "Scalpel could be launched on five days' notice. Twenty-four hours later, we wouldn't have to worry about the Russians having the bomb for twenty years."

Sage lit a cigarette. "I can't believe the discovery of the Soviet espionage ring didn't have more effect."

"Truman was shocked," Dolan said. "I think maybe the president's got enough guts to agree to Scalpel—but not without some political support. And the key to that support is Wardell."

"I tried my best to convince him to go back to Washington," Sage said. "But he insisted on going to Hong Kong."

"I'm not waiting," Dolan said. "I'm on my way to Hong Kong to see him."

"The time is that short?" Sage asked.

"The demobilization is becoming very rapid. Any day someone's going to ask why the hell haven't those planes been returned to the Russians. More and more of our best airborne units are being transferred stateside. And every day the Russian air defenses get stronger."

"My operatives tell me radar is still not a problem," Sage said.

"You keep on top of those operatives," Dolan said. "I want to know if they bring an extra pistol near that research facility. And most importantly, I have to know instantly if the Russians tumble onto the plans for Scalpel. That would be disastrous."

Sage looked at Dolan with piercing eyes. "What are the chances of launching Scalpel without the president's authorization?"

"No," Dolan snapped. "As strongly as I feel about it, that isn't the way our system works. The next step would be a military coup, and we'd be no better than the Commies. You remember that, Sage. That's an order."

"Yes, sir," Sage said.

Dolan looked at him for a moment, trying to read his face. Then he said, "I want you in Germany. Get to Berlin and strengthen that network while we have the chance. I'm off to talk to Wardell." He turned to his aides and added, "Let's go, boys."

"Good luck, sir," Sage said. He watched Dolan leave the room and walk back across the runway to his plane.

Sage's companion asked him, "Do you think Dolan can talk Wardell into supporting Scalpel?"

"Maybe," Sage said. "But we're not going to count on it. We're going to give him a little help." A thin, cold smile came to his face. "More than a little help."

They had a drink in her hotel, the Peninsula. Then they went out to the hired car. The driver used the vehicular ferry to Yaumatei Pier, then followed the coastal road east around the island, past North Point and Heung Gong, the "fragrant harbor." They left the car and took a sampan to the floating restaurant sitting illuminated and still beyond the fringe of the crowded harbor craft.

Susan ordered for them—crab meat and sweet corn soup, baked lobster with onion, dry Cantonese wine. Wardell paid little attention to what he was eating. Since that afternoon on the peak, he'd felt like he'd fallen under some sort of spell. His thoughts were no longer his own, but were controlled from outside of him.

First, there was Charley. When Charley was alive, he had hardly ever seemed as real to Wardell as he did now. As the rickshaw had taken him and Susan from the dock that afternoon, Wardell had gazed at the crowded streets, and suddenly, he was his brother, moving furtively in disguise through the alleyways, on some desperate mission against the Japanese.

That was the way to fight a war. Not in Washington, poring through stacks of tedious legislation, bickering endlessly over budgets, enduring the blustering in backrooms and the Senate floor. In his now well-established role as the dispassionate compromiser, Wardell had restrained something important within himself, a need for action, for adventure. Charley had died young, far before his time. Yet in the span he'd had, he'd lived his life to the full.

This woman was an example. There was a fire inside of her, an energy source magnetic in its effect.

After fourteen years alone, Wardell in the space of a month had found two women who stirred him. But Laura Jameson's attraction was more intellectual, a passionate commitment to ideas, to causes. Susan Gordon's was purely sexual.

65

Wardell found himself barely able to listen to what she was saying, to respond in the appropriate places. Instead, his attention was riveted on her—the movement of her sensuous lips, the casual brush of her arm against his, the delicate white skin of her arms. When her eyes met his, Wardell felt his body temperature rise.

He struggled to control his reaction, feeling more like a ridiculous schoolboy than a forty-nine-year-old man, a U.S. senator, a brother mourning with his brother's wife. He had an extra drink or two, trying to calm himself. But the bourbon had little more effect than water.

The restaurant was nearly empty when they finally left. The old woman still patiently waited outside to pole them back across the bay in the sandalwood sampan. They said little as they reached the docks, crossed to the car, and were driven back to the city.

"I can't believe it's so late," Wardell said as the car pulled up in front of the hotel.

"Do you mind walking me up to my room?" she asked.

"Of course not," he said with a smile. He paid the driver, then took her arm as they crossed the empty, dimly lit lobby. The elevator rattled to a stop, and the attendant, a grizzled old Indian man, pulled the gate open.

After they went inside, Susan said, "I checked into this hotel in November of 1941, and I've been here ever since. Before I came to Hong Kong I don't think I lived in the same place for more than two or three months since I was a teenager."

"Does it feel like home now?" Wardell asked.

Her face was suddenly somber. "No," she said.

The elevator stopped at the seventh floor. Wardell escorted her to the end of the corridor.

"I want to tell you how much this day has meant to me," Wardell said as she turned to face him.

"And me, too," she said.

"All those years of wondering," Wardell continued, "not knowing what happened to my brother, not . . ."

She put her fingers on his lips, silencing him. "No more talk," she said.

She put her hand on the back of Wardell's neck and pulled him to her. Their lips met, then opened. Wardell could feel her tongue probing his, licking at the tip.

He pulled her to him. He could feel her breasts against his chest, the exquisite silkiness of her hair brushing against his face. Then her lips traveled from his mouth across his jaw line and she kissed his neck.

Something inside Wardell said no, this isn't right. But the door to her room was open and she took his hand. "Come," she said.

The voice inside him disappeared. He followed her into the small room and stood by the bed as she lit a single candle.

He watched her glowing eyes as she moved toward him. She kissed him gently, lightly on the lips. Then her fingers began unbuttoning his shirt, and her mouth was on his chest.

She undressed him, kissing and caressing him, at times softly, at other times with an animal-like ferocity. He closed his eyes, and suddenly it felt as though she had many hands and many mouths, all passing swiftly over him to linger on the most sensitive spots. His body shivered with desire.

Then her hands were on his shoulders and he lay

back, naked, on the bed. He enjoyed her weight on him, crushing her to him as they kissed, their teeth touching.

She pulled away, her hands caressing his sides as she slid down the length of him. Her mouth reached his penis, and she began kissing all around it. He sighed. He could feel his penis shake at each kiss. He was looking at her. His hand was on her head and he pressed it downward so her mouth would engulf him. His hand remained on her as she moved up and down. Then, as he exploded with unbearable pleasure, she was still.

He lay, unmoving, breathing deeply as the warmth rippled through him. Then he sat up, took her arms, and pulled her to him. She rubbed her whole body against his, enjoying the friction. Then she fell on her side and lay there as he explored her like a blind man. With his hands and mouth he discovered the shape of her mouth, her eyes, her nose, her breasts, her thighs. He learned the texture of her hair, her skin, the moist recesses of her sex. His fingers were light as he did this, teasing and caressing.

Then she moaned, a deep, throaty signal of intense desire. Suddenly, they both became frenzied, pressing deep into each other's flesh, pawing, grasping. They coupled with a kind of fury, thrusting, thrusting until it seemed that they would make their two bodies one.

Then it was over. Wardell rolled over on his back, totally spent. He felt the brush of lips on his in the brief moment before sleep came.

Hours later, Wardell awoke with a start. He sat up, for a moment staring uncomprehendingly into the darkness.

Then he felt the woman beside him, and he remembered where he was. The candle had burned out, and only faint moonlight seeped through the curtains. As his eyes focused, he could see the outlines of a bureau, two chairs, a small lamp table—the sole furnishings of the sparse room.

He closed his eyes. The liquor that hadn't seemed to intoxicate him had evidently ravaged him during sleep. His mouth was ash-dry, his lips parched and cracked. His head felt as though someone had implanted a baseball behind his eyes, and his stomach rumbled.

He tried to lie back down, but when he closed his eyes, a wave of dizziness swept over him. He sat up again. He had to get out of the room.

He quietly got out of bed. He dressed, feeling very clumsy, his body heavy and unresponsive.

Wardell opened the door to the hall, then took a last look at the bed. Susan was lying on her side facing him, one exposed white breast rising and falling rhythmically as she breathed. He stood, staring for a moment. Then he closed the door and walked toward the elevator.

The clock in the lobby read five A.M. He had to wait nearly fifteen minutes for a car. Finally, an ancient Nash pulled up and he climbed inside.

He stared glumly out the window during the trip back to the hotel, fighting his hangover and the feeling that he'd made a fool of himself last night. How could he lose control of himself like that?

And yet, what was wrong with what he'd done? What harm had he done to his brother? In a way, considering the type of man his brother was, the most appropriate wake for him was the two people who had loved him most in the world loving each other.

The car hit a hole in the road. The jolt sent pain like a knife through Wardell's head, and he closed his eyes, fighting it.

He opened them again, breathing deeply to calm his stomach. Then the image of Susan came into his mind.

He hadn't made love with that intensity in years. When he'd entered that hotel room, he'd become a different person, shedding the skin of the somber politician he'd become. Susan's passion had uncovered his, long buried.

Soon it would have to be buried again. Maybe he shouldn't see her anymore. But maybe he should. He had two more days left in Hong Kong.

The cab reached his hotel as the first rays of dawn streaked the sky. The elevator operator was dozing, and Wardell climbed the two flights to his room. He put the key in the door, heard the lock click, then pushed.

The room was a shambles. The floor was strewn with papers and the stuffing of slit-open mattresses, cushions, and pillows. Drawers were pulled from the bureau, the bases of lamps were shattered, the paper backing of framed paintings had been ripped off.

Wardell walked into the bathroom. Even his tube of toothpaste had been cut open, the white paste smeared all over the wash basin.

He leaned against the frame of the door, staring. What in heaven's name had they been looking for? He carried relatively little money, no jewels or other valuables. He had a briefcase of papers from Washington, but he wouldn't dream of having top-secret

70

documents sent to him in a place like this.

What would have happened if he'd been in the room? A shudder went through him, and the image of the crazed Japanese with the samurai sword went through his mind.

Then he breathed deeply, and his head cleared. He grabbed the bottle of aspirin, downed two with a swallow of water, and headed for the lobby to call the police . . . and the American embassy.

SIX

A shot rang out. Then another. Wardell's heart pounded as he dove to the ground and crawled toward cover that seemed impossibly far.

"David!"

Wardell sat upright in bed. The adrenaline still flowed in him from the incredibly vivid dream.

He couldn't believe he'd fallen asleep. The Hong Kong police hadn't finished questioning him until after dawn. The hotel had moved him to another room. He'd lain down on the bed, clothes on, exhausted, but mind racing. The clock had reached six, then seven.

Now a glance told him that it was nearly eleven in the morning. From the other side of the door came another knock, and Wardell recognized the voice calling his name.

He wearily swung his legs over the side of the bed, hoisted himself to his feet, and padded over to the door.

Gen. Mack Dolan's eyes roamed over Wardell as if he were a new recruit standing inspection. He grunted, then said, "You look like you've been crawling through every dive in the Orient, David."

Wardell grimaced. "Give me a break, Mack. You don't know what—"

"I do know," Dolan interrupted. He motioned behind him. A room-service waiter appeared with a large silver urn of hot coffee and pastries. "I figured you might need this."

Wardell smiled. "Thanks." He gestured to the sitting area of the room. "I'll be with you in a couple of minutes."

Wardell went into the bathroom, splashed water on his face, then inspected himself in the mirror.

His headache was gone. But his eyes were bloodshot and every muscle in his body ached. When he took off his shirt to take a quick shower, he saw in the mirror some welts on his shoulders and neck.

A closer look revealed them to be teeth marks.

"Jesus," Wardell muttered to himself. Like a college student in heat, he'd been the night before. But as he removed the rest of his clothes and stepped into the shower, the memory of the intensely passionate night flooded over him. God, it had been a long time since he'd been stirred like that.

He let a last ripple go through him. Then he turned the control on the shower vigorously toward cold.

When he had finished showering, shaving, and dressing, Dolan was draining his second cup of coffee. The general lit a cigarette, then said, "Now you look more like a senator."

"I wish I felt more like a senator," Wardell said.

"You would if you acted like one," Dolan said. "It

73

was damn foolish making this trip at this time."

Wardell started to object.

"I know the reason," Dolan said. "I had a talk with Rachel."

Wardell grimaced. Rachel Lang, his administrative assistant, had been with him for nearly ten years. He didn't at all like the fact that she'd talked to Dolan, even if he were a friend.

Dolan knew what Wardell was thinking. "Rachel was very sensibly concerned about you. Christ, David, Hong Kong's only been liberated about three weeks. Even with U.S. security, we almost lost you in Japan. The limeys are trying, but whole goddamn divisions of agents could operate without anybody knowing. That's the way Hong Kong has always been."

"I know," Wardell said. "But I had to do what I had to do."

Dolan shrugged. "We all do. And I shouldn't be riding you on this, not after what you've been through. You're here, and that's a fact."

Wardell poured a cup of coffee. He took a big sip of the rich brew, then said, "We both know why I'm here. But I don't know why I'm looking at your mug this morning."

"Simple," Dolan said. "I came to talk to you."

"That seems a waste of time," Wardell said. "I'm scheduled to be back in Washington early next week."

"That's too long," Dolan said. "I had to talk to you now. Today."

"So talk."

"Not here," Dolan said. "This hotel isn't the most secure place in the world, by a long shot. As you found out last night."

"You know about that?" Wardell asked.

Dolan nodded.

"I can't figure out what someone was looking for," Wardell said. "They didn't touch my cash."

"You'll have a better idea later today, maybe," Dolan said.

Wardell sighed in frustration. "More of this secrecy bullshit," he said. "Can you tell me one thing? Does this relate to the conversation your friend had with me in Japan?"

"Yes."

"I thought so," Wardell said. "I'll tell you, Mack, I didn't trust that guy at all."

"He's for real. Maybe the best agent Bill Donovan had in the OSS. When the war in Europe ended, we got him. He's really a colonel, but you'll never see him in uniform. He's got his own way of doing things, but he gets results. When we're back in Washington, I can prove that to you."

"Okay," Wardell said. "I'll take your word for it." He drank the remaining coffee in his cup. Then he asked, "When and where do we talk?"

"I'll pick you up in a car in an hour. I've got to go over to the embassy to cable Washington."

"I'll meet you there," Wardell said.

"David—"

"I'm not staying locked up in a cage," Wardell said firmly. "If you want to talk, I'll talk. But you're not telling me what to do." He smiled, then added, "After all, Mack, I got discharged in January, 1920."

Dolan smiled, too. "We should never have let you

out. Too damn stubborn to be a civilian."

The hotel operator told Wardell the phone in Susan's room was off the hook. He went down to the lobby of his own hotel and made arrangements to hire a car for the day.

He had to wait fifteen minutes for the car. At midday, the streets of Hong Kong were at their most crowded, and the car crawled along at a snail's pace. Wardell sat in the back, chain-smoking. That was unusual for him, a rare sign of impatience. But then he hadn't been himself since he'd arrived in Hong Kong.

The car finally reached the driveway of the hotel. Wardell jumped out and crossed to the elevator. He was waiting when two men approached him.

The man who spoke had the build of a football linebacker. His accent was British. "Senator Wardell, we have to talk with you."

"Later," Wardell snapped.

"Now," the man said firmly.

"Who are you?" Wardell asked angrily.

"British intelligence," the man replied.

"Good for you," Wardell said. The elevator arrived. Wardell started to walk in. The British agent grabbed his arm.

"This is not a request, Senator," the man said firmly. "You're on British soil, not American. Let's not make this unpleasant."

Wardell glared at him. He'd had enough of these intelligence types in the last weeks to last him a lifetime. For a moment, Wardell considered calling the American embassy and making an issue of this.

Then he sighed. That would probably cost him twice as much time and a lot more trouble than answering a few questions.

Wardell took a last glance at the elevator, the image of Susan lying in bed above floating briefly in his mind. Then he turned to the agent and said, "Okay. Let's make this quick."

The man smiled. "Good," he said. He pointed to a door across the lobby. "This way, Senator."

The office was the hotel manager's. Wardell took the big chair behind the huge teak desk. The British agents sat in two Queen Anne chairs on the opposite side.

"I'm Worthan," the muscular man said. "This is Egan."

Wardell didn't say anything.

Worthan continued. "We wish we'd had a little notice of your arrival, Senator Wardell."

"This is a personal trip," Wardell said. "It has nothing whatsoever to do with my position or your government."

"Unfortunately, that's not true," Worthan commented. He paused to light a cigarette, then added, "I knew your brother Charles rather well. Fine man."

Wardell sat forward. "How did you know my brother?"

"He was a rather prominent chap in these parts before the war. I met him first at the races. Loved a wager, Charley did."

Wardell nodded, knowing that was true.

Worthan continued, "He knew that I was an agent. In fact, he was of more than a little help to us. He traveled quite a bit: Saigon, Shanghai, Bangkok. Picked up some valuable information about the Nips,

77

carried some documents and funds for local agents. We had to restrain him from doing too much—he would have blown his cover."

"That sounds like my brother," Wardell said. Then he asked, "What about after the occupation? What can you tell me about this resistance work he did?"

Worthan glanced over at his companion. He took a long drag on his cigarette before he said, "I don't know what you're talking about, Senator. Charley was killed the day the Japs invaded."

Wardell stared at him. Then he said, "I know that isn't true. That grave in the American cemetery is empty."

Egan spoke for the first time. "I was with him that day, Senator. We were ferrying people down to the south coast in trucks to meet boats. He was driving the truck in front of me when the Zero made a strafing pass. He was killed instantly."

Wardell didn't know what to say.

"I assume the story you've been told came from the young lady you were with last night," Worthan said.

"What if it did?" Wardell asked.

"She's the reason we wanted to talk with you. At least a large part of the reason. Did she tell you who she was?"

"I recognized her. Susan Gordon."

"She is Susan Gordon, all right," Worthan said. "But I'll bet she didn't tell you why she had to spend the war here."

"She and Charley were married," Wardell said.

"She and your brother may have met a few times. That was it. Susan Gordon came to Hong Kong in 1940 with a man who, we later found out, was a rather well-known organized crime figure in your country. The purpose of the trip was to meet with some of our finer citizens to set up a drug-smuggling route from Southeast Asia to your West coast. It seems that Miss Gordon had acquired a rather strong taste for opium herself, a taste that it's easy to indulge in Hong Kong."

"I don't believe that," Wardell said.

"You don't have to believe it," Worthan said. "Just listen. It seems that Miss Gordon and her boyfriend had a quarrel after their arrival and he split back to the States. She found herself a new friend and stayed on. Her habit got heavier and heavier, and by the time of the invasion, she was in very bad shape—too far gone to think about evacuating."

Wardell had the image of the beautiful young woman in his mind. "She certainly doesn't look like a drug addict," he said to the British agent.

"She was cleaned up during the war. You can thank your government for that."

"Wait a second," Wardell said. "This sounds more and more farfetched. If my memory serves me, the Japanese controlled Hong Kong for five years."

"They certainly occupied the colony," Worthan said. "But Hong Kong has always nurtured intrigue. Egan and I survived the occupation underground. And so did operatives of American intelligence. And one of the most valuable of their agents was Susan Gordon. As the mistress of an important Japanese general, she had access to high quality military information."

"She told me about the general," Wardell said. He paused for a moment, thinking. Then he asked, "Why would she tell me this story about marrying my brother? I don't understand."

Worthan looked at him coldly. "It was a very quick and effective way to get close to you."

"Why would she want to do that?"

"I don't know," Worthan replied. "I suggest you ask your own government that."

Wardell leaned forward, his face stern. "What do you mean?"

"I mean Susan Gordon is still working for American intelligence. The day before you arrived, she met with a man named David Sutter, the supervising OSS agent in the colony. Other agents drove her to the ferry to the mainland, and followed her when she met you."

"How do you know that?" Wardell demanded.

"We were keeping an eye on you, too. We heard, belatedly I may add, about your visit. We didn't want a repetition of the unfortunate situation in Hiroshima, so we decided to provide discreet protection. Obviously, we know our American counterparts."

Wardell's mind was spinning. He was confused and angry. If this were true, he was going on the warpath.

"I've got to talk to Susan Gordon. She's got some explaining to do."

"We'd like to talk to her, too. But she's gone—the first plane this morning."

"But why did—"

Egan broke in, "Her boss found out we tumbled onto their scam. We stepped in after your hotel room was ransacked. They can follow around anybody they want. But burglarizing an American senator makes our government look bad. We told them to buzz off. Then they told Miss Gordon to get on her bloody horse and disappear."

Wardell got to his feet. He paced back and forth

behind the desk.

His mind believed the two British agents. But emotionally he found the story hard to accept. If it were true, he was like the most naïve schoolboy who believes himself madly in love with the first girl who lets him go all the way. Wardell never doubted that he and Susan had shared something very intense the night before. He knew she was an actress, but . . .

Get control of yourself, he thought. What happened in that room upstairs is over. The far more important question is why the hell I am the target of American intelligence.

Mack Dolan had one hell of a lot of explaining to do.

Wardell's swirling emotions had coalesced into cold fury by the time he reached the American embassy. When he and Mack Dolan were alone in a soundproof conference room, he exploded.

Dolan listened without interruption as Wardell spoke. His lips tightened around his cigar and his face grew more and more red.

Finally, Wardell finished by asking, "Now, do you mind telling me what this is all about?"

Dolan didn't answer for a moment. Instead he took the cigar out of his mouth, balanced it on the edge of a large glass ashtray, and looked up at Wardell.

"David," he said. "We've known each other for nearly thirty years. I hope our relationship is such that you'll believe me when I tell you I knew absolutely nothing about this business with the girl."

"I believe you. It's not your style, Mack," Wardell said. "But I also believe your trip is tied into this mess.

And I'll bet you know who did dream up this scheme."

"I'm going to start with this local idiot," Dolan said. "But it's going to trace back to my friend Sage. He's really gone too far this time."

"That's an understatement," Wardell said angrily. "If he's the one, he's committed a very serious felony. I won't rest until he pays for that. Even if I have to go all the way to the president."

"It's not as simple as that, David," Mack Dolan said. "I'm as angry about this as you are. However, you know as well as I do how volatile the situation is in Europe. Sage personally set up and controls our entire espionage network in the Soviet Union and Eastern Europe."

"Then no wonder we're in trouble," Wardell snapped. "If the man has all that responsibility, what in the hell is he playing games with a U.S. senator for?"

"I'll have to ask him that. But I think I have an idea why."

"Well?" Wardell said.

Dolan looked up at him. "David, please do me another favor. I want you to listen to what I have to say. I wish now I could have waited until you had a chance to calm down, perhaps when we got back to Washington. But it's desperately important. And I hope you can put what has happened to you aside and weigh what I have to present on its own merits."

Wardell grimaced. "I don't know, Mack. If it's got something to do with Sage, I'm not sure this is the time."

"At the heart of the matter, Sage is a bit player. The issue itself may affect the future course of world politics. Maybe even the future of human civilization."

"It's that important?" Wardell asked.

"You'll have to judge. Just listen. Okay?"

Wardell debated. Then he sat down in a chair and said, "Okay."

Dolan lit the cigar. "If I sound pedantic at times, you'll have to excuse me," the general said. "I want to be clear. So I'll start with a basic tenet of political science—every weapons system has a political significance. The greater the weapon, the greater the political significance. If we accept that as true, then the atomic bomb is the most important political fact of our time."

"You'll get no argument from me," Wardell said. "Remember, I've just come from Hiroshima and Nagasaki."

"I know," Dolan said. "That sight has been impressed on the minds of many world leaders—especially Stalin's and he is an especially paranoid person to begin with. Our use of the A-bomb has given a special incentive to the Soviet Union to increase their national security. Unfortunately, that means nothing but trouble for the rest of the world."

"What do you mean?" Wardell asked.

"I mean that the Russians have developed a detailed plan for greatly expanding their sphere of influence. Through our intelligence system, we've found out that they expect within two years to control all of the nations of Eastern Europe. Stage Two, also to come in the next two years, is the takeover of the Allied-occupied part of Germany, Austria, Italy, and Finland. Stage Three is the rest of the continent—France, Spain, Portugal, the low countries, and Scandinavia."

"That's pretty far-fetched," Wardell said.

"Is it?" Dolan asked. "Think about it, David. You've

83

been thoroughly briefed on the European war. You know that the communists controlled a large part of the resistance forces in France and Italy. De Gaulle may be on top now, but his position is precarious. Italy is in turmoil. If the countries to the east of them fall and the Soviets mass troops on their borders, I don't think those governments can muster the wherewithal to fight."

"You may be right," Wardell admitted. "But the Soviet Union has been weakened badly by the war. They're in no position to fight another major conflict."

"Now, you mean," Dolan said. "I agree with you. But every day they grow stronger again. And the US sits idly by, unwilling to 'offend' our wartime allies, even though we know the Russians are really our enemies."

"Are you sure we know that?"

"Positive. The massive spy network uncovered by the Canadians proves the point."

"The atomic bomb spies, you mean?"

"Yes," Dolan said. He snuffed out his cigar and leaned forward, hands clasped. "David, the only advantage we have over the Russians is the bomb. And it's a huge advantage . . . for now. Until recently, the word has been that the Soviet Union wouldn't have the bomb for ten to twenty years. We now know that they have all the information they need. Their research facility has been in operation since 1934. It could be as little as two years before our advantage is wiped out. I say we've got to use those two years to make the Russians accept our design for the post-World War II order. Up to now, most of the decisions have been made by default, and that falls right into Stalin's hands."

Wardell put his hands behind his head, thinking. Finally, he said, "I agree with you that we haven't been aggressive with the Russians. I think Churchill was right and we've been wrong—we let Stalin get away with practically everything for fear of having Russia pull out of the war. But Stalin is a belligerent, stubborn, tough man. I don't think the threat of the bomb is going to make him change his plans."

"I don't either," Dolan said.

Wardell's face reflected puzzlement. "So what are you saying, Mack?" he asked.

Dolan's face was somber. "I'm saying we ought to use the bomb."

For a moment Wardell was too shocked to reply. Then he spat, "You're out of your mind, Mack. You've gone off the deep end. I thought you said you'd seen the pictures of Hiroshima."

"I have, David. And I'm determined that I don't see similar pictures of Paris or Rome or London . . . or New York."

"That's scare talk," Wardell said. "You can't be serious."

"I've never been more serious," Dolan said. "David, you promised to hear me through with an open mind."

"You promised to talk sense," Wardell said.

"I will," Dolan said. "A sense that will insure peace for generations to come. To remove the threat of communist aggression not only from Europe, but from China and Southeast Asia and the Middle East, just as a surgeon cuts a cancerous tumor from the human body."

Wardell took a deep breath, hesitant to ask the question. But he did. "And how would you do that?"

"Scalpel."

"What?"

"Operation Scalpel. A two-part military attack, completed in less than twenty-four hours."

Wardell's stomach was tight from tension. He couldn't believe what he was hearing. At the same time, he was fascinated.

"Explain," he said.

Dolan replied, "Step One. We have assembled Russian transport planes, fighters, military equipment and uniforms at a staging area within striking distance of the Soviet nuclear research facility. The pilots to fly the planes and the elite airborne units to carry out the raid are still in Europe. The Soviet air defenses are very porous and we are sure we could get to the drop zone without detection. With the advantage of surprise, we can totally destroy the facility in a few hours."

"You probably could," Wardell said. "But how long would that slow down the Russian development program? Two years? Five years? The Germans made the mistake of underestimating the Russians' capabilities. Eventually, they'll get the bomb and they'll be more likely to use it."

"That's why we go on to part two," Dolan said. "We demand that Stalin withdraw all his troops from Eastern Europe. And that true democratic elections be held in all the constituent republics of the Soviet Union. The Ukrainians, the Caucasians, many of the other peoples have been chafing under the domination of the Russians. The Soviet Union will be dismantled."

Wardell scoffed, "Stalin would never agree to that."

"No, he wouldn't," Dolan said. "But Stalin won't survive. Not after we drop the bomb."

Wardell felt a surge of anger. The image of the

wasted landscape where the city of Hiroshima once stood flashed into his mind. "That's insane," he said forcibly.

"Was dropping the bomb on Hiroshima insane? You were involved in the decision-making process, and you concurred that saving millions of lives justified the destruction. Now, if we can stop the aggression of the Soviet Union, we can save tens of millions of lives. In addition, we can insure that hundreds of millions of people can live free from the threat of a communist dictatorship in their countries, and free from the threat of a future nuclear holocaust that could wipe out human civilization."

Wardell got to his feet. His whole body trembled from the effect of the incredible plan Dolan presented.

His first reaction was to leave the room. His job was to represent in the U.S. Senate the people of Arizona. He never intended to have to be a part of military decisions that would cost the lives of hundreds of thousands of people far behind his borders. It wasn't any of his business.

But it was his business, he reminded himself. He'd made it his business when he'd sought the chairmanship of the Senate Armed Services Committee, when he'd sought and accepted the role of participant in the planning and execution of his country's defense. Deep down inside he knew how much his position meant to him.

His motives weren't just a desire for power and self-importance. He truly believed that he was the kind of logical, rational, intelligent man who should be involved in monumental decisions. He'd entered politics because he didn't think such decisions should be made by emotional demagogues like Huey Long.

Yet how could a man trust himself enough to form an opinion on a proposal like this Operation Scalpel? It sounded like playing God, this gross interference in the internal affairs of another sovereign nation.

But Stalin was a man who played God, maybe even believed he was a god. Was it moral to sit back and let a brutal dictator carry out his aggressions? Wasn't that why the U.S. had fought this long bloody war against Hitler?

Wardell exhaled. He felt totally exhausted, mentally and physically.

He excused himself to go to the bathroom. He splashed water on his face, dried himself, then came back into the conference room. He sat down opposite Dolan once again.

"Mack, exactly who formulated this plan? And who knows about it?"

"It's my plan," Dolan said. "The details are only known to a handful of senior officers, most of whom are in intelligence. I've discussed the idea in general terms with many others, including Eisenhower, Stimson, and Leahy."

"And?"

"The military people are desperately worried about our advantage. The politicians—that includes Ike in my mind—can't abide the thought of another conflict so soon. The people want peace now, so they want peace now, no matter what the future price. My only chance to get Truman to listen is to convince a respected politician to make the argument. Otherwise, it will just seem like another half-baked military scheme."

Wardell spoke slowly. "And I'm that politician?"

"You're the only one, David. The only man with the vision and the courage. And one of the handful of men the president would listen to."

"I'm flattered," Wardell said. "But I'm not sure—"

"I'm sure," Dolan said forcefully. "David, the decision has to be made now. We can't keep those planes secret for long, and if we have to stage the raid with American planes from American bases, it will have to be planned again from scratch. What do you say?"

Wardell sat silent for a long time. Then he asked, "I suppose what Sage had in mind, using the woman, was to get her to influence me?"

Dolan shrugged.

Wardell continued, "I'd like to find out."

"That's not the real issue," Dolan said.

Wardell grimaced. "No, it isn't." He paused for another moment before he said, "I need some time, Mack."

"How much?"

Wardell flashed a wry smile. "Years. But maybe we'll talk again in the morning, before I leave?"

Dolan got to his feet. "At breakfast."

SEVEN

Wardell told the driver to return to the hotel. Hong Kong, a city that he'd always loved, now seemed totally alien and hostile. He found the mass of people depressing and breathed a sigh of relief when he was alone in his room.

Wardell took off his clothes, ordered a bottle of whiskey from room service, and stepped into the shower. By the time he was out, the whiskey had arrived. He drank three fingers in a few large sips, then crawled into bed.

Tired as he was, sleep wouldn't come. When he closed his eyes he saw a swirl of haunting figures floating in his mind. Their twisted mouths opened as they pointed accusingly at him. No, they were trying to say. No.

Finally, he must have fallen asleep. The phone woke him with a start.

His first thought was to ignore the call. But the shrill sound continued. He reached over, grabbed the receiver, and barked, "What is it?"

The operator told him she had a call from the United States. As he waited for the connection to be completed, he glanced at his watch on the bedside table. 7 P.M. He'd slept for nearly five hours. His body felt as though it had been one hour.

"David, are you there?"

The sound of a woman's voice was unexpected. Wardell hesitated, then asked, "Who is this?"

"Laura Jameson, David. Are you all right? You sound strange."

Wardell breathed a sigh of relief. For a moment, he thought Susan had been on the line.

"I've been napping," Wardell said. Then he asked, "What time is it there?"

"Eight in the morning," Laura said. There was a pause before she added, "I've been furious at myself since that last night in Tokyo. I . . . I couldn't wait until you returned to apologize. I was impossibly rude."

Wardell's thoughts went back to the scene in the restaurant. It seemed to be three months ago instead of three days.

"No need to apologize," he said. "The trip had been hard on all of us. Emotions were running high."

"They were," she said. "I've been thinking a lot about that conversation, David. I'm not apologizing for what I said. More than ever I believe that mankind can't live with the atomic bomb. But the way I said it was awful. If two people like us can't reach a conclusion through reason, then there isn't any hope that nations can reach a conclusion."

"You're right," Wardell said. "But it is an intensely emotional issue."

"The dialogue here in Washington is certainly

intense. All of us have been besieged for information since we returned. The hearings we conduct to prepare our report will take a long time. The number of opinions and policy alternatives is immense. You've got a lot of work in front of you."

If only you knew, Wardell thought. He was seized by a very strong desire to discuss Dolan's plan with Laura. The responsibility of making the decision alone was almost too great to bear.

He couldn't talk, of course. Not only did she not have security clearance, but the telephone line could well be monitored.

He did say, "We have a lot to talk about when I get back."

There was a pause on her end. Then she said, "I hope those talks include other issues besides politics. David, I think the reason I instigated the argument that last night was that I was afraid of what would happen after dinner. I'm so used to shutting myself off emotionally my defenses go up automatically. The truth is that I'm terribly attracted to you. I want to see you again . . . if, of course, you still want to see me."

He did. Wardell knew that as soon as she finished speaking. In the very difficult days and years ahead, he needed a partner, someone with whom he could be open.

He realized that Laura might not eventually turn out to be that person. But he hoped she would.

"Nothing has changed," Wardell said. "I want to see you again, too. Even more after what's happened here in Hong Kong."

"What's that?" she asked, her voice showing concern.

"It's too complicated to go over on the phone. I'm flying out of here tomorrow morning. I'll call you as soon as I get back in the capital."

"Thank you, David," she said.

"Thank you," he replied. "I can't tell you how much this call has meant to me."

He heard the click on the other end of the line. He put down the phone, then went into the bathroom.

Mack Dolan was sitting with two of his aides in the corner of the nearly empty hotel lounge. Wardell approached his table.

"Let's talk, Mack," Wardell said.

"Boys," Dolan said.

The two junior officers got up and moved to seats at the bar.

Wardell sat down. Dolan raised his glass to him, "Well, here's to nothing. At least you listened."

"How did you know what I was going to say?" Wardell asked.

"I could see it in your face," Dolan said. "You're going to chicken out, like the rest of them."

"It's not as simple as that, Mack," Wardell said. "I want to . . ." He let his voice trail off as a waitress approached. Wardell ordered a bourbon.

As the waitress moved away, he turned back to the general. "I listened to you this afternoon. Now you listen to me. All right?"

Dolan shrugged.

"I don't trust Stalin any more than you do. I was at SHAEF for several staff conferences near the end of the war, and I had more than my share of arguments with Eisenhower. I thought he was handing too much of Eastern Europe and Germany to the Russians for what amounted to minor tactical reasons. I believe what you told me about Stalin's plans."

"So," Dolan asked, "why aren't you with us?"

"Because of the monumental impact of the decision to drop a nuclear bomb outside of wartime—especially considering the timing. Even you admit that it will be at least two years before the Russians have a working bomb."

"But the raiding force is in place now. And the Russians can seize a lot of territory and rebuild a lot of their military capability in two years."

"I took that into consideration," Wardell said. "Believe me, Mack, I realize the effect of not moving now. The least important reason to move now is the Russian planes and equipment—that's a little like saying 'I happened to find a gun so I guess I have to use it to shoot somebody.'"

Dolan's face was grim. "I think this is a mistake, David. By the time the politicians in Washington get done with their thousands of task forces and committees and study groups, the nuclear cow will be long gone out of the barn. We'll have totally lost our chance to take the initiative, instead of taking it on the jaw like we did at Pearl Harbor—only an atomic Pearl Harbor will be a thousand times worse."

"I recognize that danger," Wardell said, "so I'm presenting a counter plan."

"Which is?"

"Just as you asked, I want to brief the president, in private, on Operation Scalpel. I'm going to ask him to authorize it as an official contingency plan. In addition, I'm going to ask him to approve a secret appropriation for Scalpel. I want fully developed operational plans, continually updated, based on the very latest intelligence. I want sufficient troops periodically drilled in the type of assault Scalpel would require, and I want those troops to be available to move on forty-eight hours notice. And I want pilots trained and aircraft on stand-by to transport those troops and provide fighter support."

Dolan chewed on his cigar as he looked at Wardell appraisingly. Finally, he said, "I don't know if we could provide tight enough security."

"We'll have to. I want Scalpel to be as top secret as the Manhattan Project. You'll report to me, and I'll report in private directly to Truman."

"That could work," Dolan said. He studied the cigar for a moment, then added, "I still think we should attack now, David. A year from now, two years from now, we're going to be operating from a weaker position. But I must say that your plan is a lot better than a total refusal."

"I think it's the intelligent way to proceed," Wardell said.

"Tell me one more thing," Dolan said. "Are you proposing this contingency plan just to get me off your back? Is this some intellectual masturbation you're going through. Or do you really believe that you could recommend to the president that we make a preemptive nuclear attack on the Russians?"

Wardell's face was somber. He looked directly into Dolan's eyes and said, "I think it would be the most terrible decision any world leader ever had to make. But considering the terrible alternatives, I think

Truman is tough enough to do what has to be done. I think, I hope, at the time I will be, too." He paused for a moment, then added, "It's one of those things you can never be totally sure of, Mack. Like how you're going to react the first time in combat. It's a lot different when you've got to pull the trigger."

Dolan smiled for the first time. "Well, I remember you were damn good and damn quick pulling the trigger in World War I. I guess I'll have to trust you now."

For the first night in weeks, Wardell got a good night's sleep. He was up early the next morning to pack.

As he moved around the hotel room, he reflected again on how pleased he was with the compromise he'd arrived at after Laura's phone call. He was also pleased at Dolan's reaction. The contingency plan was the right, the rational way to approach the very serious problem of Russian aggression.

The only unsatisfactory part of the affair was the blatant attempt by John Sage to manipulate him into accepting Scalpel. The thought that Sage, because of his importance to the intelligence network in Eastern Europe, would escape punishment galled Wardell.

He didn't bring up the subject with Dolan last night because he didn't want him to know that he was going to talk to the president about legislative supervision of intelligence activities. There had been numerous discussions about transforming the wartime OSS into a peacetime intelligence-gathering organization, the Central Intelligence Agency. Wardell realized the dangers of allowing agents like Sage, who were used to operating in the freewheeling wartime atmosphere, to have the same freedom in peacetime. Wardell was determined that Congress would have the opportunity to review major covert activities and personnel. Maybe he'd have the chance to see that Sage got booted out as soon as there was a suitable replacement.

In any case, that was in the future. Wardell closed his suitcase, called for a porter, then accompanied his baggage to the lobby. He went to the desk to check out. With his bill, the desk clerk brought a plain white envelope with his name on the outside.

Wardell slit the envelope open with his index finger. He read the short handwritten message. "I'm terribly sorry, David. I hope I have the chance to make it up to you someday. Love, Susan."

He continued to stare at the note as an unexpectedly strong wave of emotion passed through him.

Then he turned back to the desk clerk and asked in an abrupt tone, "Who delivered this?"

"It was in your slot when I arrived on duty this morning, sir."

"Is the night clerk still here?"

"He won't be in until eight this evening."

Wardell grimaced. Then he thought, What's the use anyway? It's over.

He crumpled the note and envelope into a ball and threw it at a wastebasket. Then he followed the porter carrying his luggage out to the waiting car.

EIGHT

June, 1948 — Laura sat in the fighting chair next to Wardell, in the cockpit of the sports-fishing cruiser trolling eastward into the Gulf Stream, out from Bimini atoll. She had turned up the collar of her light jacket so the lower part of her face was concealed. But her dark hair, blowing free in the starboard breeze, and the profile of her face, inclined upward toward the azure sky, stirred Wardell.

Once again, he was reminded about how badly they needed this vacation. Two years after their marriage, they'd become almost like strangers living in the same house.

No, Wardell cautioned himself. Strangers wouldn't have fallen into the habit of brief but bitter outbursts over the most minor differences.

How could things have gone so wrong so quickly? Wardell couldn't answer. All he did know was that he still loved her. And this vacation, now near the end of its first week, seemed to have brought them closer together.

Laura looked over at Wardell and smiled. "This is a far cry from my usual bamboo pole and bent pin," she said. "Then again, we didn't have many blue marlin in my fishing hole back home."

"I didn't know you were a fisherman," Wardell said.

"It was a way to impress the boys," she replied. "Only problem was I usually caught bigger fish. So I had to learn to be shy and demure instead." She saw the look on Wardell's face, reached over to take his hand, and added, "I guess I could use a few more demureness lessons, huh?"

Wardell squeezed her hand. "Not a one. If you hadn't been the person you are, I wouldn't have married you."

"Are you sure you were right?" Laura asked. "I've been doing so much thinking the last few days. I can't believe the shrewish . . ."

Wardell gently put his hand over her mouth. When she stopped, he bent down and kissed her on the lips. "That's all in the past," he said. "It's been a very difficult time for both of us. And it would have been difficult even if we weren't two stubborn, set-in-their-ways people trying to make a marriage work."

Laura looked up at him. "But—"

He interrupted her. "No buts today. Let's take it out on the marlin."

She smiled. "Aye, aye, Wardell."

He kissed her again. Then he turned to look up toward the flying bridge, where the captain, his hand light on the auxiliary controls, was scanning the water for signs of game. Nothing yet.

Wardell next checked the way the two baits were trolling. The small, bait mackerel, into which the giant

13/0 hooks had been set, were moving freely. Having read a book on big game fishing before the trip, Laura had made a fuss over having her bait rigged in the New Zealand manner, with the hook free, preceding the lure fish on the leader. That had greatly impressed the captain, and Wardell had taken pleasure in watching Laura smile to herself.

He sat back down in his chair, closing his eyes to bask in the tropical sun. He couldn't remember the last time he'd been this relaxed. What he had said to Laura had been true—the postwar years had been more difficult and conflict filled than World War II. At least during the war everyone knew exactly who the enemy was, everyone shared a common goal of destroying that enemy.

Once the war had ended, however, conflict had set in. The armed services fought bitterly for their share over the vastly reduced manpower and funds appropriated by a Congress elected by a country tired of war. The Allies quarreled incessantly over war reparations, over the rebuilding of Europe, and over Communist aggression in Eastern Europe, in Greece, in Turkey. And above all was the vital issue of the atomic bomb, and whether to share the secret.

Gradually, progress had been made on the first two problems. The National Security Act of 1947 had created the new cabinet position of Secretary of Defense, to whom the secretaries of the Army, Navy, and the newly independent Air Force would report. The Act also created out of the wartime OSS and other intelligence departments a new Central Intelligence Agency. In addition to his chairmanship of the Senate Armed Services Committee, Wardell had assumed the important but burdensome role of Congressional overseer of the CIA.

Progress had been made in rebuilding Europe and confronting communist aggression. In March, 1947, in response to the fighting in Greece, the president had issued the Truman Doctrine, around which the free countries rallied. In June of that year came the announcement of the highly successful Marshall Plan. The communists responded by forming Cominform in October, 1947, and completing their takeover of Eastern Europe with the coup in Czechoslovakia in February of 1948. But in March the Western European nations had concluded agreement on the Pact of Brussels, a defense organization that, Wardell hoped, would soon broaden to include the United States and Canada in what was being called the North Atlantic Treaty Organization.

The issue of international control of atomic weapons was still unresolved however. And it was this issue that was causing the greatest strain in Wardell's marriage. The visits to Hiroshima and Nagasaki had had a profound effect upon Laura. She had become an ardent believer in world disarmament, especially the destruction of all existing nuclear weapons. Wardell's arguments about the need to counter Soviet aggression fell on deaf ears, and she in turn resented that the vast majority of his time was devoted to military planning and intelligence operations. The more they tried to reason, the more they became polarized, until much of the time they spent together was passed in awkward, heavy silence.

Yet somehow, they had avoided a split. And this time together, away from the pressures of Washington, had revitalized their relationship. Wardell rediscovered what he had always believed—that as man and woman they belonged together. As the intense pressure of politics eased, they'd be able to place their work in the proper perspective.

Wardell felt a hand on his arm.

"You look so somber," Laura said. "Remember, this is a vacation, Senator. Relax."

Wardell put a hand on hers. "I am. Washington seems a million miles away."

"Let's never go back," Laura said. "We'll buy a boat like this and spend our days chasing after marlin and tuna."

"You mean it?" Wardell asked, looking into her dark eyes.

For a moment something dark passed over them. Then she smiled again and said, "No. And you don't either. But for now let's pretend—"

"Miss!" The captain called. "It's a marlin."

Wardell and Laura shaded their eyes, looking out over the boat's wake. They both saw the dark shape just under the surface, moving with incredible speed. The speed of the boat dropped off suddenly.

"Get ready," Wardell said to Laura. "They trail bait for some time, and he seems to be coming up on your line. If he strikes, you'll be in for a fight."

"Oh, dear," Laura said.

Wardell grinned. "Must be the New Zealand baiting."

Laura shot him a grimace. Then she sat down in the fighting chair.

The mate had taken the wheel on the bridge, and the captain was standing beside Laura.

"When he takes the bait, miss, ease up on the drag," the captain explained. "Then count to five and smack him."

The deck, beneath the lathework mat, was covered with rivulets of swirling wash, running from the scuppers under the transom corners and washing over their wet feet.

They waited in tense silence. Suddenly, the shape under the water exploded through the surface. The white trailing bait vanished, and they heard the click of the clothespin as the line dropped from the tip of the extended outrigger. Wardell moved forward and cut his own line. Then he turned to see the captain helping Laura ease the drag wheel on the huge reel. He saw her lips moving, knew she was talking silently to herself.

"Now!" the captain said sharply.

She screwed the drag down tight.

"Ease up and hit him again," the captain almost shouted. "It might make him run."

Wardell took a moment to look up at the bridge. The mate, following the action, had cut the port engine. The boat spun in a clockwise turn.

Laura had eased the drag, the rod tip shivering now. The line streamed out from the reel with a high keening sound. Her face set in a look of strong determination, Laura then struck the drag tight again and eased it.

They could see the marlin, beneath the surface, swim south in the beginning of his run. The boat turned to follow.

"He'll take out all the line if we don't chase him," the captain said. "Are you comfortable, miss? This hasn't hardly begun, you know."

Laura looked up at him. "I'm ready," she said.

Despite the speed of the boat, the line was still screaming off the reel. The mate accelerated to full power and for a moment the line disappeared. The boat was bouncing heavily now, chasing diagonally across the waves.

Wardell noticed the sound of the screaming reel soften. Looking at the reel, he saw that more than half of the reserve line had been paid out. Fortunately, the giant fish was slowing.

"Now screw the drag back tight," the captain instructed. "And start reeling in line. He's going to begin jumping."

"I think I've lost him," Laura said. "It's dead weight I'm reeling."

"The weight of the excess line, Miss. Reel in. It'll be easier now than later."

"Easier? I feel like I'm hooked to the bottom of the ocean right now."

The boat was still chasing south. Laura had reeled in perhaps fifty yards of line when the marlin broke the surface and rose into the air. It fell off to the side, the leader trailing from its huge jaw, and once more vanished beneath the waves.

"He'll jump again, Miss," the captain said. "He's a beauty."

"You doing all right?" Wardell asked Laura. "You need a break?"

"I'm going to land him," she replied, reeling in more line.

Wardell gazed for a moment at the fierce look on her face. She was a born fighter, he realized. She was not the kind of woman you changed. The harder things became, the more stubbornly she resisted.

The fish exploded through the surface once more, his wildly lashing tail seeming to hold him erect for an instant before he dove again.

"Tail walking," the captain explained.

Laura once more reeled in line. Her face was flushed with excitement and exertion. Wardell thought she looked more beautiful than ever.

The fish jumped several more times, then began to circle the boat. Laura continued to reel, although she'd been fighting the fish for more than half an hour.

The circling marlin was pulled closer to the boat with each circle. The captain and the mate had exchanged places. The mate, eager to have a hand in the finish of the fight, reached over the gunwale and tried to grasp the end of the leader wire.

"He's still green," Wardell shouted. "Watch it!"

A killing hatchet was attached to the inside of the transom below the roller. Wardell pulled it from its prongs and stood close beside the mate, waiting. He placed a reassuring hand on Laura's shoulder, feeling her muscles strain as she continued to drag the fish closer.

"A bottle of champagne for this, Laura," he said.

"Make that two," she called back.

Then Wardell heard a buzzing overhead. Looking up, he saw the broad wings of a PBY Catalina, white stars beneath each wing. The huge amphibian was circling low overhead, and an Aldis signal lamp was blinking from the right cabin port.

"Be ready!" Laura shouted.

Wardell turned his attention back to the fish that was slowing as it circled very close to the boat. The shining leader wire was coiling widely, most of its length now visible above the surface, the end barely ten feet out from the boat's side. Laura reeled in more line. The leader stretched taut just over the surface of the water, and the mate reached out again and seized its end.

Then the Catalina roared in low in a sudden rush. The mate had taken the leader end and was pulling in hand over hand. The massive length of the marlin lay unmoving just below the surface of the water.

Suddenly, the amphibian plane roared in just overhead. The fish reacted, erupting in a flash of white spray. Wardell saw the mate's hands on the wire, coiled tightly for a good hold. He reacted instantly, raising the hatchet and swinging down sharply. He cut the leader just out from where the mate's hands were coiled in it. The giant fish disappeared rapidly.

The mate looked at Wardell, his face ashen. "Thanks," he mumbled.

Wardell nodded, then looked up. The Catalina was still circling their position, signaling with the Aldis lamp.

"Damn!" Laura said.

Wardell turned. She was standing beside him, her expression angry.

"That plane cost me my marlin," she said fiercely. "Who in the hell does he think he is?"

"I don't know," Wardell said.

The boat's engines dropped off to a low rumble. The captain climbed down from the flying bridge.

The captain said to Wardell, "That was fast thinking. You saved my mate."

"And lost my fish," Laura said. "The sound of the airplane spooked him. Who is that up there?"

The captain replied, "He's signaling us back into Bimini."

"A storm coming up?" Wardell asked.

"No, sir," the captain replied. "It's a message for you, Senator. A Navy plane is waiting for you on the airstrip on Bimini."

"I should have known," Laura said. "What do they need him for this time?"

The captain shrugged. "All they told me was to head back in."

"We'll have to go," Wardell said. As the captain climbed back up to the bridge, he turned to Laura. "I'm sorry," he said. "I'll find out what this is all about the minute we dock."

She kept her eyes down for a moment. Then she sighed, "I'm sorry, David. I know it's not your fault. But everything was going so perfectly for a change. And now . . ."

Her voice trailed off. He pulled her close to him, and kissed her.

The trip back in to the dock took nearly two hours. Laura and Wardell spent most of the trip sitting in silence on the deck, staring off at the horizon. Wardell could feel the old tension setting in the closer they got to Bimini.

By the time they tied up, Wardell was angry, too. He jumped down on the dock. A Navy lieutenant was waiting for him.

"What's this all about?" Wardell demanded.

"Sorry, sir," the lieutenant said. He handed Wardell an envelope. "Message from Washington."

Wardell turned and ripped the envelope. Inside was

a decoded cable:

SOVIETS BLOCKADED BERLIN THIS A.M.
18 JUNE 1947. REQUEST RETURN TO
WASHINGTON IMMEDIATELY. WE NEED
YOU, DAVID.

H.S.T.

"What is it, David?"

Wardell handed the cable to Laura.

She read it twice. Then she asked, "What does this mean?"

"We've been expecting the Russians to make a grab for all of Berlin. I guess this is it."

"What do they need you for?" Laura asked. "Isn't this a problem for Marshall and the others in the State Department?"

"I assume they want to discuss military and intelligence options," Wardell said.

"Oh, no," Laura said with great concern. "David, this is not an excuse for war. Nothing is."

"I didn't say anything about war," Wardell said. "But you know as well as I do that in a crisis, it's wise to get as many opinions as possible. I can assure you I'm going to recommend negotiation. Then I'm going to get back here as quickly as I can. It's Friday now—we'll reserve the boat for Sunday."

"I don't know," she said in a low voice. Then she added, "I'll go back with you."

He shook his head. "There's no reason for your vacation to be interrupted. I haven't seen you this relaxed since I've known you. You can sit here in the sun and sip those fancy rum drinks. I'll be back before you know it."

She was silent for a moment. Then she said, "All right."

He kissed her. "Don't worry. I'll try to do what's right. Trust me."

II

BERLIN

NINE

The streets of Berlin were crowded. The tension in the city, already high, had been exasperated by a large communist demonstration in front of American military headquarters.

John Sage waited patiently in a café, drinking coffee until the crowd had finally melted away into the night. When he entered the imposing headquarters building, he used a rear entrance. The lone guard didn't recognize him. Sage stood by until he made a telephone call.

An aide appeared shortly to escort him to Colonel Wheeler's office. Sage entered, nodded to the colonel, and sat. Then he saw there was another man in the room.

Colonel Wheeler gestured to the man, asking, "John, have you ever met Lieutenant Richie?"

"No," Sage replied.

Wheeler said, "The lieutenant has a story to tell you. I thought it was worth your time to listen."

"That's good enough for me," Sage said. He turned to look at the lieutenant. Richie was a tall, lean man in his mid-twenties. He had dark hair, dark eyes, and a businesslike manner. He was dressed in civilian clothes.

"Does the name Rudi Fraenkl mean anything to you, sir?" Richie asked Sage.

"No," Sage said. "Should it?"

"He knows you," Richie said. "Or, rather, of you."

Sage lit a cigarette. Then he asked, "What does this man look like?"

"He's a small man, about fifty, wiry, dark mustache. He wears a belted black raincoat, even in warm weather. He hangs out with the pimps and black-market types, around the Am Zoo, the Rollenhagen Stube, some of those dives along the Ku-Damm."

Sage leaned back, taking a thoughtful drag on his acrid-smelling Turkish cigarette. He shook his head. "That description could fit a lot of people. What does this have to do with me?"

Richie replied, "We first picked Fraenkl up around the Reichschancellery months ago. He was trafficking in penicillin. But we turned him loose, because he made himself useful. I buy information from him, troop movements and personnel changes in the Russian Zone. We're certain, of course, that he's got a two-way business going, selling the Russkies bits of information about us. A true postwar German entrepreneur—he'll sell you cigarettes, medicine, his sister."

Richie paused for a moment. Sage's eyes were fixed on his face.

He cleared his throat and continued. "Two nights back Fraenkl called me. I hadn't seen him for weeks. I met him at a *Nachtlokal* near the Russian Zone. He told me a peculiar story, claiming he could set up a

114

secret rendezvous with a high-ranking Russian officer who had information to sell. He does not know the officer's name. Only that he wanted to make a connection with an American—someone named Jason Tulley. I didn't know who this Tulley was, and I suggested alternatives. Fraenkl insisted that Tulley was the only man the Russian would talk to."

"What else did Fraenkl say? What other proof is there that this is a real contact?"

"He wouldn't say anything else. He insists on talking to Tulley personally."

Sage studied his cigarette for a second. Then he said, "Thank you, Lieutenant. If you don't mind, I'd like to talk to Colonel Wheeler alone."

Richie stood, saluted, and left the room.

"Well, John," Wheeler said. "What do you think?"

"It's probably nothing. I wouldn't bother, if it weren't for the name Tulley."

"And this goddamn blockade," Wheeler said. "We need all the information we can get about what in the hell the Russians are up to. I half expect to see tanks rolling out of their zone tomorrow."

Sage shrugged. "We'll see." He got to his feet, then said, "Ned, have Richie set up a meeting with Fraenkl. But not in the Kurfürstendamm or anywhere near the Brandenburg area. Somewhere away from the Russians, northwest Berlin. Near the Saatwinklerdamm. Let me know the place by tomorrow morning. I'll meet with this Fraenkl tomorrow night."

"Security?" Wheeler asked.

"I'll take care of that, Ned," Sage said. "But have Richie there. He knows Fraenkl. And he seems to have a head on his shoulders."

Wardell's Navy plane had mechanical problems. Wardell spent four hours on the ground in Pensacola, Florida before continuing on to Washington.

He'd missed the evening meeting at the White House. Instead, the limousine took him to the Pentagon. A young captain escorted him through the darkened corridors to the office of the secretary of defense.

James Forrestal, the first man to hold the newly created cabinet position, was sitting in an armchair, sipping coffee while he read a long memorandum. When Wardell entered, he set down the coffee and came forward to greet him.

Wardell spoke first. "I'm sorry to keep you here so late, Jim."

"It's not you, David. It's our friend Stalin." He looked over Wardell's shoulder at the captain. "Son, please get the senator some coffee."

The officer saluted and left the office. As they walked toward the chairs, Forrestal said, "I hope Laura wasn't too upset at our calling you away like this."

"She wasn't pleased," Wardell said. "She knows my responsibilities, of course. But considering our schedules, it's so damned difficult to find a time when we can both get away. My flying up to Washington for a couple of days wasn't in the plans."

"This situation wasn't in our plans either," Forrestal said. "And I'm afraid the president has a request for you that's going to put a bigger dent in your vacation."

Wardell grimaced. "I don't know, Jim. I—"

"Let me brief you first," the secretary said. "Then you decide. Fair enough?"

Wardell sat. "That's what I came up here for."

A Filipino steward brought a tray with coffee and sandwiches. When he'd left the room, Forrestal began.

"I know that you've been briefed previously on the increasing number of travel restrictions the Russians have been imposing since April. It's all part of their not very veiled plan to include Berlin in the East German state. A few days ago, as part of that plan, they introduced currency reform into East Germany. The main purpose was to make their new ostmark the sole currency in Berlin. Yesterday the Allies countered with the announcement of the First Currency Reform Act, which establishes a West Germany currency. The currency reform act was a clear signal that the British, the French, and we Americans are determined to see that a strong West German nation survives."

"And the Russians don't like that idea."

"Not a bit," the secretary said. "Ostensibly, cutting off access to Berlin was to prevent the new tainted currency from polluting the East German economy. But in reality it's the power play many of us have expected for a long time. Marshal Sokolovsky, the Soviet military governor, said as much this morning in an announcement that clearly included all of Berlin as part of the Soviet occupied zone."

Wardell's face was somber. "We set the stage for this when we failed to include an airtight legal clause guaranteeing access to Berlin in the German occupation agreement during the war."

"I don't know if that would have helped," Forrestal said. "Who's going to enforce the law? The plain truth

117

is that the Soviets are grabbing for Berlin just as they did with Czechoslovakia in February."

"So what action is the president considering?" Wardell asked.

Forrestal scowled. "We're not in a good position, David. Our conventional forces are matchsticks compared to the troops the Soviet Union has available. There was such a goddamned uproar after the war about getting our boys out of uniform that we denuded the Army. Our total ground reserves are now slightly over two divisions, only one of which could be mobilized with any speed. The Russians have twenty divisions within two weeks' travel of the demarcation line."

Wardell thought for a few moments. Then he asked, "We must have other alternatives?"

Forrestal replied, "We discussed four at the White House earlier this evening. One, we can present the situation to the United Nations. The problem there is the Russians are certain to veto any meaningful resolution. We'll probably introduce the subject for propaganda purposes, but it's like spitting in the wind."

"I agree," Wardell said.

"Two, we can send an armed convoy down the autobahn to try to break the blockade. But if the Russians attack, we'll be up a creek without a paddle. We don't have the manpower to fight."

That thought distressed Wardell. Then he asked, "Number three?"

"Airlifting supplies to Berlin. That will keep the city functioning, at least temporarily, while we attempt to negotiate."

"That sounds reasonable," Wardell commented.

"It's a hell of a logistic problem," Forrestal said. "There're over two million people in Berlin. Just to get enough fuel—coal or oil—is a monumental task, much less food, clothing, and the multitude of other supplies. But we're probably going to give it a try."

"I agree," Wardell said. Then he asked, "You mentioned a fourth option?"

Forrestal took a deep breath. "I almost hate to bring it up, because I believe it's what got us into this situation in the first place. The bomb."

"What do you mean?"

"The reason we've stripped away our ground forces is that so many of your colleagues in the Congress seem to believe that we can stop the Russians simply by threatening to use the atomic bomb. Well, I don't think our friend Stalin is very susceptible to saber rattling. At least he hasn't been, up to now. If we threaten to drop the bomb, we'd better mean it. In my mind—in the mind of every rational man—we're nowhere near the stage yet where that drastic a response is called for."

Wardell looked away. Suddenly, Operation Scalpel jumped into his mind. Even Forrestal didn't know about the very secret contingency plan.

But it wasn't time to bring it up now. Wardell agreed with the Secretary of Defense. This blockade could be lifted in a week, for all they knew.

Wardell discussed his reactions with Forrestal. Then he asked, "So what is the request the president wants to make of me?"

The Secretary leaned forward. "David, we're going to need a hell of a lot of support in the Congress whatever way this crisis moves. An airlift is going to require a massive amount of money and the shifting of men and equipment. At the same time, the president, the Joint Chiefs, and I all feel we have to move as quickly as possible to beef up our ground forces in Germany, in case the military alternative is forced upon us. Considering the mood of the country and the recent voting patterns of the Congress, we're going to have to do a hell of a job of persuasion."

"You are," Wardell said.

"That's why we need your help, David. The president would like you to fly to Europe immediately. We'd like to review the situation in Berlin firsthand with General Clay. Then we'd like you to inspect our ground forces, and talk with the leaders of West Germany, France, Britain, and our other allies. Your stature is such that your colleagues are much more likely to be swayed by your report than by all the briefings from the administration—especially since this is an election year. It would be tragic if our hands were tied by accusations that Truman is making too much of this crisis just to help his reelection campaign."

"I see the problem," Wardell said. He lit another cigarette, then leaned back, thinking. There was no doubt in his mind that the president's approach was absolutely correct. Wardell had to review the situation firsthand in order to fight the certain battle in the Congress. Beyond that, Wardell wanted to go, wanted to inspect the situation for himself should certain monumental decisions face him in the weeks and months ahead.

But there was Laura. It was precisely these kinds of situations that were tearing their marriage apart. No matter how much people loved each other, they had to spend time together nurturing the relationship. It was sort of like planting a garden—no matter how carefully you prepared the soil and planted, nothing would grow if you didn't constantly water and weed and prune.

He and Laura had been brought closer by that first week together. But they had a lot more talking to do. God only knew what effect this interruption would have.

Forrestal broke into his meditation. "What do you say David? I told the president I'd call him tonight."

Wardell exhaled. Suddenly, he was tense. He sighed again, then said, "I have no choice, Jim. I have to go."

Laura sat by herself, in a far corner of the terrace of the small hotel. The time was shortly after noon, but she'd given in to temptation and ordered a third rum and coke.

David's call had come early this morning, and she'd been filled with resentment ever since. Rationally, of course, she knew she couldn't blame him—no one took the responsibilities of office more seriously than she did, and she knew that his position required such a trip in a crisis. Emotionally, however, the situation once again reminded her of the deep fundamental philosophical difference between them.

She should have known two and a half years ago at Hiroshima. That trip to postwar Japan had been the most profoundly shocking experience of her life. Not the attack by the madman—that could happen anywhere. Rather, it was the vision of that blasted landscape, like a vision of the dark side of the moon.

The most appalling thing was that the destruction was caused by man. Supposedly sane, rational, responsible men had sat together and calmly made the decision to murder two hundred thousand people in the most awful possible way.

Men had been making those kinds of decisions since the dawn of civilization. History was a tapestry of the most hideous wars and destruction. But as weaponry became more sophisticated, the capacity of one man or a few men to wreak havoc on others increased. Now, in the atomic age, the end of civilization could result.

Laura was convinced that a profound change in attitude had to take place throughout the world. The vast majority of the public who'd given power to the men who ruled them would have to raise their collective voices to shout, "Stop. We will not accept war as an alternative ever again."

The mildest reaction Laura received from her colleagues to that statement was a bemused grin. Other reactions ranged from "crazy" to "traitorous." Laura didn't care. The people she talked to on her travels, the people she met in parks and department stores and PTA meetings—they listened.

David was one of the people who didn't listen. Not that she considered him a warmonger. He did pay her the courtesy of hearing her arguments fully and without interruption. Laura knew that David hated the thought of another war and would work to prevent one.

But deep down he accepted the possibility. Indeed, in his position as head of the Armed Services Committee and policy advisor to a Democratic president, most of his working hours were devoted to preparing for that eventuality. And no matter what Laura said he couldn't see that such preparation was a self-fulfilling activity.

Arms would build to a critical point, like the mass in an atomic pile, then war would suddenly break out.

Laura knew she loved her husband as she'd never loved another man. But more important was the future of mankind. That they'd drifted apart emotionally was half her fault. She'd hoped that this vacation would bring them back together so that she could begin anew to win him over.

Then this crisis came. Now she was discouraged about ever succeeding with David. After this another problem would arise, and a third, ad infinitum.

"Can a fellow buy a lady a drink?"

The voice startled Laura. "What?"

"You look like you're a million miles away."

Laura looked up. It took her a minute to recognize Carl Waldman. "Why . . . how did you get here?"

Waldman said, "I was out on a fishing charter. When we got back the other night another captain happened to mention that the Wardells had chartered his boat. Where is the senator?"

"He had to go back to Washington."

"Berlin?"

Laura nodded.

Waldman shook his head. Then he asked, "Mind if I sit down?"

"Of course not," she said.

Waldman pulled out the chair and sat. He was a tall, lanky, sandy-haired man with fair skin and bright blue eyes that always seemed to have a hint of amusement in them. Those eyes were so compelling that many people didn't notice right away that he was missing his right arm.

Waldman had lost the arm in a kamikaze attack

during the war. Before he'd been drafted, he'd been a reporter for the *Washington Post*. His experiences during the war had radicalized him. He now worked as a speech writer for Henry Wallace, and was a regular contributor to several small leftwing publications.

Laura and Waldman had previously found out that they shared many of the same opinions about disarmament and other military issues. Even David Wardell, although he disagreed with Waldman's beliefs, respected his intellect.

"How about another drink?" Waldman asked.

"I shouldn't," Laura said. "I've probably had too many already. I'm afraid I'm upset about our vacation being ruined."

"If you've had too many, one more won't hurt," Waldman said. He motioned to the waiter. Then he added, "This Berlin situation seems very serious."

"I don't really know the facts," Laura said. "It's hard to get information down here."

"I'm not fully informed on the details of what caused this confrontation. But I know that the Russians are very worried about a strong German state."

Laura said, "And we're worried about the communists seizing power."

"Communists," Waldman scoffed. "That label. It's nations, not political parties, that cause wars. And Germany caused unprecedented suffering."

"Does that mean the Russians are allowed to dominate independent nations?" Laura asked. "We suffered, too."

"The US lost four hundred thousand soldiers. Twenty million Russians died."

Laura's face went white at the thought.

124

"I'm sorry," Waldman said. "I didn't mean to plunge into this on a beautiful day. I'm just worried that the warmongers are going to use this as an excuse to rant about their beloved bomb."

"I am, too," Laura said. "I can't stop thinking about it. I'm afraid David's tiring of hearing about it."

"Your husband is a man who gives me some hope. I think he listens to reason. I'd like to talk to you more about the subject. But not here."

Waldman stopped as the waitress arrived. He hoisted his glass then toasted, "To vacations."

Laura touched his glass and took a sip. "I'm afraid mine is nearly over. As long as David's out of Washington, I might as well put the time to good use. I'm going back to Iowa for some campaigning."

"What about tonight? Dinner?"

Laura hesitated.

"Come on," Waldman said. "I promise I won't lay a hand on you." He paused, then said with a smile, "I can't risk the only one I have."

Laura laughed. "All right. But I'm afraid the heat is getting to me. I'm going back to my room for a siesta."

"Eight o'clock, then? Here?"

She nodded.

Waldman watched her walk across the terrace. The smile on his face was now a look of intense reflection.

She was an important woman to him, he thought. And she could be far more important in the days ahead.

TEN

The balmy tropical breeze was scented with hyacinth and jasmine. They had cocktails on the hotel terrace as the sun, bathing the palm trees in blood-red shadows, was going down. Then the red ball dissolved in the still, blue sea, and the sky was black and full of stars.

Laura didn't want to move. So they sat while lanterns were lit; then they dined on fish so fresh it seemed to have leaped from the sea to their plates. After, they lingered over fruit and snifters of Armagnac.

All the time, Laura talked. She felt a wonderful freedom, as if she'd suddenly been released from years of solitary confinement. In her everyday life, her colleagues and constituents, lobbyists, reporters, even her husband, all wanted to convince her of something. Carl Waldman just sat for hours, listening, nodding agreement, looking steadfastly at her with his intense, magnetic blue eyes.

The waiters began moving about the terrace, lifting chairs onto tables in preparation for closing. Suddenly self-conscious, Laura said, "I'm sorry. You shouldn't have let me ramble on like this."

He smiled. "I enjoyed it. There are so few people in Washington I can say that about. We all need somebody we can talk to freely."

"Yes," she said. She lifted her hand to her face. It was dry, but she felt flushed and warm. It was probably the cocktails and the wine and the brandy. But she felt intoxicated by something else, too.

"Your husband," Waldman asked. "Who does he confide in?"

"Not me," she said. "Not really. The poor man, so much burdensome secret information."

"That much?"

"All that CIA information. He has to be so careful with his phone calls, and shredding notepaper in his office. It's so bizarre."

Waldman sat, thoughtful for a moment. "I didn't know he was the Senate liaison with the CIA. A major responsibility." He paused, then asked, "Is there anyone he's close to?"

"I can't think of anyone, really," she said. "His brother, before he died in the war. But that's . . . I forgot. Mack Dolan."

He leaned forward with interest. "General Dolan?"

She nodded. "They huddle together for hours in the den. I don't know why they can't get together in David's office. I don't like the man at all. He practically ignores me."

"Hmmm," he said.

They sat in silence. Then a waiter came up and stood patiently just behind them.

Laura said, "I think we'd better go."

They rose. The moon had come out, bathing the hotel in a soft light. He took her right hand in his left.

The lobby was deserted. They climbed the stairs. Her room was at the end of the corridor.

She unlocked the door, then turned to face him. "Thank you for a wonderful evening, Carl. I—"

He pulled her to him and kissed her.

For an instant she was stunned. Then she began to struggle. But his one arm was like iron, holding her close.

Finally, his lips left hers. "No," she stammered. "This isn't right."

He kissed her again, holding her so tightly she could barely breathe. She started to pull away. But a heat was rising within her. As her chest heaved, her nipples rubbed against him, sending shivers up and down her spine. She felt his hardness, and her hand moved downward toward it, as if it had a life of its own.

Then they were in her room, in the darkness. She was on her back, her skirt thrown back. His lips were on her, moving up her legs. Her whole body vibrated, and she was breathing hard, expelling air in gasps. Her mind tried to tell her this was all wrong, but from somewhere else in the depths of her body came another far stronger animal desire that seemed to sever the connection between her brain and the regions below.

She felt her panties moving down her legs. Then, for what seemed like an eternity, the only sensation was his hot breath on her, tingling her pubic hairs, caressing her inner regions in a way she'd never felt before.

She couldn't stay still. She began moving her legs back and forth, gently squeezing his head between her soft thighs. As she did so his tongue flicked out, licking gently. Waves of intense pleasure began rippling through her, and now she found moans escaping her lips. "Please," she cried. "Please."

His mouth was on her. Her moans became sharp cries. She reached down and put both hands on the back of his head, pulling him into her. She rocked back and forth on the bed, shuddering with pleasure. She took in a giant gulp of air and held it as she got closer and closer and closer.

Then she climaxed, exhaling air and sound in one loud, exquisite cry. She lay back, her body totally drained, arms at her side as she tried to get her breath back.

Suddenly, his weight was on her, his lips on hers. Before she could react she felt him in her, hard and deep. Once more she began to move, rocking with him as her passion mounted again.

At first, the sound was like an echo in the back of her mind. Gradually, Laura realized it was the phone. She turned and crawled across the bed toward it, feeling as if she were swimming through viscous air.

A woman's voice informed her it was seven A.M. She grunted, replaced the receiver, and lay back.

What had happened to her? Suddenly, a mass of disjointed memories of the night before tumbled about in her mind. She sat up, looking around.

The room was empty. There was no trace of him. Had it been a dream?

Then her body suddenly felt warm. She knew that it had really happened. She'd been unfaithful to her husband. How could she have done that?

There were reasons, of course. Her resentment at his sudden absence, the tropical night, the liquor. And Carl. He had practically taken her, as if . . .

No, she told herself suddenly. She couldn't blame him. It was her fault.

She reached over and took her watch off the bedside table. She had less than a half hour to dress and pack before she had to leave to catch the plane. With a sigh, she forced herself to get out of bed. As she stepped into the shower, her one thought was a wish that Carl Waldman would not be on the same flight. She never wanted to see him again.

John Sage sat in a dark corner of a coffee bar on the first floor of a *Gasthaus* in the Saatwinklerdamm, near the canal. Lieutenant Richie sat across the way, smoking a cigarette. Outside, three of Sage's men covered the darkened street, waiting for the appearance of the battered prewar Opel Rudy Fraenkl used to deliver his women and his black-market goods.

Finally, the car drove into the light of the street lamp. A figure climbed from behind the steering wheel, crossed the street, and entered the café. Sage saw that Richie's description of the man had been accurate, down to the sharp chopping stride and fluttering eyes. The man even walks with a German accent, Sage thought.

Fraenkl approached Richie, who nodded toward Sage's table. The German walked over. He moistened his lips before he spoke.

"Bitte," he said. *"Herr Tulley?"*

"Sit," Sage replied in German. He motioned to the

waitress, who brought two steins of beer.

Fraenkl tested the beer, his eyes on Sage.

Sage finally said, "Tell me your story."

Fraenkl moistened his lips again. "It was a small matter. There was a dispute with a customer over a woman. Nothing, really. The Russian military police came by. Such things have happened before, they pay little attention. But this time they arrested me."

He shook his head grimly at the memory, then drank more beer before continuing. "Two days they held me without interrogation. Then they bring me to the Falkenberger Strasse, you know. I am alone, locked in a cell. And all for nothing."

He looked over at Sage, as if expecting a sympathetic response. The American was looking at him impassively.

Fraenkl dropped his eyes and moistened his lips. "Finally, a Russian officer came into my cell. I think he was an officer—he acted like one—but his uniform bore no insignia. The Russian ordered the guard to lock the cell behind him and go back to his post at the far end of the corridor. For the longest time he sat inspecting me as if I was a piece of meat.

"Then he spoke. He said he knew I had contacts with American intelligence agents. My heart leaped to my throat. Then he told me he wanted me to go to the Americans and arrange a meeting with a man named Jason Tulley. He told me if I agreed to arrange this meeting, he would have me released immediately. If I said no, if I tried to tell anyone else this conversation took place, he would have me shot."

Fraenkl took a sip of beer. "I believed him. He was that type of man."

131

"What did he look like?"

Fraenkl shrugged. "Like a Russian officer. Bigger than you, heavier. Dark hair. More than that, I cannot say. The cell was poorly lit, and I was frightened. All I wanted to do was get out of there, so I agreed."

"How do I meet him?"

Fraenkl replied. "First I must be sure you are Tulley. The Russian told me to be careful to . . ."

Sage reached across the table and grabbed the German's wrist. He applied viselike pressure. "There's a state of war in Berlin now, Fraenkl," Sage said. "There's no need for vermin like you unless you're useful to us. Do you understand?"

The German's eyes had practically disappeared into his skull. He started to reply, but the words were stuck in his dry throat. He nodded vigorously.

Sage maintained his grip a moment longer. Then he released him and sat back. "How do I meet this man?"

"There is a bombed-out house in the Friesenstrasse, just inside the Russian zone. He drove me there to release me. If I park my automobile at a certain corner tomorrow, he will be there an hour after midnight tomorrow night."

"I want to meet in the American zone," Sage said.

"I don't know how to reach him. I don't know who he is. I don't think he would—"

"Enough," Sage said in disgust at the German's rambling. He leaned back and lit a cigarette, thinking. Then he asked, "You sure you don't know this Russian's rank?"

"No," Fraenkl said. "But it must be high. The way he acted, the way the guards responded when he spoke."

Sage sat back thinking again. Falkenberger Strasse

was the Russian intelligence headquarters. Using a scum like Fraenkl was an unusual way for a high-level officer to make contact.

Then again, these were unusual times. With the onset of the blockade many of Sage's sources had dried up. He was under heavy pressure from Washington to find out anything he could about the Soviet Union's plans.

Enough pressure to take the risk, he decided. Even the risk of entering the Russian zone.

Sage snuffed out his cigarette. He looked at Fraenkl and said, "I'll meet tomorrow night."

"Yes, sir," the German said.

"We'll leave from here. In your car. I want you here by eleven, so there's no rush. You understand?"

The German nodded. He started to rise.

"One last thing," Sage said in a low, hard tone. "I know we pay you for information. We're raising the price for this. If everything goes right, you live."

ELEVEN

The C-54 transport was routed through Frankfort to the Berlin air corridor. As the plane banked into the final landing pattern, Wardell looked out over the strange ruins of the city. He saw below the cemetery, a swath of green between two rows of new apartment houses. Then the cemetery gave way to concrete, and Wardell felt the wheels of the aircraft hit the runway.

The C-54 taxied to Tempelhof aerodrome. When the plane came to a stop and the engines were shut down, Wardell was surprised to hear the sound of a military band.

He walked to the open hatchway. Gen. Lucius Clay, military governor of the American zone of Germany, was waiting to greet him.

Wardell shook hands warmly. "What's this all about, Lucius?" he asked.

Clay replied, "Morale. You're a symbol that Washington hasn't forgotten about us. That's important now." He paused, then added with a smile, "Not that we don't consider you a VIP anyway, David."

"Thanks," Wardell said. "I appreciate the honor. And it's been awhile since I've reviewed troops. Let's get at it."

A half hour later, they were riding in the back of a buff-colored Chevrolet command car. Wardell said to Clay, "What's your view of the situation, Lucius?"

Clay's face was grim. "The president and the cabinet must realize that this is more than a cold-war ploy. If we back down here, Berlin will fall and then West Germany will fall."

"You mean by military action?"

"Yes," Clay replied. "They know our weakness in conventional forces as well as we do. I don't think they'll march tomorrow or the next day—starving us out is less costly politically as well as economically. But down the line I don't think we're going to negotiate our way out of this."

"What negotiations are going on right now?"

"Precious little. The Russians claim they closed the autobahn to repair an unsafe bridge over the Elbe river. I've tried to get a statement from Sokolovsky on how long the repairs are going to take, but I might as well be talking to myself. The Russians had previously stopped all rail and river traffic, so we're cut off."

"Except by air."

"Right," Clay said. "But the logistical problems involved in an airlift are astronomical."

"We've solved big problems before," Wardell said. "We'll solve this one."

They rode in silence for a few minutes. Then General Clay said, "You know, David, that a tenth of all the bombs we dropped on Germany during the entire war fell on Berlin. The level of destruction of the city as a whole was seventy percent. In the center of the city it was ninety-five percent. These people have suffered terribly."

"I realize that," Wardell said.

"That's why I believe we must take action immediately to end this blockade. We must demonstrate to the German people, and to the other countries in Europe, that we're prepared to meet the threat of communism head on."

Wardell turned to face Clay. "What do you recommend?"

"I want to send an armed convoy down the autobahn."

"But you said a few minutes ago you think that would bring Soviet military retaliation."

"It would. But the conflict would be brief if we had bombers ready to fly. Bombers with atomic weapons aboard."

Wardell suddenly had a hollow feeling in his stomach. Scalpel, he thought. He knew Clay wasn't one of the handful of men who had been briefed on the secret operation. He wondered if he'd found out about it anyway.

"That's a pretty serious suggestion, Lucius," Wardell said.

"The atomic bomb is our only advantage. But it isn't doing us a damn bit of good. Right now, I feel like we're playing baseball without a bat. Stalin doesn't take us seriously. He only will if there's a plane in the air over Russia with an armed nuclear bomb."

Wardell didn't respond for a moment. Ultimately, he knew Clay's suggestion might be the only answer. But not now.

"I'm sympathetic to what you're saying," Wardell said. "But the implications are so profound that we have to approach the situation carefully. Frankly, I don't think any major decisions are going to be made between now and the election in November. Truman is in enough trouble without having to deal with the additional label of warmonger. And I have a suspicion that Stalin is going to wait to see if Dewey is easier to deal with. Berlin might have to hold on until then."

Clay grimaced. "November is the limit. An airlift will be difficult enough in good weather. When winter comes, it will be a nightmare. Not to mention the vastly increased need for fuel."

Wardell knew Clay was right. He looked out the window as they passed row after row of apartment buildings. Each one of them would use a planeload of coal during the long winter.

The car turned a corner. Clay said, "We'll be at my headquarters shortly. I've got a map that—"

The pavement twenty meters in front of the command car erupted. Four MP's on motorcycles leading the command car were hurled into the air by the ball of flame and debris. Shattered glass raked Wardell and Clay. Wardell grabbed for his face as the command car skidded. He dimly heard automatic weapons fire and he instinctively ducked for cover. Then his head slammed against the car door and he blacked out.

John Sage stood on the sidewalk outside the café. Beside him, a nervous Lieutenant Richie lit another cigarette.

Finally, Richie said, "Sir, do you really think you

137

should go? After the attempt on General Clay and Senator Wardell, the Russians could—"

"I don't think there's any more danger," Sage said calmly. "If the KGB wanted to kill Clay and Wardell, they'd be dead. My guess is that one of the Communist-oriented labor groups that have been conducting the demonstrations in the Western zones is responsible. Whoever had his finger on the command detonator got too jumpy and pressed the button too soon."

"Thank God for that," Richie said.

Sage didn't reply. He continued to stare down the road.

They heard the decrepit Opel before they saw it. Then the car came into the dim light of the street lamp and pulled to a halt.

Fraenkl started to get out.

"Don't bother," Sage said.

He opened the passenger door. Richie crawled into the tiny back seat. Sage got in front.

Fraenkl said nervously, "You must go alone. The instructions were—"

"Drive," Sage ordered. "Let me do the worrying."

The German stared at him.

"Drive."

Fraenkl put the car into gear.

The car reeked of cheap perfume and cheaper cigars, and engine fumes poured in through holes in the floorboard. Sage opened the window for fresh air. Then it started to rain.

The windshield wipers didn't work on the driver's side. Fraenkl craned his neck to the right as he navigated through a maze of broken roads. Finally, they neared the boundary of the Russian zone.

Fraenkl stopped the car on a rubble-strewn side street. "The Russian sector is fifty meters ahead. There is concertina wire across the road, but a section has been pushed together at the left-hand side. Go another hundred meters to a cross street. The third building on the left-hand side is the one you want."

Sage nodded without looking at the German.

Fraenkl struck a match to check his watch. "It's nearly midnight," he said. "You must go."

"I'm waiting," Sage said.

"But . . ."

The look on Sage's face cut off the German's protest.

Ten minutes passed, then fifteen. The rain intensified, drumming incessantly on the thin roof of the small car. The air inside was thick with the smoke of cigarettes.

Sage opened the car door. The warm damp air smelled sweet. He turned to the back seat and said to Richie, "You stay here in the car. If I'm not back in exactly one hour, you shoot Fraenkl."

"No!" the German protested. "I haven't done anything but what you asked."

"Then you've got nothing to worry about," Sage said.

"Do I come after you if you don't appear?" Richie asked.

"No," Sage replied. "Report back to Colonel Wheeler. There'll be others to handle the Russian zone."

"Who?" Richie asked.

Sage slammed the door shut without answering. He reached under his raincoat to adjust the automatic pistol in its holster. Then he turned up his collar against the rain and moved down the street.

The area had been totally destroyed in the wartime bombing and as yet no reconstruction had taken place. There were no streetlights and the darkness was total. The pavement was pockmarked by bomb craters and strewn with rubble vomited from the gutted buildings. Sage had to pick his way carefully, and he was soon thoroughly soaked.

He was almost on the roll of concertina wire before he saw it. The gap Fraenkl had mentioned was narrow, and Sage had to flatten himself sideways against the wall. His coat caught on a barb, then ripped as he pulled himself free.

He was in the Soviet sector. He moved more carefully now, straining to hear through the sound of the rain. He stopped ten meters from the crossroad, waited a couple minutes, then dashed across the intersection. He saw no traffic.

The top floors of the third building on the left had caved in. But the rubble had been partially cleared in front of the gaping opening where the doorway had been.

Sage stood still. All he heard was the sound of water running, a rivulet of rain draining into some subterranean opening.

Sage drew his pistol. He cautiously stepped into the blackness of the bombed-out building.

He'd traveled a dozen steps when he was suddenly blinded by a tight beam of light shining directly into his eyes. He clicked off the safety of his pistol.

Then the light clicked off. A voice called out, "*Podidyeh, podidyeh*, Sage."

The voice was familiar. When a flame broke the

darkness, a match lighting a cigarette, Sage confirmed his guess.

"Penkovsky," he said.

The Russian lit a candle. He led the way down a flight of stairs to the cellar of the ruined building. He stood the candle upright in its own drippings on the lid of a ruined crate.

"My dacha in Berlin," Penkovsky said in a gesture toward the bleak, damp hole in the ground. "It's been a long time since I have entertained you, my friend."

"I'm not that entertained yet," Sage said. "I'm more confused. I'm wondering why a KGB general resorted to using a scum like Fraenkl to pass along a message. Not to mention what he's doing in a place like this to begin with."

"I could ask the same of you, my friend," Penkovsky said. "Your rank is roughly equivalent to mine. You're here for the same reason I am—our countries are at each other's throats, and once again war looms." He paused for a moment, then said, "We will talk of that soon. But first, for old times' sake, I brought a bottle of vodka. Let's drink to each other."

Sage's eyes had adjusted to the gloom, and he saw a bottle of vodka and two small glasses on a table to his right. Penkovsky filled the glasses, passed one to the American, and raised his.

"To all who fought against the Third Reich!"

They drank. Sage filled the glasses the second time, and toasted, "To peace."

Again they emptied the glasses. Penkovsky filled them a third time, but let the glasses stand on the table.

Penkovsky looked at Sage, his heavy face somber. "I don't know what has gotten into our politicians, my

141

friend. Twenty million of my countrymen slaughtered in war, our country ravaged, our people starving. And that madman in the Kremlin cannot resist risking millions more deaths."

Sage didn't reply for a moment. He studied the Russian, then asked, "What do you want from us? Are you considering defecting?"

"Defecting? No, I could never do that. I am a Russian and a proud man. But I do want to prevent a war between our two countries. If war comes now, you will drop those atomic bombs of yours. Or if you back down, we will have our bombs ready and that monster Stalin will use them. I guarantee you, he will."

"I agree with you, Igor," Sage said. "In this kind of atmosphere, hotheads take over. Unfortunate things happen, like the bomb that almost killed General Clay and Senator Wardell today."

"We had nothing to do with that," Penkovsky said.

"I didn't think so," Sage replied. "I would like to see a lesson administered to the idiots who did."

Penkovsky thought for a moment. Then he said, "That is a reasonable sign of my good faith. My men are already looking for the culprits. I think something public, perhaps an unplanned detonation of explosives they're carrying in an automobile?"

"Fine," Sage said.

"Good. We will cooperate."

"What else will we cooperate on?" Sage asked. "I'm still not sure what you're doing here. We could have arranged the matter of the would-be assassins on a lower level."

Penkovsky picked up one of the full glasses and drained it. Then he said, "For now, my only purpose was to open a direct line of communication. Not just to you, but directly to your president. There is every possibility that in such a major power confrontation as our blockade a sudden decision will be made by our premier that would have very drastic consequences. In order to prevent war, your president may have to act very quickly. I want to know that accurate intelligence will reach him directly and immediately."

"That's a tall order," Sage said. "I'm not sure I trust you, and it's going to be much more difficult to persuade Washington that a KGB general is suddenly becoming cooperative, especially under the circumstances."

"I anticipated that reaction," Penkovsky said. He unbuttoned his coat and produced a small manilla folder which he pushed across the table.

"I've brought a present for your government," he said. "This file folder contains the blueprints for our two newest fighter aircraft, the Yakolev 15 and the Mig 9. The Yak 15 is basically a Yak 3 airframe modified to take a Junkers Jump turbojet. The Mig 9 is a new all-metal, mid-wing monoplane powered by two BMW turbojets mounted side by side in the nose. The fuel is carried in the thin wing sections. The Mig 9 has a speed of five hundred sixty miles per hour and a top altitude of forty-two thousand feet. As you see, the technology we captured from the Germans has been put to good advantage."

Sage picked up the packet. "We have much of the information on those aircraft already," he said.

"I know precisely what you have," Penkovsky said. "My people arrested the agent who passed it on to you, and I personally ordered his execution. However, you don't have any reports on the operational tests of the aircraft, vital information for planning combat procedures. That is the proof of my good faith."

Sage pondered for a moment. Then he said, "This is a first step, Igor. I'll pass it along and we'll have to see how it's received."

"And you, my friend? What do you think?"

"I think I'll reserve judgment, too," Sage replied. "No offense intended."

"None taken," the Russian replied. "We will meet again soon. Time will prove what bond we shall establish. For now, let us drink vodka and talk about old times."

"I have to be out of the zone an hour after I left the car. Or our courier Fraenkl will be shot."

Penkovsky consulted his watch. "We have some time left. Besides, I'm not so sure that Fraenkl's usefulness hasn't come to an end. His future discretion may be in question, especially with his propensity to get himself into trouble."

"I'd already thought about that," Sage said. "I shouldn't have any trouble finding an excuse to have him detained for as long as we need."

Penkovsky's smile broadened. "A true professional. Now, let us toast again."

TWELVE

Wardell remembered more about that day than almost any in his life, even though it was seventeen years ago.

He'd had to leave for Tucson before dawn. As always, he woke without an alarm. He used the guest bathroom in the other ell of the huge ranch house so he wouldn't wake her. He dressed, made coffee, then wrote a note to his son.

Amanda was taking Charlie to the orthodontist that afternoon to be fitted with braces. A common childhood occurrence, but Wardell's ten-year-old son was resisting stubbornly. Wardell felt bad over having to be away and leaving Amanda to fight the battle. She was certainly up to it, but he had taken a few moments to try to help by explaining in writing to Charlie why he had to be a man and face necessities.

One of those unpleasant necessities had called Wardell away that day. Twice in the past week shots had been fired at his trucks hauling phosphates from a chemical company outside of Tucson. There'd been a lot of that in the early twenties when Wardell and his brother had set up their trucking operation. In those days Wardell had never gone anywhere without a revolver on his hip and a shotgun in his car.

Now the Depression was bringing out the cowboys again. It could be union trouble at the plant, a disgruntled ex-employee of Wardell trucking taking revenge, or a gypsy trucker or two looking to horn in on the business. Whatever it was, it would be dealt with immediately. That was Wardell's style, and it had served him well.

He'd finished the note as he saw the headlights of a car approaching the ranch house. He opened the front door to tell Johnny Blair, his driver, to wait. Then he walked back into his bedroom. Amanda was sleeping on her side, her dark hair over most of her face. He brushed a lock aside and touched his lips to her cheek. She stirred slightly, but didn't waken.

If he'd known what was going to happen that day, he'd have never left her side. Eleven hours later, after a frantic seventy-mile-an-hour dash back from Tucson, he was pacing frantically in a drab hospital waiting room. His wife's car had been swept off the road and down a steep embankment. Charlie had been thrown from the wreckage and killed instantly. Amanda had been pinned in the car when the gas tank exploded. A passing motorist had risked his life to pull her out, and she'd been brought to the hospital alive.

Barely alive. The doctors were working frantically, and Wardell got no news for an hour. When a doctor did come out, he was somber and brief. Amanda had suffered severe smoke inhalation and seventy percent of her body was covered with second and third degree burns. Her condition—"extremely critical."

Wardell had resigned himself to her dying. All he hoped for was to see her again once before she died. If she was conscious, he wanted to tell her . . . tell her what? His mind was choked with swirling emotions.

A nurse called him.

After the dimly lit waiting room, entering the intensive care unit was like walking into a sunspot. The bank of overhead lights blinded him. As he waited for his eyes to adjust, he had become aware of the slow, mechanical hiss of a respirator. The sound had been mournful, desperate, infinitely sad.

He had taken a deep breath to compose himself. Then he'd pulled aside the green curtain around the bed.

What he saw had pierced his heart like an arrow. He had involuntarily gasped, then stepped back.

Like the victim of a medieval torturer, Amanda had been spread-eagled on a steel-arched Stryker frame. Her body had been covered with ice bags in a desperate attempt to lower her body temperature. Wardell had averted his eyes, and they'd come to rest on a chart. He saw the latest temperature reading had been 104.2 degrees.

He'd forced himself to look at his wife again. Before he could bring himself to look at her face, he'd noticed that even the tips of her toes and fingers were charred and oozing.

Suddenly, the fingers of one of her hands had uncurled, reaching out to him. He'd stepped forward to lightly touch those fingers. They had closed around his.

Finally, Wardell had looked at Amanda's face. He'd shuddered. Her hair and eyebrows were gone. Every inch of her skin had been covered with a thick white cream. All he recognized were the dark eyes of the woman he had loved more than anyone on earth.

"Amanda," he'd said. "Amanda, I . . ." Emotion had choked off his voice. He had felt tears running down his cheeks.

She hadn't been able to speak. The respirator continued to hiss as it forced air slowly, insistently, into her dying body.

But she didn't have to talk. He'd been able to read her eyes. And he knew whatever he had to say was surely written on his face for her to see.

Then, with what he would see later as uncanny communication, he'd bent to kiss her. He breathed in a sweet-sour smell, like that of a dying orchard. His lips touched her eyelids.

Then they closed. He called for a nurse, who took a quick look and pressed a buzzer. Feet had pounded in the hallway and figures in white brushed by him.

He'd turned and walked woodenly away, knowing that she was gone.

"Senator?"

Wardell opened his eyes. A nurse was standing by his bed.

"Time for your medication," she said.

He slowly sat up. The movement sent sharp pains through his head. He winced, then let the nurse help him.

She handed him four pills and a small cup of water. He downed the pills, then sat with his eyes closed, fighting the headache as she took his blood pressure.

After she left the room, Wardell checked the watch on the table next to his hospital bed. A little after four in the afternoon. He was surprised to find he'd dozed since lunchtime.

The sleep helped. Wardell considered himself lucky to have escaped the assassination attempt with such relatively minor injuries—several cuts, bruises, and a pretty severe concussion that had knocked him out for nearly six hours. For the first twenty-four hours after that he'd been very uncomfortable, but now his headache was more tolerable. The doctors told him he'd be released after another forty-eight to seventy-two hours observation.

He couldn't read, however, so he had nothing to keep his mind from wandering. The sounds, the smells of the hospital constantly kept pulling his mind back to the death of his wife. He knew it was natural that those thoughts would occur, but they depressed him. Time passed very slowly if he wasn't sleeping. He'd asked for a radio, and he hoped that the embassy would send someone over to . . .

The door opened.

He turned his head too quickly and he closed his eyes against the pain. Then he heard, "David. Oh, David."

"Laura," he exclaimed.

She bent down to kiss him. He reached up and stroked her hair. She put her head on his shoulder. He could feel her crying.

"Hey," Wardell said. "I'm all right. Really, I am."

She pulled away to look at him. Her eyes were red. "I've been so worried," she said. "The first report said . . . said you and General Clay had been killed. I nearly went crazy until the White House called and said you were alive. The Air Force sent a car for me and got me on the first plane out to London. I've been traveling for nearly a day. I . . ."

He reached out, pulled her to him, and kissed her again. "Thank you," he said. "You don't know how happy I am to see you. It's been—"

"I can imagine," she said. Her face was white, and she nervously bit her lower lip. Then she added, "David, I felt so guilty. After that last day in Bimini. I was like a foolish, spoiled little girl, whining and moaning because I didn't have a playmate. And all the while you were here in Berlin risking your life. If you'd been killed, I don't think . . . I don't think I could have survived."

He squeezed her hand. "I think you could have. You're stronger than you think."

She wiped at her eyes with the corner of a handkerchief. "I used to think so. I used to think I had all the answers. Now I'm not so sure. Why can't I be like a normal woman, worrying about my kids and re-decorating the living room and the dance at the country club on the Fourth of July? Instead, I . . . we've got the weight of the world on our shoulders. Married couples are supposed to argue about taking out the garbage, not how to handle the atomic bomb."

"I know what you're saying," Wardell said. "That's the responsibility we assumed when we took office. Somebody has to represent those millions of other couples who don't want to have to think about life and death matters all the time."

"But why us?" she said, her voice high-pitched. "Maybe we've done our work. Maybe it's time we left Washington and became one of those couples."

Wardell didn't reply for a moment. He stroked her forearm. Finally, he said, "Maybe you're right."

"What?" she said in surprise. "David, do you mean that?"

"I'm going to tell you what I've been thinking about as I've been lying here in this hospital bed. Don't get upset, because it has a point. I've been thinking about Amanda and my son."

She didn't say anything. She looked into his eyes somberly.

He continued, "I haven't talked about them much. And I'm not about to now, I've dealt with it long ago. But the conclusion I've come to is that I want another son. Or a daughter. I owe it to myself, we owe it to ourselves. We've been fighting a long war. I think you're right. It is time we spent some of that money I've been accumulating all those years."

Her eyes filled with tears again. "Oh, David," she said. They embraced, holding each other tight.

They didn't speak for a long time. Then Wardell said, "Of course, we can't take off into the sunset right now. Especially not until this Berlin situation is resolved. And you're committed to this reelection campaign."

"That doesn't matter," she said. "The party can—"

"Hush," he said. "I've got a proposal. My term ends in 1950. You accept one more term. After the election, after this Berlin crisis eases, I'll resign from the Senate. That'll give the governor a chance to appoint someone to serve the last year or so of my term, and that will give a Democrat a head start on winning a six-year term in 1950. I'll get my business affairs in order and work on getting the ranch spruced up. And I'll have plenty of time to spend with you in Washington, before your term expires."

"It sounds wonderful," she said tentatively, "except, I don't know about . . . about the ranch."

"You mean, about living in Amanda's house? I think you'll love it. When I get back to the States, we'll get away for a few days and go out there. Just the two of us, alone. Deal?"

She smiled. "Deal. In fact, we can fly back when you're released from the hospital."

He grimaced. "I'm afraid not. This incident has delayed my trip, not canceled it. I've still got to go on to Rome, Paris, and London before I can go back. I've got two or three weeks, at least."

She started to protest, but she stopped herself. She looked down at her hands. "You have to do what you have to do," she said. "I'm happier than I ever imagined I could be, before I walked into this room. We'll have a wonderful life, David. I promise."

"I'm sure we will," he said. "In fact, I—"

"Mrs. Wardell, I'm afraid you have to leave."

Neither one of them had noticed the nurse enter the room. "Doctor's orders," she said.

"I'll be back in the morning." Laura got to her feet. "Now, I want to go in to pay a call on General Clay. How is he?"

"About the same as I am. Restless and bored. He'll be delighted to see you."

She bent and kissed him gently on the lips. "I love you. I'll always love you."

THIRTEEN

Wardell adjusted the volume of the radio. Then he sat back and resumed listening.

More than the eyes of the world are focused on Berlin. Yesterday the communists, Grotewohl and Pieck, following the model of Hitler and the example of Prague, tried to seize power in Berlin by terror. But they miscalculated. Berlin will remain free; it will never become communist.

The words of Berlin Social Democratic Party Chairman Franz Neumann were drowned out by the roar of the eighty thousand Berliners jammed into the soccer stadium. Neumann gave way to acting Berlin Mayor Louise Schroeder, and more thunderous applause could be heard over the radio.

Wardell turned to General Clay, "Lucius, that statement of yours yesterday that we would never allow the Soviet Union to take Berlin by force seems to have stiffened the heart of the Berliners."

Clay grunted. Then he said, "We had to try to put an end to those rumors that we were planning to pull out. It's incredible how fast a story spreads. Like the water shortage."

Wardell nodded. Two days previously housewives all over Berlin had rushed to fill every available container with water after a broadcast on Soviet radio had stated that the West Berlin water system was about to fail. Because of the rush the prediction almost came true. Then the American radio shrewdly urged Berliners to use all the water they wanted, explaining that there was plenty. The demand returned to normal.

More difficult to counter was a demonstration by a communist mob in front of city hall the day before. The demonstration became a riot, and Berlin city assembly-men had to sneak out of the building to meet elsewhere.

General Clay slowly got to his feet, moved across the office, and poured himself another drink. Ignoring the painful bruises and cuts from the bombing attack, he'd gotten out of bed after two days and flown to American headquarters in Heidelberg to plan the American reaction to the Russian blockade. He'd arrived back in Berlin on Friday, June 25. Wardell, who'd been released that morning, joined him at the embassy.

Clay returned to his chair. He asked Wardell, "You read Truman's official statement announcing the air-lift?"

"Yes," Wardell said. "And it was about time. Indecision would have cost us a lot."

Clay grimaced. "You mean the support of our valiant allies. I'll tell you, David, I expected the French to dance around like this—they've got problems with their own commies at home. But I expected the British

154

to have more backbone. I got wind of the report Brownjohn sent back to the Atlee government. Our deputy military governor practically said that we'd either have to reach a compromise with the Russians or get out of Berlin entirely. Now that Truman's acted, and now that the Berlin city government has taken a strong stand, the British are going to have to go along. At least for the time being."

"I hope that time frame will be as long as it takes to back the Soviets down," Wardell said. "That's why the president has asked me to go on to Paris and London. I've got a feeling I've got a lot of hard talking to do."

"I don't envy you," Clay said. Then he asked, "When are you leaving Berlin?"

"Tomorrow. I'm going to inspect air force bases at Lübeck, Celle, Fassberg, and maybe the British fields at Wunstorf and Schleswigland. I've got to be fully briefed on the details of the airlift before I go on to the French and British capitals."

"Before you leave," Clay said, "I wish you'd stop by to see Colonel Wheeler in my headquarters. Do you know him?"

"Ned Wheeler? Of course."

"There's something happening that could be very important to the future course of events in Berlin, something I'm uncomfortable about going through channels about. I'd like you to listen and judge for yourself if it ought to be brought to Truman's attention."

Wardell's interest was caught. "What is this?" he asked.

"I'll let Wheeler explain. When can you see him?"

"Why not now? Call him and tell him I'll be there

within an hour."

Wardell listened for nearly an hour. He asked a few questions, but Colonel Wheeler anticipated most of his queries, interrupting with asides.

Finally, Wardell said, "Ned, I've got a favor to ask you. Could you leave the two of us alone for a few minutes?"

Wheeler looked puzzled. But he said, "Certainly, Senator. Tell the guard outside the door if you need me again."

There was a heavy, tension-filled silence in the office. John Sage spoke first. "I've got the feeling that Hong Kong is more on your mind than Berlin, Senator. It's time we cleared the air."

"The air can't be cleared," Wardell replied. "Two and a half years later is far too late for an apology. Not that I'm sure I'd accept one."

"I'm not apologizing," Sage said. "If Scalpel had been carried out in the fall of 1945, we'd be talking in a free Berlin now. And we'd be looking eastward toward a free Czechoslovakia, a free Poland, a free Hungary, a free Rumania. Instead, we've let the Russians take the initiative in pushing us across the continent."

Wardell lit a cigarette. "Hindsight's always easier, Sage. Especially for people who don't have to bear the decision-making responsibility. And freedom's a funny word in the mouth of an American intelligence officer who's run covert operations against those elected officials."

"I may have gone too far, Senator," Sage said. "But that was a critical time. And you forget I saved your life at Hiroshima."

"Did you?" Wardell asked. "I've often wondered if that whole attack was another one of your stratagems. And what about this bomb which conveniently went off early enough to save General Clay and myself, but close enough to scare the shit out of us? Is this another attempt to get me behind the decision to implement Scalpel?"

Sage stiffened. He said angrily, "Those are accusations of attempted murder, Senator. If you believe that, bring me up on charges."

"Charges? Don't be ridiculous, Sage," Wardell scoffed. "How in the hell am I supposed to get any evidence? That's the problem with this cloak and dagger stuff."

"So now I'm a symbol of what's wrong with intelligence gathering?" Sage said.

Wardell leaned forward. "You know I have access to the CIA files. I know all about you, Sage. I've made it my business. And I also know your value. But I'll tell you that one of my long-term goals is to train enough new people so that we can boot you and others like you out of our service entirely."

They sat in silence again. Finally Sage asked, "Is that it, Senator? Is that why you wanted to talk with me alone?"

"No," Wardell said. "Remember, I'm not the one that brought up Hong Kong. For the time being, that isn't the issue. Rather, I'm trying to decide what to make of this Russian general who's suddenly decided to become a good citizen."

Wardell paused to light another cigarette. Then he said, "I'm not sure exactly how and why your relationship with this Russian began."

Sage replied, "If you've seen my file, you know what my job was in Moscow. I did set up a network to gather information about the Russians, but the Germans were our primary enemy. And we had to depend upon the Soviet government for logistical support for intelligence gathering and covert activities in the German occupied territories. Penkovsky was my primary KGB liaison. He arranged, among other things, for us to carry out interrogations in POW camps, to recruit Germans and other Eastern European nationals, and to insert individual agents and sabotage teams behind German lines."

"And you trusted him?" Wardell asked.

Sage's face was stern. "I don't trust anybody, Senator," he said. "If I did, I wouldn't be alive. All I can say is that my relationship with Penkovsky was productive. He's a very shrewd, capable intelligence officer, a giant step above most of the pompous morons that clog the upper ranks of the KGB."

Wardell thought for a moment.

"Do you think he's serious about defecting? Or is this a ploy?"

Sage sat forward in his chair. "I'll tell you what I think. I think Penkovsky's ass is on the line. He's so bright and he's risen so fast that he's made a lot of those other morons very nervous. I think he's in Berlin because his superiors want him out on a limb. If anything goes wrong with this blockade gamble, it's Penkovsky who'll be the sacrificial lamb."

"So?"

"So I think Penkovsky's evaluated the situation and decided there's an excellent chance that the Western

158

Allies won't back down. He's decided to make friends on the other side, just in case he's got to save his neck."

"If that's the case," Wardell said, "if he's just trying to ease his way for a defection, why go to all this trouble? Considering his rank, we'd welcome him with open arms if he simply walked into our headquarters. He'd be a treasure trove of intelligence information."

"True," Sage said. "But I think Penkovsky doesn't simply want to be on our side, I think he wants to be on the winning side. If a serious military confrontation takes place, Penkovsky wants to be able to tip the balance firmly in our direction. He'll have a lot less looking over his shoulder to do for the rest of his life if the Russians are humiliated and Stalin falls."

"I see," Wardell said. He leaned back, reflecting. Then he got to his feet.

"What are you going to tell the president?" Sage asked.

"I haven't decided to tell him anything," Wardell said. "I might wait until we hear from Penkovsky again."

"That might be too late," Sage said.

"I doubt it," Wardell said. "I think it'll be months before we come to the crunch point. And at that time, I might want to be more sure of where this Russian general really stands."

"And how do you do that?"

Wardell looked hard at Sage. "By meeting him myself."

Sage kept his eyes locked on Wardell's. "I can arrange that. Let me know."

"I will," Wardell said. "And in the meantime, let me give you a warning, Sage. If I get the slightest hint of any attempt to influence me, General Clay, or any other key military or government officials, I'll go to the director of the CIA and get you pulled. I don't care how many agents you're running. You understand?"

"I've always understood, Senator," Sage said. "And maybe some day you'll understand."

Laura Wardell was walking across the hotel lobby when she heard her name called out. She turned.

Carl Waldman was walking across the broad, carpeted room toward her. When he reached her, he bent and kissed her on the cheek. "It's good to see you," he said.

Laura felt her skin turn warm at his touch. She had tried hard to erase the memory of that night in Bimini.

"Carl," she said somewhat tentatively, "I didn't . . . I mean, I'm surprised to see you here."

"Where else would a concerned journalist be these days? I can't think of a more important story since V-J Day. What's happening in Berlin could change the future course of European government."

"I know," she said somberly .

The smile vanished from his face. He put his hand on her forearm. She resisted the urge to pull away. "I'm sorry," Waldman said. "Callous of me, not to remember the reason you're in Berlin. How's David?"

"Fortunately, he's fine. He was very lucky."

"Emotions are very high here," Waldman said. "I've spent two days talking with labor leaders, city officials, journalists. They're very afraid that the course our government is taking is going to lead to war."

"The course the U.S. is taking?" Laura said. "It was

the Soviet Union that caused this crisis."

"Was it? That's the position of Truman, General Clay, and those hardliners. But if you look past the physical fact of the blockade, you find some very disturbing facts about the way we've tried to manipulate the German currency and the German political parties toward our own ends. Many people think the Russians had to step in to prevent economic and political chaos."

"David doesn't believe that," Laura said.

"His information comes from those who don't want him to believe that. I'm not repeating to you just what Berlin communists and leftists are saying. The French and British governments have very serious doubts about Truman's hard line."

"I know," Laura said. "David is going on from here to Paris and London."

"And you?" Waldman asked.

"I have a reelection campaign, and a series of delayed hearings in my subcommittee to run. I'm stopping in London for two days; then I'm going back to the states."

Waldman smiled. "That's a coincidence. I'm going to London tomorrow myself."

A jolt of concern went through Laura. "Oh," she said.

Waldman moved closer to her. He put his hand on her elbow and said in a low voice, "Laura, I'm sorry for what happened between us. I had no right to force myself on you. I gave in to an overwhelming attraction, and I caught you at a vulnerable time. As far as I'm concerned, it's totally over. I mean that."

"Good," she said.

"I want to put that behind us for an important reason, Laura. We share similar opinions on a wide variety of very important issues. We've got to keep our lines of communication open. We don't have that many allies in these troubled times."

"No, we don't," Laura admitted.

Waldman dropped his hand from her arm. "One of those issues is the possible drastic overreaction to this Berlin crisis. Already I've heard rumors that Truman is going to send bombers and atomic warheads to Great Britain."

"I don't believe that," Laura said with concern.

"The U.S. has a lot of ways to put pressure on the British," Waldman said. "I think you owe it to yourself—and to your husband—to hear the whole story."

"How do I do that?"

"I'd like to introduce you to some people in London. There's going to be an informal conference the day after tomorrow. All it would cost you is a few afternoon hours."

The idea of seeing Carl in London, no matter what he'd said about their brief affair, was disturbing to Laura. But then she said to herself, that's ridiculous. David and she had never been closer, especially since he'd made the startling, wonderful decision to leave the Senate. If she was so weak that she couldn't be in the same city as an attractive man, she wasn't the woman she thought she was.

Waldman's mention of atomic weapons did raise a concern in her. With Truman in trouble politically, he was forced to keep up the image of a strong, anti-communist leader. Hiroshima never left Laura's mind, and she couldn't forget that it was Truman who had made the decision to drop the bomb there.

She thought for a moment, nervously biting her bottom lip. Then she said to Waldman, "Leave a message at my hotel. The Savoy. I'll get back to you as soon as I know what my schedule is."

Waldman pressed her hand. "Thank you, Laura. I know you'll be glad you met these people." He hesitated a moment, then asked, "I have another request. A favor. Perhaps when you and David are back in Washington, I could take you both out to dinner. I'd like a chance to talk with him about the situation. I'd like to give him my perspective."

"Of course," Laura said. "David is always willing to listen."

Waldman said seriously, "I hope so, Laura. There are a lot of men in Washington who aren't. And if they're allowed to have their way, we'll be looking at photographs of Atomic Domes from all over Europe."

FOURTEEN

As they strolled down the rue de Constantine, Wardell's glance was drawn to his right. He stopped. Beyond the landscaped lawns and rows of lime trees of the Esplanade des Invalides, the Eiffel Tower, back-lit by the descending sun, was a gleaming silver spear thrusting majestically upward into the reddening evening sky.

"Beautiful, *mais non*?" asked Wardell's companion.

"Yes," Wardell said. "I can't think of a more beautiful city in the world than Paris." He turned and looked at Henri Philaix, defense minister of de Gaulle's government. "I can imagine what it must have been like marching victoriously back into this city after so many years of war."

Philaix smiled. "*Oui*. But most of us, we had little time to enjoy ourselves. The threat from the communists, who had been the most organized of the resistance forces, was so very grave. We were barely able to obtain control of the government." He paused for a moment before adding, "Even now, there is the constant threat. The riots, demonstrations, speeches. So many problems."

"And now there is Berlin," Wardell said.

"Yes," Philaix said. He stopped walking.

They were near the huge Hôtel des Invalides. In front of them was the majestic façade, over six hundred feet long. At the center was a magnificent doorway, flanked at either end by pavilions. Decorations in the form of trophies surrounded the dormer windows and in the equestrian statue of Louis XIV, supported by Prudence and Justice, in the rounded arch above the entrance.

They took in the sight. Then Philaix commented, "It was through that doorway that the body of the Emperor Napoleon passed. It was 1840. After seven years of negotiation with the British, Louis Philippe was able to dispatch his son to collect the remains. After a long sea voyage from Saint Helena, the coffin was disembarked at Le Havre, then brought up the Seine to Paris. The funeral was December 15, and for that occasion the skies opened with a blinding snowstorm. Still, our countrymen turned out in throngs, standing silently, in great sadness, as the hearse passed beneath the Arc de Triomphe, down the Champs-Elysées, across the Place de la Concorde, to the Esplanade. And then the emperor's body was laid to rest, and along with it, the greatest glory of France."

The story moved Wardell. He could almost see the funeral procession in front of him now. Paris always affected him that way—it was a city of ghosts.

Philaix said to him, "Perhaps you wonder why I tell that story. The reason is that when we Frenchmen think of Russia, we first of all think of Napoleon and the futile attempt at conquest that was his downfall."

"I see," Wardell said. He considered this for a moment, then asked, "So this is the reason for your hesitancy to support the Berlin airlift?"

"You misunderstand me," Philaix said. "It is not that we are afraid to confront the Russians. There is no world leader as staunchly opposed to communism as de Gaulle, I can assure you. However, there are times when confrontation is not the best course of action. Stalin, like Hitler, like our Emperor Napoleon, dreams of conquest. We believe those dreams will bring him to ruin. The Russians can no more conquer Europe than Hitler or Napoleon could conquer Russia."

"I see what you mean," Wardell said. "That certainly may be true in the world of conventional warfare. But now, with the atomic bomb, the old limits may not hold."

"Ah, the bomb," Philaix said. They walked in silence again.

Then Wardell asked, "I assume my meeting with de Gaulle has been arranged as planned?"

"*Oui*," Philaix replied. "And I can tell you our government will not oppose your airlift, although for political reasons we will not provide logistical support. But I want to send a message to your president through you, my distinguished friend. Beward of the fate of Napoleon. Even with your bomb, you may find Mother Russia a burial ground for your ambitions. Beware."

For the first time in the six days since he'd left Berlin, Wardell had an evening free. He'd declined Philaix's offer of dinner and returned to his hotel.

166

The hectic pace of his trip had exhausted him, exacerbated as it was by the lingering effects of the injuries he'd suffered in the explosion. He ordered a bottle of bourbon and an ice bucket from room service; then he filled the huge bathtub and soaked for nearly an hour.

When he emerged from the bathroom, more relaxed than he'd been in days, the liquor had arrived. He poured a drink and settled down in a chair to read a packet of cables from Washington.

Everything he read confirmed his previous opinion that Truman's short-term goal was stabilizing the situation in Berlin so that he could concentrate on his reelection campaign. If the complex planning for the airlift could be completed in time to assure a steady supply to the besieged city for the rest of the summer and fall, the U.S. would be content to pursue negotiations and initiatives at the United Nations. Only when he had a free hand after November would he consider more drastic action.

The question in Wardell's mind was would the Russians be content with the status quo until then. He suspected that they thought the blockade would be effective, and they could be right. But if the airlift did work, there was the chance that Stalin would get impatient. In that case, the American intelligence system had better provide sufficient warning.

Or British intelligence. During the war, Wardell had developed a great deal of respect for the British intelligence agencies. One of his main objectives in London, his next stop, would be to reestablish his relationship with the powerful, shadowy men who ran that very effective network of spies.

Wardell made some notes about his upcoming British trip, then put the foreign policy cables aside. He picked up a stack of papers dealing with constituent problems that Rachel Lang, his administrative assistant, had forwarded. He was a third of the way through the stack when there was a knock at the door.

He opened the door. A hotel employee stood outside with an envelope on a silver tray. Wardell got some change off the desk, tipped the man, and closed the door.

He sat down and opened the envelope. Inside was a single sheet of paper. He read, "David. I'm in Room 1437. Susan."

An hour later he was in the hallway of the fourteenth floor. In the moment or two before the door opened, he almost changed his mind again for the tenth time.

Then the handle turned, and she was standing there. "David," she said.

She was even more beautiful than he'd remembered. Her hair was longer, cascading down over her bare shoulders to the middle of her back. Her blue satin dress was cut low, and her skin had a luxuriant creaminess that made him want to reach out and touch her.

But he didn't. He stood silently.

Then she said, "Come in. Please, David. I want to talk with you."

He followed her into the small but elegantly appointed single room. He crossed to one of the two armchairs. She sat in the other.

"Did Sage tell you I was in Paris?" Wardell asked.

She looked down at her hands, her face somber. "No. Though you have every reason to suspect that he did. But I . . . I paid off my debt to him in Hong Kong. He's contacted me two or three times, but I've ignored him. I've resumed my career."

"I haven't seen your name," Wardell said.

"I've been working on the continent. Primarily here in Paris, and in Brussels. It's not as lucrative as film work but it's more . . . more stable. The quieter life suits me."

"It must," Wardell said. "You look even lovelier than I remembered."

A brief smile flashed onto her face. "I'm surprised you remember at all. That charade . . . it was disgraceful of me. The bottom rung of a ladder I'd been climbing down for years. It was a nightmare."

"I appreciate your apology," he said. "But I realized long ago it wasn't your fault. Those were extraordinary times, and you were in extraordinary circumstances. You did what you had to do."

"That's the way they always put it," she said. She ran her tongue over her red lips, then added, "I've had enough of men like that to last me a lifetime."

"If you mean that," Wardell said, "then maybe the lesson was worth the price you paid."

She looked at him directly for the first time. When her eyes met his, he felt a long-buried stirring inside him. Paris, he said to himself. The city of ghosts.

She leaned over and kissed him on the cheek. "Thank you," she said. "That was a very nice thing to say."

He didn't reply.

She broke the silence. "How have you been, David? I

suppose I should know, but I find myself avoiding the newspapers."

"Busy," he said. He paused, then added, "I was married two years ago."

"Happily?" she asked.

He took in a short breath. "She's a member of Congress, too. The responsibilities make it difficult to spend any time together. I think I'm leaving the Senate shortly."

She smiled, "I'm glad to hear that. Life is too short. When I realized later the years I threw away . . ." She shook her head. "How is it we never learn until afterward? When the mistakes are already made?"

"If you want the answers to questions like that," Wardell said with a gentle smile, "you're going to have to go out and talk to one of these French philosophers. I'm just a beaten-down old politician from the ranch country. I've run out of answers myself."

She laughed. "I meet enough of those philosophers in the theater. Thank goodness most of their plays are written for two men wandering about talking on a bare stage. I start yawning after ten minutes. I'll take decadent Molière or Racine any day."

"Me, too," Wardell said.

She looked at him with sparkle in her eyes. "David, have you eaten? Could we have some supper somewhere?"

He hesitated.

"I promise I'll be a good girl," she said. "I'd just like your company."

"Okay," he said.

*   *   *

He got back to his suite a little after 4 A.M. He had no idea how so much time had passed, and he had little memory of what they'd talked about. But it seemed like only an hour or two until the waiters were making preparations to close the café, and he and Susan had strolled back along the deserted quay to the hotel.

Wardell took off his suit and put on his robe. He had a busy and very difficult day ahead of him, beginning with a breakfast at the American embassy at 8:30. But as much as he needed the rest, he knew he wouldn't sleep.

She was like an enchantress to him. During the entire evening, she hadn't made one gesture of flirtation; there had been no deep searching looks, no touches on the arm, nothing. It might have been better if she had, for Wardell was prepared to resist any overt gestures.

Instead, she had simply been herself. And for Wardell she radiated an intense magnetism. He'd never experienced anything like it with another woman. He didn't understand it because it touched a part of him that reason didn't control. And that frightened him.

His relationship with Laura was different. He loved her, he was attracted to her physically. But the relationship was based so much more on mutual respect, on shared intellect, on a feeling of partnership.

He needed to be reminded of that right now. He glanced at his watch. 4:28. Washington was six hours earlier. Laura had been scheduled to return from London the morning before. She might be in bed, still adjusting from the time change.

He decided to call her anyway. He picked up the phone, gave the number to the hotel operator, and lit a cigarette.

He was on his second cigarette when the phone rang. Wardell's housekeeper was on the line. Laura had not arrived in Washington. No, there had been no communication about when she was expected.

Wardell hung up, puzzled. That wasn't like Laura. Of course, she could certainly have been delayed by business in London, but . . .

He stood when he heard the knock at the door. There was a second knock, and he crossed to open it.

Susan Gordon was standing there, dressed in a simple cotton shift.

"Susan? What are you doing here?"

She stepped inside and closed the door behind her. She put her hands on Wardell's shoulder and kissed him on the lips.

"I've been a good girl all night," she said. "Now it's time to be a bad girl."

Wardell saw her reach around her back with both hands. He heard the sound of a zipper. Her shift fell to the floor. She was naked beneath it.

Wardell took in one sharp breath. Then she was in his arms again. This time her mouth opened, and her tongue searched out his. His left hand stroked her body, then cupped around a breast. Her skin felt hot to his touch.

Her lips left his, moving to his neck, then his bare chest. Her hands played inside his robe as she licked and kissed and gently bit his flesh. He closed his eyes for a moment, feeling the heat build within him. Then he took her head in his two hands, tilted it upward, kissed her on the lips, and said, "Let's go to bed."

She went to the bed, pulled down the spread, and lay on her back. Wardell dropped his robe and moved to her.

Crouching over her, it seemed to Wardell she bloomed beneath him like some hothouse flower, odorous, moist, with the most intense erotic eyes and wet lips. He lowered himself over her, the tip of his penis touching her. He entered her slowly, gradually, carefully. She didn't move at all, breathing in short, almost silent breaths.

When Wardell made his first full thrust, she suddenly energized. Her hands dug into his back, nails clawing at him. He could feel her teeth as she bit his neck, his shoulders.

Her wildness sent a fire through him. He felt her breasts crushed beneath him, rolling under his chest, her ivory-skinned belly heaving under his, her hips against his, her moist vagina engulfing him. Each time she groaned, he felt her turmoil as well as his.

The bed swayed as they rolled, clutching and folding, ripples extending from the roots of their hair to the tips of their toes, which sought each other and intertwined. Susan's moans now mounted in endless spirals, widening, expanding. He answered every cry with a deeper plunge. They rolled again and she was now over him, and her fingers were everywhere and her breast was in his mouth.

Then Susan let out one last cry. Wardell exploded, surprised as a savage grunt passed his own lips. He lay back and her body collapsed, her head on his chest.

"I love you," she said. "I love you more than you'll ever know."

FIFTEEN

The meeting room was in the back room of a storefront stuck incongruously in a row of Victorian houses in north London. Laura sat alone at the scarred, round wooden table, sipping a cup of tea while she made notes on a yellow legal pad.

In the last four days, she'd experienced the most remarkable awakening of her life. Since her high school days, she'd been hard working and determined, but now she realized that she had always lacked the kind of clear sense of purpose that led to true accomplishments.

Of course, she'd had some minor successes, amendments to legislation that made real, if small, contributions to the advancement of human rights. But in terms of truly effecting change, of altering for the better the lives of Americans and other peoples, she'd had little effect.

Carl Waldman's British friends, however, had opened her eyes. She couldn't believe that after Hiroshima she'd still been largely blind to the incredible and imminent danger that the atomic bomb posed to world peace, indeed to the course of human civilization.

The door opened. Laura smiled when Waldman walked in. He bent to kiss her cheek. Then he introduced a rather pale, thin young man in a gray, striped suit.

"This is Mr. Baker," he said. "Mr. Baker has some documents and other information that you should know about before you go back to the U.S."

Laura rose and shook the man's hand, which felt cool to the touch. Then she sat down and waited until he opened his briefcase.

"Mr. Baker is a staff member of the Technical Committee of the British Atomic Energy Authority," Waldman explained. "I should also tell you that his presence here is unauthorized."

Baker cleared his throat nervously as Laura's eyes moved toward him. "Some may call it treasonous, what I'm doing," he said in a rather dry, high-pitched voice. "But better treason than what may come if something doesn't stop them."

"Them?" Laura asked.

"Those that want to use these bombs they're building. It's inhuman, to use a power like the atom to destroy whole cities and countries."

The man's face was reddening, and already perspiration appeared on his brow. He wiped at his face with a yellowed handkerchief. Then he looked at Laura and said, "You should know I went to work for the government because I thought atomic energy was a miracle that could fuel power plants and ships and maybe even planes. The power of the sun on earth, a new age of prosperity that would finally end poverty and suffering."

He took in a deep breath. "But all they're concerned about is their bomb. It's bad enough, the ones in our government. But your government continues to make demands that will drive us to war."

The man's intensity made a vivid impact on Laura. She'd been uncomfortable at first with the fact that he was there without the permission of his government. But his passionate feelings made her curious about what he was going to tell her.

"What demands are those?" Laura asked.

The man cleared his throat. Waldman spoke first.

"You're familiar with the McMahon Act?"

She nodded.

"That bill, in addition to setting up our Atomic Energy Commission, also prohibited our sharing new nuclear information with any country, including Britain. It did not, however, preclude passing along declassified research or shipping raw materials. As a result, the U.S. contributed to the development of the British plutonium pile at Windscale in Cumberland."

"I didn't know the British were making plutonium," Laura said.

"They have," Baker said. "But the bomb research at Harwell is coming along more slowly than expected. Too slowly for your government, I understand. I have found out that scientists from your atomic research program are on their way to Britain now."

"But I thought you said they are prohibited from passing along technical information?" Laura asked.

"They are," Baker said. "However, there is a loophole in your legislation. It says nothing about them

176

coming to England to actually put together nuclear bombs using British plutonium."

Laura was shocked. "I can't believe that. Aren't we making our own bombs?"

Waldman answered. "Not quickly enough to suit the government, not with the situation in Berlin. The disagreement over currency reform in Germany seems to have set off Truman and the others almost as much as Pearl Harbor did in 1941. The red baiters and warmongers are having a field day."

"That's awful," Laura said.

Baker nervously cleared his throat again. "There is something that is worse. I managed to obtain information that an abandoned World War II airfield within fifty kilometers of Windscale is undergoing massive construction, including facilities for storing nuclear weapons. I also have heard from a reliable source that in July a force of more than fifty B-29 Superfortress bombers are being sent to that airfield."

Laura didn't reply.

"The B-29," Waldman said, "is our longest range bomber. Long range enough to reach the Soviet Union carrying nuclear weapons."

"My God," Laura said. "They can't be serious about starting an atomic war."

"They are serious enough to stock bombs on British soil. That's an outrage," Baker said vehemently.

"What are you going to do?" Laura asked.

Waldman replied, "Mr. Baker cannot do anything. He has taken considerable risk in coming here today. If what he has told us here were known, he would be tried under the Official Secrets Act and executed. He certainly cannot broadcast the information to create a public outcry."

Laura looked at the almost emaciated man. "Why did you take that risk? What can I do? If I try to use the information, they might trace it back to you."

"We don't expect you to do anything in public," Carl Waldman said. "I've arranged for Mr. Baker to meet you for two reasons. One, if the contingency plans of the U.S. government do become public knowledge, some American leader must be ready to lead a lobbying campaign against them. You have the reputation and integrity to do so."

"I don't know," Laura said. "I'm not exactly the most popular member of Congress."

"That isn't the most important reason," Waldman continued. "The second is that you're married to David Wardell."

Laura sat back in the chair. "David? What does this have to do with him?"

"I don't have to tell you about your husband's position. As Chairman of the Senate Armed Services Committee, he's fully briefed on all military affairs. He's the sole Senate member who is kept informed of major intelligence activities of the CIA. If Truman didn't need your husband in the Senate, he would probably have been named secretary of defense, and the president listens to him as if he were a cabinet member. Finally, there have been rumors of certain top-secret military preparations that even top Defense Department officials are in the dark about. The name I've heard connected with these shadowy plans is General Dolan."

"Mack Dolan," Laura repeated to herself. That would be the reason he comes to the house, and why

David and he lock themselves away.

She was lost in thought for a few moments. Then she leaned forward and said, "I still don't understand. David never talks to me about classified military information, and I wouldn't dream of asking him."

Waldman exchanged a brief glance with Baker. Then he said, "Laura, that's not what we mean. What we want you to do is talk to your husband whenever you can. The only information he gets is from all those generals and defense department types who are itching to use those bombs. No one will ever change their minds. Our only hope is that the few responsible influential men like David won't let them. You've got to take every opportunity you can to provide him with perspective, to give him the other side of the story."

"I already do," Laura said. "I can't say I've had any effect on him."

"I think you would if you truly make yourself an expert on the subject. Laura, the issue of atomic warfare is so new that almost all the experts are those who've been involved in atomic research. Naturally, they want to build more and more bombs. It's about time there were equally well-informed people who could counter their arguments."

Laura took a deep breath. She felt an excitement growing in her. All her life she'd been looking for *the* mission, the one purpose to which she could devote herself that would have a profound, lasting effect.

The issue of the survival of the human race in the face of the creation of atomic warfare was such an issue. Beside that issue, everything else paled.

What she could do was less clear. The way Carl Waldman described David and his power, he seemed like a stranger, a remote figure she barely knew. He never talked in any detail about his work, his meetings, the issues under discussion. And she never probed.

Her husband was a man, however, who did listen. He might not approve of her antinuclear activities at first. But if he respected her knowledge of the subject, he would hear her out. And, possibly, if the momentous decision to use atomic weapons again was imminent, he might consult her beforehand.

Laura turned to Baker. "Thank you very much," she said. "If you took any risk in coming here today, you won't face any additional risk in the future from me."

Baker nodded.

Laura said to Carl Waldman. "I'll do what I can."

"That's all we can ask," Waldman said.

Baker got up and left the room.

"I guess I should be going, too," Laura said.

Waldman took her hand. "Laura, one caution. We're going to have to be careful about being seen together too often back in Washington."

Laura reddened. "You mean . . ."

He interrupted, "I mean, I'm well identified with a variety of leftwing organizations, many of which have been labeled communist by all the red-baiting that's so popular in Washington these days."

"I never pay any attention to those idiots," Laura said.

"But other people do," Waldman said. "And when you start speaking out on the issue of atomic energy, you're going to come in for a lot of heat. If the red baiters can connect directly with people like myself, they'll drown you in rhetoric. Your arguments will be automatically dismissed before you get a chance to express them."

"I thought free speech was guaranteed in the Constitution," Laura said. "I'm certainly not a communist, and I won't stand for guilt by association."

"Guilt by association is a favorite tactic. We can't let our opponents use it, even if it's deeply morally wrong."

Laura looked into his blue eyes. Then she lowered her gaze and sighed. "I suppose you're right."

"That doesn't mean we won't be able to communicate," Waldman said. "We can of course chat at parties and other events like we have in the past—even the worst of the anticommunists talk to me. However, for other communication I'll set up a drop."

"What's that?"

"A place where we can leave messages and material for each other. A safe place."

Laura frowned. "That sounds like a spy novel."

"We are spies, in a way. Or at least we're engaged in covert warfare," Waldman said. "We're fighting against those who would doom our civilization for idiotic, nationalistic short-term gains. Our end justifies far greater means than being cautious and discreet."

"You're right," Laura said. "I've always been a person who got in trouble airing my feelings in public. I'm going to have to change that if I'm going to survive in the climate that's building in Washington. I'll be spending most of my time in front of that awful House Un-American Activities Committee if I don't."

Waldman patted her hand. "Good. I knew you'd understand. I'll get information to you about the drop."

"One question," Laura said. "What if there is

something very important we have to talk about?"

"Then you'll send me a message. Don't worry, even in Washington we can find places to meet without eyes on us." He stood, leaned over and kissed her on the cheek. "I'll leave first," he said. "You wait a few minutes."

The door closed. And suddenly, Laura felt very alone.

Her mouth was dry. She took a sip of the cold tea left in her cup and then gazed around at the peeling paint on the walls of the small back room. What was she committing herself to? What had brought her to this shabby back room where she listened to half-whispered secrets from a man committing treason against his own government?

She knew what, of course. She knew that not devoting herself to eliminating the threat of nuclear warfare was unthinkable. But she also, at this moment, remembered her conversation with David in Paris. She remembered their decision to leave politics; to become private citizens, raise a family, and spend time with each other.

Was she betraying that commitment? Not yet, because her reelection campaign was still ahead of her, and after that a two-year term in which she would work as hard as she could. After that term, however, the decision would have to be made. And she could already tell it was going to be difficult.

She rose and gathered her things. Put the decision out of your mind, she told herself. If you don't, every moment with David is going to be difficult. And the future would be difficult enough as it was.

SIXTEEN

November 2, 1948 — Wardell had flown out to Phoenix from Washington the night before. He caught a few hours of sleep in the small apartment he kept in the city, then rose early the next morning to vote.

His press aide arranged for heavy coverage of the senator at the polls. He posed for nearly half an hour, pretending to mark blank ballots and drop them into the ballot box. When the photographers had enough shots, he cast his real vote and went outside to hold an impromptu press conference.

Public opinion polls called Dewey a sure winner. Wardell made a strong statement forecasting Truman's "certain" reelection. He reiterated that prediction despite a barrage of questions. Then he went on to make the required courtesy calls on other Democratic state and local candidates.

It was nearly noon by the time he returned to the apartment. He called Laura at her campaign headquarters in Des Moines. They only had a chance to talk for a few minutes before she had to leave for a meeting.

She sounded confident about the election, but very tired. She'd been in Iowa campaigning all but a handful of days in the last six weeks.

Wardell was depressed when he hung up the phone. He was exhausted, too. Every leading Democrat had been pressed into service to help whittle away at the giant lead Dewey had after the conventions. Wardell had sandwiched campaign trips between endless public hearings and private meetings centering around the Berlin crisis.

But little had been accomplished. The airlift was a logistical miracle, but the difficulties had continued to grow as winter settled in. Absolutely no progress had been made in direct negotiations with the Russians, and on October 25, just a week before, the Russians had vetoed a UN Security Council resolution calling for a lift of the blockade.

The result was a stalemate. And the longer the stalemate lasted, the more the tension increased. Wardell was possessed by the certainty that the postelection months would bring the crisis to a dangerous breaking point.

Wardell's strength had also been touched by personal tension. For all their closeness during that week in Berlin when he was recuperating from the assassination attack, he and Laura had returned to Washington to find themselves living together like two strangers.

Something had happened to her in London. Wardell recognized the difference immediately. He could see the fire, the determination in her eyes. She'd poured herself into research on atomic physics and atomic weaponry. At first Wardell welcomed the opportunity to talk with her about a subject that concerned him very deeply. But soon he realized that the purpose of her conversation was to win him over. She wouldn't budge an inch, no matter what contingencies he brought up. She had the missionary zeal of a fanatic. From the time he'd been exposed to Huey Long, Wardell had had a deep distaste for fanatics, and he knew that contributed to the deterioration of his relationship with Laura.

And their sex life had dropped off to practically nothing. The sexual tension was primarily Wardell's fault. He felt guilty about it, but he couldn't help it.

He was obsessed with Susan Gordon. That first night in Paris had been followed by three more. It was a tribute to his self-discipline that he could concentrate during his difficult sessions with de Gaulle and members of the French government. Emotionally, all he'd wanted to do was go back to that hotel room.

Susan had made the parting easy on him. Sometime during the last night, she'd left him alone. When he arose the next morning, she'd checked out. In a brief note, she said she thought it was better if she went to Brussels for a few days. It would eliminate the temptation to go on to London with him.

In London, he'd driven himself to work even more than usual, to forget her. But going to bed at night didn't become any easier when he went back to Washington.

Then, in early September, he opened his morning mail to find a note from her. He'd canceled a subcommittee hearing to fly to New York to meet her. The weekend in the suite at the Plaza had been, if anything, more intense than Paris.

Wardell had never experienced a physical attraction

that was so consuming. All his long-term relationships had been with women to whom he'd been drawn by their intellect as well as their beauty. With Susan, he rarely talked of anything more serious than what to eat or drink.

He'd concluded that escape from the increased burdens his position placed on him was the primary reason for his infatuation. The pressures of the crises his country faced would overwhelm him if he didn't get release. He told himself that when he left the Senate, the weight would be off his shoulders and the obsession would pass.

That's what he told himself. He didn't know if he truly believed it. And the way Laura and he were getting along these days, married life together seemed as much of a pipe dream as world peace.

The phone rang, and Wardell snapped himself from his thoughts to answer it. He replied to a few questions from a *Washington Post* reporter calling long distance. When he was through, he held the receiver for a few moments, then depressed the button and dialed his ranch.

An hour and a half later, Wardell's 1937 Packard convertible pulled up outside the apartment building. The driver's door opened and Johnny Blair stepped out. Blair had worked for the Wardell family for most of his sixty-seven years. He had a touch of arthritis now, and the Arizona sun seemed to have dried him up and baked his skin as hard as the desert floor. But he still put in twelve-hour days as rigorous as those he'd worked when Wardell was a boy.

Wardell embraced him, a big grin on his face. Then Blair asked, "Where to, boss?"

"Feel like driving?" Wardell asked.

"Long as you want," Blair said. "Climb in."

In a half hour, they'd left the city far behind. The big engine hummed as they followed the winding two-lane highway through towns with names like Horse Thief Basin, Bumble Bee, and Broken Arrow. The road trailed up into a broad country of deep red-rock formations and spirelike pinnacles standing high and slender against the sharp blue sky. Across the expanse of country they drove, in sight of an open ridge of cliffs which the sunlight painted with an array of wild colors.

After a couple hours, Blair pulled the Packard off the road into the shade of a small bluff. "You mind, boss? I need me a rest."

"Course not," Wardell said.

"Then open up that glove compartment there. We'll have a little refreshment."

Wardell turned the knob and pulled out a full quart of Jack Daniels bourbon. He broke the seal, unscrewed the cap, and took a big swig.

He smiled and handed the bottle to Blair, saying, "You always knew how to pack a lunch."

Blair took a couple swigs, then burped with satisfaction. "Man can dry out in the desert real easy," he replied. He took another swig, then handed the bottle back to Wardell. Then he asked, "Want me to keep the engine on so you can get election reports on the radio?"

Wardell shook his head. "We won't know anything until late tonight. I'd just as soon forget the blow by blow."

"You think Truman's going to win?"

Wardell shrugged. "Don't know. If he doesn't, life will be a lot easier for me. You'll have an extra hand around the ranch a lot more of the time."

"Wouldn't mind that at all," Blair said. "You might, though. You're like your daddy. Never met a man who despised having things easy as much as him. He had to tackle the hardest jobs, ride the meanest horse, and chase the orneriest women in the state." Blair took another swig, then added with a smile, "Caught most of them, too."

Wardell chuckled. "I remember." He sat in silence for a while, the happy memories of his boyhood flooding back. Then he said to Blair, "How about some more driving? I don't get my chance to drink my fill of Arizona very often. The desert and the smell of those ponderosa pines are like champagne."

"Wouldn't know about champagne," the grizzled cowboy said. "But if it's driving you want, it's driving you'll get."

An hour later they stopped to eat at a diner in a small town off the main highway. By the time the moon rose, they were at the edge of the Painted Desert. The bottle of Jack Daniels was gone.

"Think it's time to head back?" Blair asked.

"Guess so," Wardell said. He felt more than a little the effects of the bourbon. But he also felt more relaxed than he had in a long time. The prospect of Truman's defeat, his resignation from the Senate, and a quiet life on the ranch seemed more and more appealing. Even a life on the ranch without Laura.

He turned to Blair. "Let's go back. Anytime you feel like stopping for a rest, though, do it. We're in no hurry."

"I can drive for days, boss. Don't worry."

The night air was crisp and cool, and the sound of the engine was like a lullaby. Wardell soon fell asleep.

He woke abruptly when the car came to a stop. He looked up, covering his eyes against the harsh light of a service station.

"Where are we?" he asked Blair.

"Outside of Phoenix. You been asleep five or six hours."

Wardell shook his head against the thick cobwebs. "Feels like a month," he said. He opened the car door, and headed for the gas station. He used the toilet, splashed water over his face, then walked into the office to get a soda from the vending machine.

A radio was playing. Wardell stopped abruptly as he heard, ". . . of the most startling surprises in American politics. Although a Chicago newspaper had been so confident that they printed a headline announcing Dewey's victory, President Harry S. Truman has not only recorded an upset victory, but has achieved a Democratic landslide. Right now Mr. Truman has carried twenty-eight states and accumulated three hundred four electoral votes, compared to sixteen for Mr. Dewey."

Wardell was stunned. He stood, listening as the announcer went through the roll of states whose returns were in. Finally, the announcer turned to local elections. Wardell marched back out to the car.

"Let's get going, Johnny," he said. "I've got to get back to Washington pronto."

III

SCALPEL

SEVENTEEN

Penkovsky was late. Very late.

Sage stood just inside the shell of the bombed-out building in the Russian sector of Berlin. The rubble-strewn street was silent, except for the occasional scurry of rats or a scavenging stray dog.

He'd been waiting well over an hour. Twice Sage had retreated into the depths of the ruin to light a match to check the time. He would have left already if Penkovsky hadn't gone to great lengths to set up this meeting, which was eight days earlier than their next scheduled encounter. The risks Penkovsky took in getting word to Sage must mean information of great importance.

The risks also could have resulted in Penkovsky's arrest. In that case, Russian troops could be closing in on the meeting spot right now. Sage knew he would be quite a catch for Soviet intelligence. That's why he found his hand drifting toward the waistband compartment where he kept his rubber-coated cyanide capsule.

Sage picked his way back through the rubble once more, then squatted. In the flare of the match, he saw that it was nearly two A.M. More time had passed than he thought. He had to get back to the American zone.

He was barely a couple of steps from the building when he heard the sound of a motor. Headlights appeared as a vehicle turned the corner onto the street in which he stood. He dove for cover back inside the ruin.

He scrambled out of the line of sight of the doorway, crouching behind a shattered wooden cabinet. He was slightly surprised to discover that his pistol was in his right hand, drawn instinctively as he moved.

It had been a number of years since Sage had been an active agent. Almost all his time was spent running other agents, not handling the cloak and dagger stuff himself. He hadn't even had time to get to the pistol range since early in the war. He hoped that his once-considerable skills hadn't totally deteriorated.

The vehicle pulled to a halt in the street outside. Sage clicked off the safety of his Walther. He strained to hear the sounds of boots hitting the pavement and moving in on his hiding place.

But all he heard were the footsteps of one man. He inched cautiously forward, peering intently into the darkness.

The footsteps stopped at the gaping hole that served as an entrance to the ruin. Sage heard a match being struck, then he saw the flame rise.

The match stopped at chin level. In the orange light, Sage recognized Penkovsky.

"Igor," he said, rising from his crouch and stepping forward.

"I was hoping you were still here," Penkovsky said.

"I'd just decided to leave."

"That would have been very unfortunate," Penkovsky said. "Come. Let us go downstairs to talk. I was barely able to slip away, and we do not have much time."

Penkovsky turned on his powerful flashlight. Sage followed him to the basement of the bombed-out building.

Penkovsky lit a candle. When he turned to face Sage, the American could see deep circles under his eyes. The KGB general looked ten years older than the last time they'd met.

Penkovsky lit a cigarette. Then he said with a grave expression on his face, "We are on the brink, my friend."

"The brink?"

"Of another war. Unless, of course, your country chooses to capitulate and deal with a Europe made up of Soviet satellite nations."

Sage looked at him skeptically. "That's a bit apocalyptic, isn't it, Igor? After all, we do have certain strategical advantages."

"You mean the bomb," Penkovsky said. "The super weapon that your president and politicians have been using since 1945 instead of developing a realistic defense policy. Well, I called you here to tell you that your monopoly on atomic weapons is at an end."

"I don't understand," Sage said.

"I'll make it clear. I have just obtained information that our atomic research team will explode the first Russian nuclear bomb in two weeks."

A jolt went through Sage. He stood in silence for a second. Then he asked, "What proof do you have of this?"

"I am afraid I have nothing at this moment. I have been monitoring the research Professor Kurchatov's team has been conducting at Kasanov. The information obtained from sources inside the Canadian and American atomic research programs drastically reduced the development time. As recently as two months ago, the most optimistic projection was the explosion of the first test bomb in late 1949."

"How could things change so rapidly?" Sage asked. "Maybe your information is wrong."

"No," Penkovsky said. "You know our system well, my friend Sage. Stalin is an impatient man who is obsessed by the atomic bomb. If Kurchatov had given him a projected completion date and missed by one day, he would be a dead man. Like all of our prudent program heads, Kurchatov gave himself generous leeway. And even he was surprised by the speed of the work."

"I see," Sage said. He thought for a moment, then asked, "What implications does this have now? Why couldn't you have told me this at our meeting next week, when you may have had some documentation?"

"Because now that the atomic bomb is almost in our hands, Stalin is ready to take action here in Berlin. The airlift has been enormously frustrating to him, but he waited until your election was over. He sees Truman's election as a referendum on the airlift, and he realizes that your government will not give up West Berlin. So he's going to take it."

"How?"

"Two armored divisions are already on their way from Poland. Six more will be in place in two weeks. The East German factories are producing fighter aircraft at a record rate. If the first atomic test is successful, those divisions will move into Berlin and expel the Western Allies by force."

Sage protested, "Truman won't stand for that. And we will still have far more nuclear weapons than your country."

Penkovsky replied, "What difference does that make if we have only one? A single atomic bomb that could make Washington or New York another Hiroshima. Would any president be willing to risk that cataclysmic event for two-thirds of Berlin? I doubt even a man like Truman would make that decision. You and the British do not have sufficient ground forces in Europe to resist, and the French don't have the stomach for another battle. Your government would back down. And as our stockpile of nuclear weapons grows, we will take the rest of Germany. Then Italy and France. At some point, the aggression will become unacceptable to your government, or to the British, and the bombs will start falling. And the world as we have known it will be no more."

Sage felt as if a profound weight had suddenly been placed on his shoulders. What Penkovsky was saying was so horrible that his mind rebelled against it. But in his years in Moscow, he'd come to know the mind of Stalin well—too well. Penkovsky's scenario was chillingly realistic.

Penkovsky broke the silence. "This information has to get to your president immediately. There is no time to waste."

"I'll try," Sage said. "But I'm afraid with no documentation they might not believe it. Our politicians have been saying that your country won't have the bomb for five years. The only thing that will change their mind is the actual test itself."

"That will be too late," Penkovsky warned. "You must act now, and act aggressively. That is why I have come here tonight."

"I have one idea," Sage said. "Could we meet one more time? The only chance we have is for me to bring a man to meet you. A very influential man that Truman would listen to."

Penkovsky sighed. "I don't know. The risk is very great. With the confrontation so near, everyone is being watched."

"I'll place a classified ad in the French newspaper. Monsieur Tulley looking for a bilingual secretary. That will mean we'll be here at midnight that evening. We'll wait for an hour, then return the next night."

Penkovsky was silent for a moment. Then he asked, "This is necessary?"

"We're talking about a decision that could lead to war. I can't see my government acting without some sort of confirmation. And even after this meeting, I'm not sure they will act."

Penkovsky spoke in a voice heavy with meaning. "They had better, my friend. Or the future will be bleak for all of us."

Wardell rose as the maître d' led Laura to the table. He took her hands and kissed her on the cheek.

"Congratulations," he said. "Another very comfortable victory."

She smiled. "Thank you. You know, I must be getting blasé in my old age. The first time, I was so excited, so high, I thought I'd fly right out of my headquarters and up into the sky. Now elections seem more like an annoying duty, like going to the dentist."

"Annoying, but necessary," Wardell said. He motioned to the waiter and ordered a bottle of wine. Then he turned back to Laura and said, "We're celebrating tonight. Mouton Rothschild '34."

"David, that's extravagant," Laura said.

"It's a time to be a little extravagant. We've both been working hard. We ought to treat ourselves better."

"Is that what the trip to Arizona convinced you of?"

"Partly," he said. "I'd forgotten how much I missed it. You'll love it, when we leave all this behind."

Laura looked down, avoiding his eyes. There was a moment of awkward silence. Then she said, "Have you talked to the president?"

"I saw him today, with the other Congressional leaders. I've seldom seen a happier man. The pundits had him dead and buried, but he survived. I was surprised, too. I didn't think he could be the kind of effective campaigner that he turned out to be."

Laura frowned. "Tough talk. Unfortunately, the people seem to feel we need an iron fist at this time."

Wardell said, "Evidently, you don't. You really feel Dewey would have been a better choice?"

"I don't know," she said with a sigh. "I don't think I trust either one of them."

"Trust them to do what?"

She looked at him with a determined expression. "To publicly forswear the use of nuclear weapons now and forever. To negotiate a permanent, lasting prohibition of such weapons all over the world."

Wardell had a reply on his lips, but he decided not to speak.

Laura said, "You were going to say that's totally unrealistic. That I'm an idealistic dreamer."

"No," Wardell said. "You know I respect your opinion. But I don't agree with it, either." He looked directly at her as he added, "And I have to assume that's one of the main reasons our marriage hasn't been working."

At the mention of marriage, Laura's face colored.

The wine steward approached the table. He uncorked the bottle. David inspected the cork, nodded, then approved the taste the steward offered him. The steward filled both glasses, then walked away.

Wardell raised his glass. "A toast."

"What shall we toast?"

He thought a moment. "To communication."

She drank. When she put down the wineglass, she said, "David, I'm sorry. Not for the way I feel. But the way I've been acting. I don't mean to accuse you. It's just that this issue has become very, very important to me. And I would like it to become important to you."

"It is," Wardell said. "Believe me. I don't know if I can support the position you take. Is that what's necessary to bring us back together again?"

"No," she said. She hesitated. "I . . . I don't think so. But I do have to feel that you fully understand my position."

"I want to," Wardell said. "Believe me, I do. So where does that leave us."

"Let's take a day," she said. "Now. Just the two of us. So you can sit down and listen until I've had my say.

Then we'll talk."

"Okay," he said.

She leaned forward, her face intense. "I don't want to feel that you're just humoring me on this, David. The issue is far too important for that. Now that the election is over, I think there's great danger that this Berlin situation could lead to something very much bigger."

"I won't humor you," Wardell said. "From the moment we met—from the moment I fell in love with you—I've always respected your intelligence. And that's still true today."

She reached across the table and took his hand. "Thank you, David. Not only for this, but for putting up with me. I know how wrapped up I get."

"People have to care," he said. He smiled, "And I'd like to care about dinner. I'm starved. I refused to touch what they tried to pass off as food on the airplane."

"Good idea," she said.

They picked up the menus. Wardell was studying his so intently that he was startled when a gruff voice said, "David. I have to talk with you."

Wardell looked up. Mack Dolan was standing next to the table.

"What are you doing here?" Wardell asked.

"Could I talk with you in private for a few minutes?"

"I'll go to the powder room," Laura said.

Dolan turned to her. "I'd prefer it if we went outside," he said. "And, Laura, I'm sorry I have to interrupt this dinner. It's important."

Wardell was on his feet. He said to his wife, "I'll be

right back."

Laura watched them leave the dining room of the Jockey Club. She tried to go back to the menu, but suddenly she was too nervous to read.

The expression on Dolan's face had been deadly serious, even grim. She remembered what Carl Waldman had told her in London about Dolan's involvement in some sort of secret war preparation. The implications of his sudden appearance, which was clearly not a social call, were frightening.

Her tension grew the longer David was away. She drained her wineglass, then poured another.

David came back alone. He didn't sit down.

"Laura, I have some very bad news for you. I have to leave you here to finish dinner by yourself."

She rose. "Where are you going?"

"Berlin," he said. "A plane is waiting for me at Andrews Air Force Base right now."

"No," she said. She touched his arm. "David, tell me. What's happened?"

"I don't know anything," Wardell said. "Believe me. Mack Dolan has asked me to go to Berlin right now. Considering our past relationship, I have to trust him that it's important. I can't say no."

"David, this scares me. We were going to have a talk, about the crises we might be facing."

He leaned forward and kissed her. "We will talk. I'll be back in Washington as soon as I can. Don't worry."

"How can I not worry?" she said. She picked up her purse. "I can't eat. Can you drop me off on your way to the airport."

He grimaced. "There's no time. You'll have to take a cab."

They walked out of the dining room and through the front door of the restaurant. A military command car was waiting outside.

Wardell kissed Laura again. Then he got in the car. As she watched the car pull away, tears formed in her eyes.

EIGHTEEN

Wardell turned to Mack Dolan as the command car sped toward Andrews Air Force Base. "Now, can you tell me what this is all about?"

Dolan noted the strain in his friend's voice. "I'm sorry I had to do this, David. I really am." He paused for a moment, then added, "Laura looked very upset. I've got the suspicion she doesn't like me."

Wardell sighed. "It isn't that, Mack. There's been a lot of strain in our marriage, trying to combine our careers with a private life. And it's . . . it's . . ." His voice trailed off.

"I shouldn't have brought it up," Dolan said.

"Perfectly all right," Wardell said. "That's what friends are for. But let's get on to the matter at hand. Why in the hell are you dragging me off to Berlin?"

"It's time."

"Time for what?"

"Scalpel," Dolan said.

Wardell saw that the general was deadly serious. "That's a pretty startling statement," he said. "Explain."

Dolan reviewed John Sage's meeting with Penkovsky. Wardell was silent as the car drove them onto the airfield and up to a waiting Air Force DC-3. They boarded.

"This is one of the planes assigned to the Joint Chiefs of Staff," Dolan explained as they entered the section of the passenger compartment that was furnished like an office. "We'll have it all to ourselves on the way over, so we can talk."

"I take it you've briefed at least some of the service chiefs about this situation."

Dolan shook his head. "No. Of course, we've reviewed in detail numerous possible scenarios, which have included such a situation as we're facing now."

"You mean, as we may be facing now." Wardell corrected him.

Dolan replied, "Your skepticism, which is perfectly justified, rests in why I haven't gone to the service chiefs. If Sage's information is accurate, the man who has to be informed is the president. The ball's going to be in his court."

"I don't envy him that decision," Wardell said. He leaned back in the padded chair, fastening his seat belt as the warning light came on. The pitch of the DC-3's engines increased as the plane accelerated down the runway.

Scalpel, Wardell thought to himself. In the last two and a half years, since that day in Hong Kong when Mack Dolan had first presented the plan, for him the word had lost much of its emotional content. It was simply one of many code names and contingency operations about which he was periodically briefed and for which he approved operation budgets hidden from the scrutiny of other members of Congress and the public. Even Laura's obsession with disarmament hadn't given him a sense of urgency about the immediate prospect of atomic conflict.

Now, for the first time since Hong Kong, Scalpel had a visceral effect on him. As the Air Force plane lifted off, Wardell felt as if it was propelling him into the most momentous crisis of his career.

The plane climbed, then leveled off. An Air Force steward came into the compartment, took an order, then returned with coffee.

"Mack," Wardell asked, "what verification have you been able to come up with from other sources about Penkovsky's story?"

"We have no other direct sources about the progress of the Soviet atomic research program. They were able to penetrate our program with ease, and we're totally in the dark about theirs. I have verified, however, that the secret information passed on to them was very detailed and very complete. For your information, a former top researcher now working for the British is under constant surveillance. If he was in fact an agent, the Soviets know everything."

Wardell grimaced. "I've been briefed on that. You mean Karl Fuchs?"

Dolan nodded. "He's made no contact with Soviet agents since he's been in Britain. That's why he hasn't been pulled in."

"I hope they're keeping a close eye on him now," Wardell said.

"They are," Dolan said. "And we're attempting to get information from Moscow. We have received reports of an unusual number of meetings involving top Soviet military officers. And the movement of additional armored divisions into Germany has also been verified. Actually, there's been a steady build-up of all types of forces since the beginning of the blockade in June. We were outnumbered badly then, and the situation is a lot worse now. If the Russians start something, we're in trouble."

Wardell pondered for a moment. Then he asked, "What if they do only have one or two bombs? Do you really think they could penetrate our air defenses and drop them on New York or Washington?"

Dolan replied, "I don't know. After all, we haven't exactly been tested. They could send fleets of bombers over the polar ice cap. We'd be so busy that a single plane could sneak in from almost anywhere. And remember our original plan in 1945—we were going to use captured Russian planes to carry our Scalpel force. For all we know, they have a Pan American Clipper that could masquerade as a charter flight landing at Idlewild or Washington National. The sum of the matter is whether we can afford to take that risk. As Sage said, despite Truman's recent election, could he get away with risking millions of American deaths to fight for part of Berlin, a city that until a few years ago meant the heart of Nazism to most Americans. The answer is, I doubt it."

Wardell doubted it, too. The Soviets had taken possession of most of Eastern Europe in the same manner, never making the stakes quite high enough for the U.S. to risk war. The American government had decided Poland wasn't worth fighting for, or Rumania or Bulgaria. Then Hungary, and earlier this year, even the brave Czechoslovakians. Stalin had proved a master poker player, and the U.S. had dropped out of every hand.

The stakes in Berlin were higher. That city would represent the first direct U.S.–Soviet confrontation. If Berlin were handed to the Soviets, it would be a severe, perhaps fatal, blow to U.S. prestige in Europe. It would probably doom an independent noncommunist West Germany, and might tip the political balance enough for the already strong Communist parties to seize power in France and Italy.

Despite all that, however, would the U.S. risk massive destruction on its own soil to stop the Russians? Wardell couldn't begin to say what he would do, much less what the man from Missouri who sat in the Oval Office would do.

Dolan tapped Wardell on the arm. He handed him a manilla file folder. "I'd like you to review the latest operation plans for Scalpel. I've just updated them recently, in light of the latest intelligence."

Wardell took the folder. Without opening it, he asked, "How quickly could we move, Mack?"

"Five days."

Wardell raised his eyebrows. "I thought the last time we talked you said two weeks?"

"We successfully negotiated with the British for two former airfields. The fleet of sixty to seventy aircraft we'll need are all overseas and all have been modified for their role in this mission. We have sufficient nuclear armaments on site to carry out stage one, and more are being prepared."

"And the troops?"

"On twenty-four-hour call at Fort Sumter, South Carolina. Most of the three-thousand-man force

208

recently returned from a joint war-games exercise with the Canadians in British Columbia. The training mission was an outstanding success. They're the best men we've got."

Wardell handed the folder back to Dolan. "That's all I need to know for now, Mack. If I have to go to the president, I'll read that in detail on the flight back. I'm exhausted, and I have a suspicion I'm going to need all the energy I can muster in Berlin. I'm going to get some sleep."

Their plane landed in midafternoon at the British air field at Wunstorf. As the aircraft taxied, Dolan explained to Wardell, "We're going to have to hop a ride on a transport to get into Berlin. Now that winter's coming, every single planeload of supplies is precious. Unless the president comes in, no plane that isn't full of supplies can take up space in the long shuttle of aircraft."

"This is a British base," Wardell said. "Are we going in on a British airplane?"

"Two squadrons of American C-54's are stationed here. Most of the four-engine transports come out of Wunstorf. It's easier to maintain them that way. In turn, other British planes fly out of American bases."

"Sounds intricate," Wardell said.

"It is," Dolan replied. "I think you'll find the next hop interesting."

The plane halted by a corrugated-metal hut. They got off and went inside for coffee. Wardell mingled with the crews inside the hut, asking questions about the airlift. One cheery Scottish pilot with a big handlebar mustache answered most of his queries.

"Worst cargo is coal. Bloody stuff," the pilot said. "Dust gets everywhere. Your pilots have a little ditty about it. Goes something like, 'Here's a Yankee with a blackened soul/Heading for Gatow with a load of coal.' Bloody right, too."

The pilot took a swig of coffee as Wardell chuckled. Then the man said, "Most dangerous is liquid fuel—kerosene, gasoline. Flying bombs, that's what those planes are with twelve thousand pounds sloshing around inside. The Brits hired a civilian company to fly that stuff—at least the pilots get paid handsome for taking the risk."

"What's the biggest problem?" Wardell asked.

"Believe it or not, salt. Berlin needs thirty tons per day. But the stuff seeps through the packages, corrodes the floor of the plane, and eats its way to the control wires. Only way to haul it is on the flying boats. They fly out of salt water, so their hulls are salt resistant. Plus their control wires run down the roof of the aircraft. Problem is that ice is starting to form in the rivers. Another few weeks, the flying boats won't be able to land at all."

Wardell started to ask another question. Dolan interrupted him. Their plane was ready.

They walked out onto the runway and hopped into a British lorry with a British crew. The lorry joined a line of trucks carrying sacks of flour to the RAF York in which they were flying.

Dolan explained to Wardell, "The key to the whole airlift is precision timing. The crew's been given a time at which they have to be over the Fohrau radio beacon, just north of Gatow. They have to hit the beacon with an allowed margin of error of plus or minus thirty seconds, out of about a fifty-minute flight. If they miss the time, they have to circle back. A plane takes off from here every three minutes, and this isn't the only base sending aircraft into Gatow."

"My God!" Wardell exclaimed. "What happens in bad weather?"

"They've got radar, and a ground controller talks the pilot down. If the pilot overshoots the runway, though, that's it—he joins the line of planes heading back to the west."

Wardell shook his head in amazement. Then he got out of the lorry and climbed aboard the York. He and Dolan strapped themselves into two cramped seats forward in the cabin filled with sacks of flour. Fortunately, the seats were by a window.

The plane waited its turn in the line at the end of the runway, then took off. Dolan, shouting over the roar of the engines, pointed out landmarks in Russian territory below.

Finally, the plane began to descend. Below, Wardell saw a big tower brightly lit with red lamps.

"The Kaiser Wilhelm I memorial," Dolan shouted. "The pilots call it the 'Christmas Tree.' Those lights ahead are Gatow."

Wardell craned his neck. Ahead, in the gathering dusk, he could see the lights of a just-landed plane leaving the far end of the runway. Behind it, another aircraft was beginning its takeoff.

Their York was now close to the ground. Wardell had a brief flash of worry that the plane ahead of them was still on the runway. But the York's wheels touched, bit, and the big transport slowed and turned off the runway onto the unloading apron.

The plane had barely stopped moving before German unloading crews swarmed over the craft. Dolan told Wardell that the flour would be taken off and an outgoing shipment of electric lamps, valves, or other products manufactured in Berlin loaded on. The plane would be on its way back to Wunstorf in thirty to sixty minutes.

Wardell stood on the apron for a few minutes, watching the sleek silver planes take off and land against the panorama of the red sky behind. The movement seemed artistic and exquisitely choreographed, like a ballet.

Dolan touched his arm. "Our car is here."

They crossed to a Ford sedan. The driver was a civilian. "I'll take you to your quarters to drop off your luggage," the driver said. "Then I've been ordered to drive you to headquarters."

"Can't we be briefed in the morning? We've had a long flight."

The driver replied without looking back, "I've been told that you're going into the Russian sector tonight."

Tonight, Wardell thought to himself. For a moment, a wave of exhaustion flooded over him. Then he told himself, why not? The sooner the better.

NINETEEN

Wardell's irritation grew the longer they waited. They had gotten to the gray building housing American intelligence shortly after eight. Now it was nearly eleven, and John Sage had still not appeared.

Wardell turned to Colonel Wheeler. "Ned, can't you send someone out after him. It's not as if this was a social affair he's late for. I've got important questions that have to be answered before we go out."

"I know," Wheeler said. "I talked with him by phone just before you arrived. He said he was on his way."

"More games," Wardell snapped to Mack Dolan. "I don't know how in the hell I can believe anything Sage says."

Dolan replied, "David, this isn't Washington. This is practically a war zone. Problems can occur. I think you've got to keep an open mind."

Wardell just grimaced. He began to pace.

He knew he was overreacting to the situation. The prospect of having to make up his mind about an operation with the implications of Scalpel was making him far more tense than usual. And the immediate prospect of stealing into the Russian zone to meet a KGB general certainly didn't help to quell his anxiety.

Wardell, Wheeler, and Dolan spent the next half hour in silence. Then the door opened and John Sage walked in.

Sage's appearance was uncharacteristically disheveled. His shoes were covered with mud, the knees of his suit were stained, his hands dirty. And there was blood on his right coat sleeve.

"What happened, John?" Colonel Wheeler asked.

Sage's face was grim. "I got a radio message just as I was leaving. One of my operatives in the Russian zone was outside a café when he saw Rudy Fraenkl's automobile pull up. Fraenkl started inside, but four men in dark suits were waiting for him. They shoved him into a black sedan and drove off."

"Who's this Fraenkl?" Wardell asked.

"The contact Penkovsky used to reach me. He's a pimp and black-market operator."

"Does this mean the meeting with Penkovsky is off?" General Dolan asked.

"Let me finish the story," Sage said. "My operative has a taxi. He managed to follow the car to a warehouse near the river."

"I assume the men were KGB," Wheeler said. "I wonder why they didn't take him to Falkenberger Strasse."

Sage turned to him. "That's the most disturbing part. The only reason I can think of is that they didn't want Penkovsky to know they'd picked Fraenkl up for questioning."

"Then the meeting is definitely off," Wardell said.

"I don't know," Sage said. "My man slipped out of the Russian zone and reached me. I took four of my men to the warehouse and we blasted our way inside. We killed three of the Russians. The fourth was wounded, but he managed to get away. We barely missed grabbing him—I hope to hell the blood he was losing prevented him from getting back to his superiors."

"What about Fraenkl?" Wheeler asked.

"The Russians shot him when we broke in. He was in pretty bad shape anyway. They weren't too subtle in questioning him. His body was battered and he'd been burned with cigarettes in a half-dozen places."

"So you think he talked?" Dolan asked.

Sage shook his head. "Fraenkl was a coward. I doubt he had much of a stomach for torture. On the other hand, I'm sure he was at least as afraid of us as he is of the Russians. And he may have held on longer than he would normally have, figuring Penkovsky would rescue him if he was arrested."

The four men were silent for a few moments, thinking. Finally, Wardell asked, "What's the bottom line? What are the chances that Penkovsky will be at the meeting place tonight? The chances, that is, that he'll be there without company?"

Sage didn't reply right away.

"Fifty-fifty?"

Sage shrugged again. "There is a chance that everything can go as planned." He paused for a moment, then turned to face Wardell directly. "Senator, the reason you're here is of monumental importance to our government—hell, to the rest of the free world. Without talking to Penkovsky, are you likely to go back and

215

recommend Scalpel to the president?"

Wardell pondered for a moment. Then he said, "I was hoping to find more conclusive proof of the Soviet Union's plans. I don't know what I think."

"Then you've got to take the chance Penkovsky will manage to get to the meeting place. Even if it's less than a fifty-fifty chance."

Colonel Wheeler stood up. He said to Sage, "John, it could be a damn sight slimmer than a fifty-fifty chance. Maybe one chance in ten that you both won't end up in the hands of the Russians. Think of what that would mean. A U.S. senator caught spying."

Wardell was silent.

General Dolan asked, "Can't you provide security?"

"I can use three or four men," Sage said. "But that won't be enough if the Russians are setting a trap. And moving more men would alert them, for sure."

Dolan looked over at Wardell. Then he said to Wheeler, "Ned, I'd like you two to leave us alone for a few minutes."

"Sure," Wheeler said. "John."

Sage said to Wardell, "Senator, we've had problems in the past. I hope to hell you're not going to let them lead you into bad judgment now."

Wardell stiffened. "I don't need a lecture on decision making, Sage," he said.

Wardell's retort didn't faze Sage. He said, "We need to know soon. We have to get started."

Wheeler and Sage left the room. Wardell stood looking at the door after it closed.

Dolan spoke first. "David, I'm sorry this is working out like this."

Wardell turned to him with a slight smile. "Why should I expect to escape, Mack? I can't forget World War I. I learned that a leader has to be the first one out of the trenches. He can't sit back under cover and send everybody out ahead of him."

"This is different, David. You're a hell of a lot more important than an infantry lieutenant. Your country needs you."

"My country needs a decision made. A decision that's more important than a man's life—even my life. Now, I can't abide Sage. I think his methods and his independence are very dangerous. But he's right when he says that I can't let my personal feelings get in the way. This is far too important."

Dolan studied the senator for a long time. Then he said, "You sure?"

"I couldn't be more sure. You can go out and tell them to get ready. I'll be with you in a minute. I want to use Ned's phone to place a call."

"The States?"

Wardell nodded.

"I'll tell them," Dolan said.

Wardell picked up the phone as he left the room. He gave the operator the number of Laura's Congressional office. She told him to hold the line.

It would be nearly 6 P.M. in Washington. After five, Laura invariably spent two hours or so catching up with her correspondence. He should be able to catch her.

The operator came on the line to tell him it would be a few minutes more.

What do I say? Wardell asked himself. He knew he

wanted to apologize for leaving so abruptly. And, he supposed, he wanted her to forgive him.

But what would that do? He had some notion it would put his mind at peace in case . . . in case things should go wrong.

Suddenly, Wardell felt foolish. He was making entirely too much out of this.

The phone finally rang. After a dozen rings, the operator came on to ask if he wanted her to continue trying. He thanked her, hung up, and walked out to meet Sage.

Carl Waldman waited for Laura in the lounge of the Marriott in Fairfax County, Virginia. When she approached, he could see she was upset.

"All the way out here," she said, "I kept asking myself what I was doing? Why couldn't we meet in Washington?"

"I explained to you in London," Waldman said. "We shouldn't be seen together. At least not alone."

"That's ridiculous," Laura snapped. "I'm a member of Congress. I meet with lobbyists all the time."

"That's true," Waldman said. "But the issue we're both so concerned with is so sensitive, we can't give the other side any more weapons than they have. I'm taking the precautions for your sake. A lot of people brand me a communist, and you can't afford to have that label placed on you."

Laura looked into Waldman's eyes. "Are you a communist?" she asked. "I really want to know. I have to know."

His gaze never faltered. "No. Of course not. I believe in a different kind of government than we have now, a government more sensitive to human beings, to their problems and suffering. But that doesn't put me into the camp of someone like Stalin. That's what all these red-baiters ignore, how obviously repressive the Soviet government is. No one who truly cares about human rights can be happy in either camp."

The answer pleased Laura. "That's the way I feel, too. I guess the war stirred deep emotions that are hard to restrain. After all the propaganda, after all the years of war movies, we can't get away from the black-and-white, us-against-them mentality."

Waldman took her hand. "You're a rare woman, Laura. And you're important to the future of our country."

His touch made her uncomfortable. She pulled her hand away and sat back.

The waitress brought drinks. Then Laura asked, "I've got a lot of paperwork to do tonight. Suppose we get to the reason for this meeting."

Carl Waldman's face grew somber. He leaned forward, lowering his voice. "As you know, with my reputation, I'm approached by people whose ideas are a lot more radical than mine. People whose purpose is destruction, without any thought to the hurt it might cause. Fortunately, I'm often able to prevent that destructive activity."

His tone of voice made Laura concerned. "What exactly are you talking about?"

Waldman hesitated to take a breath. Then he said, "Last week the editor of one of the magazines I write for came to me. I won't tell you which magazine, but it's one that's often a little sensational in its content. He had an envelope with him—some pictures an American photographer living in Paris was trying to sell."

"What kind of pictures?"

"Pictures that could be very damaging to the reputation of a prominent American politician."

Laura suddenly felt a desire to get up and leave the lounge. She took a moment to pull herself together, then asked, "What politician?"

Waldman took a manilla envelope from his briefcase. He opened the clasp, removed a small stack of eight by ten glossy prints, and passed them over to Laura.

She gasped. The top photo showed David walking toward the camera, his arm around the shoulder of a stunning young blond woman.

Waldman put his hand on her arm. "If you don't want to look at these, don't."

She felt herself trembling, and her mouth was dry. She shook her head, then managed to say, "I want to see them."

She picked up the top photograph and put it under the stack. The second photo showed David and the woman laughing at a table in a nightclub. The rest of the photos were also of the two together.

When she'd seen them all, she leaned back in her chair. She was quiet for a long time. Then she looked up at Waldman and asked, "Who is this woman?"

"According to the editor, her name is Susan Gordon. She's an actress who does stage plays in Europe, primarily Paris. Before the war she had a promising

American film career, but somehow she was interned in Hong Kong for the duration. Evidently that ended her interest in movies, or the movies interest in her."

"Hong Kong," Laura repeated, almost to herself. The more she thought about it, the more angry she got. David must have met her there. Or maybe he went to Hong Kong to meet her. How could he have lied about it so convincingly?

Laura looked at Wildman. "I'm glad you showed me those pictures. But I don't understand why you're concerned if David's name is dragged through the mud. It would serve him right."

Waldman said, "I know you're upset, Laura. But you're not thinking. Your name would inevitably become involved, and we can't afford that. The papers would have a field day with a scandal involving an attractive young female congresswoman. That's all some people need, another excuse not to take you seriously. Besides, there may be an innocent explanation for these pictures. They could be old friends. Or she could be the daughter of friends. I think you should give David the chance to defend himself."

"Maybe," Laura said. But she was thinking, what if this sudden trip to Europe is to see this woman? Mack Dolan was the type of man who'd be attracted to an actress, maybe he'd helped David find an excuse.

Suddenly, Laura found herself too upset to stay in the lounge. She rose and said, "Carl, I'll call you in a little while." She paused, then asked, "What are you going to do with those pictures?"

"Nothing," he said. "I don't believe that scandals belong in serious journals, even if I didn't know and like the parties involved. Although David may have given in to temptation, I respect him as a politician."

Laura's lips were pressed tightly together. "Maybe," she said. Then she turned and walked purposefully from the room.

Waldman stared at her retreating form, and slowly a smile of satisfaction came to his lips.

TWENTY

Sage stood in the doorway of a boarded-up building, scanning the rubble-strewn road ahead. The moon had risen shortly after midnight and was now at its apex. Despite the lack of street lamps, the street was bathed in a soft light that would have revealed any pedestrians.

Sage saw nothing and heard nothing. He called back over his shoulder, "Let's go."

He moved out cautiously. He was dressed in a black sweater and black pants, and in his hands he held an M-3 submachine gun. Wardell followed, similarly dressed. His right hand rested on the butt of the Colt .45 automatic in the holster around his waist.

They'd gone half a block when Wardell heard a sound behind them. He pulled the pistol from the holster and spun.

Sage put a hand on his arm. "It's just Richie," he said.

Wardell exhaled. Then he nodded, a trifle embarrassed. He knew Lieutenant Richie was trailing them by fifty meters to cover their rear. But he was so tense now that even the shadows seemed to have voices.

Inevitably, his mind flashed back to World War I. He could almost smell the noxious mixture of gunpowder and mustard gas and the stench of decaying bodies. Longer than the nightmares about men shrieking and dying, that odor stayed with him, as if it had permanently permeated his skin, his pores.

It was only years later that he realized what he was really smelling was his own fear. Wardell had grown up in the West, and from early childhood it had been drummed into him that a real man is never afraid. When he'd been Davy Crockett chasing imaginary Indians over the ranch with his brother Charley, he'd totally accepted the childhood belief that he was and would always be invincible.

Then came the war. And the stark, naked fear that had taken him by surprise. At first he was ashamed. Then he saw that no man on those entire battlefields— no sane man—lived without dread. Intellectually, he came to understand that. Emotionally, in the subconscious world of dreams, it had taken him many more years to accept it.

Now he realized that in its place fear could be the healthiest of emotions. The reason he was stealing down this street in the Soviet sector of Berlin was really his fear of the kind of future mankind would have if aggression was coupled with the capability of destroying entire nations with atomic weapons. That was worth the risk. Worth it, that is, if he could control the tension that had his heart pounding so loudly he was afraid it echoed through the empty buildings. All he could do was breathe deeply, and concentrate on the back of Sage in front of him.

They were now nearing the last intersection before the rendezvous point, the third house on the left on the other side. Sage halted, and Wardell came up beside him. He strained, but all he could hear was the faint rumble of planes far overhead.

"How does it look?" Wardell whispered to Sage.

Sage grimaced. "Can't tell."

He waited two or three minutes more. Then he picked up a stone in his right hand and threw it as far as he could.

In the silence, the sound of the stone landing was unnaturally loud. But it brought no response.

Sage turned to Wardell. "I'm going across first. You wait sixty seconds, then follow. If you hear anything, turn and run back toward Richie."

"Okay," Wardell said.

Sage sprinted across the road and disappeared into the shadows of the buildings on the other side.

Wardell stared at his watch, concentrating on following the sweep of the second hand in the moonlight. Then he took a deep breath and began to run.

As he reached the other side of the intersection, he saw Sage squatting by a gaping hole in a bombed-out building. As he chugged to a halt, Sage rose and turned to him.

"What is it?" Wardell asked.

Sage held out his right hand. The tips of his fingers were dark and wet. "Blood," he said.

Wardell stared. Before he could say anything, Sage wiped his fingers on his pants and took out a big flashlight. "We're going inside," he said. "You hold the light. I need both hands for the M-3."

Wardell holstered his .45 and took the light. They

moved into the blackness of the ruin. When they were out of sight of the street, Wardell switched on the light.

A trail of crimson led back to the stairs to the cellar.

"Shine the torch down," Sage directed.

Wardell did. There was the body of a man at the bottom of the stairs.

They descended quickly.

"Is it . . ."

"It's Penkovsky," Sage said. "Help me get him to that table."

The Russian was heavy. Wardell grunted as he and Sage pulled the man across the room.

Sage put his head on Penkovsky's chest. "He's still alive," Sage said. He rubbed the Russian's face, slapping him gently. "Igor, Igor."

Penkovsky groaned. Then his lips moved as if he were trying to speak. But nothing came out.

"Search him," Sage told Wardell.

Wardell opened the heavy gray woolen overcoat. Beneath, the shirt was soaked with blood.

"My God!" Wardell explained. "I can't imagine how he had the strength to get here."

"It's amazing what dying men can do," Sage said. "Especially when they have a reason. He must have been carrying something."

Wardell probed the pockets. He hesitated as the Russian groaned again. Penkovsky tried to turn, but Sage restrained him.

Then Wardell found an envelope in a pocket inside the overcoat. He showed it to Sage.

"Open it," Sage said.

Wardell did. He scanned the sheet of paper inside. "It's in Russian."

"Let me see."

Sage grabbed the sheet. Then he smiled. "This is it. A cable from Moscow. Alerting KGB station chiefs to activate all possible sources to monitor Western reaction, should the atomic bomb test be discovered." Sage folded the sheet and put it in his pocket.

A ripple went through Wardell. The information must be true. He might still have suspected a ruse, if it wasn't for the bleeding man in front of him.

Then the thought struck him—was this Penkovsky? He probed the man's jacket until he pulled out a leather wallet. He put it in his own pocket.

Penkovsky let out one last groan, and his body shuddered. Wardell saw a bubble of frothy blood on his lips.

"He's dead," Sage said. "Let's get out of here."

He led the way up the stairs. When they reached the top he told Wardell to turn off the flashlight. He paused to let his eyes adjust to the darkness and then picked his way through the rubble toward the street.

The crackle of automatic weapons on the street outside sent them to the floor. Other weapons fired in response. A deadly staccato rhythm.

Sage called to Wardell, "It's coming from the intersection. It must be Richie."

"What'll we do?"

"We've got to go the other way and circle back later," Sage said. "Now."

They ran through the gaping hole. A squad of six soldiers was sweeping the street. Sage dropped to his knees and triggered his machine pistol in a ninety degree arc. A crimson seam was stitched across the chest of the two nearest Russians. A third was hit in the

227

legs and tumbled to the pavement, screaming. The others dove for cover in buildings across the street.

Wardell heard a sound to his left. He saw a shape running at him. Instinctively, he aimed and fired. The figure dropped.

He turned back to see Sage crouching by the body of one of the dead soldiers. Then Sage screamed, "Come on!" He took off running to his left. Wardell followed, crouching as low as he could. Behind him weapons opened up, cartridges ricocheting off the pavement around him.

They reached another intersection and ducked left. Sage flattened himself against the wall. He waited a moment, then darted out from cover to spray the pursuers with fire. Wardell heard another scream amidst the answering fire as Sage ducked back next to him.

Sage reached into his belt and handed a metal object to Wardell. "Take this," he said, panting hard. "A Russian hand grenade."

The grenade consisted of a four- or five-inch handle, at the end of which was a rounded cylinder, like a small tin can.

"Where's the pin?" Wardell asked.

"There isn't any. Throw it hard. There's a spring in the handle that will snap back and trigger the firing pin. But don't use it unless we're trapped."

Wardell nodded. Sage stuck the barrel of his M-3 around the corner, fired a short burst. Then he ejected the magazine and clapped a new one in.

"Let's go!" he shouted.

As Wardell ran, he could hear the whine of an engine somewhere behind. The sound grew closer. They crossed a more major road, then veered left down a curving, narrow residential street. Most of the buildings were bombed out; in only one did lights pop on.

The street came to a dead end at a six-foot-high chain link fence. On the other side were railroad tracks.

Sage turned to Wardell and said hurriedly, "We're in luck. The British zone is only a few hundred meters down this siding. It's not blocked off, because the rail yard to the right hasn't been rebuilt since the war."

"Great," Wardell said.

Sage ordered, "You go over first. I'll cover this side. Then I'll toss the M-3 over."

Wardell holstered his pistol and stuck the grenade in his belt. He started to climb the fence, slipped back to the ground once, then climbed again. He pulled himself up to the top and got one leg over.

Then he heard Sage open up. He swiveled his head to see a squad of soldiers running toward them. A couple of them fell, but the others kept coming.

"Hurry!" Sage screamed. Wardell dropped to the ground on the other side. He pulled out the .45 and emptied the clip in the direction of the Russians.

Sage yelled at Wardell to get his attention, then tossed the submachine gun over the fence. Wardell snatched it in the air, stuck the muzzle through the fence, and pulled the trigger. The weapon bucked in his hands as he poured lead at their pursuers.

Then, as the Russians began to fire back, the firing pin clicked on an empty chamber. Sage was carrying the ammunition. Acting on some long-buried instinct instead of reason, Wardell dropped the weapon, pulled the grenade from his belt and threw it as far as he could. He dove to the ground as the grenade exploded in a flash of orange-red light. He could hear gravel and shrapnel spank the ground on the other side of the fence, but none reached him.

Wardell jumped to his feet and looked up. "Sage, hurry!" he yelled.

Sage was draped over the top of the fence, motionless.

A jolt of concern rippled through Wardell. "Sage!" he called again.

"I'm hit," came the weak reply.

Wardell was a tall man. He was able to reach up and grab the CIA agent under the arms. Grunting, he managed to pull him over the fence.

Wardell looked down the street on the other side of the fence. He saw headlights. He bent down, picked up Sage again, and with great effort hoisted him over his shoulder. He took a few steps, then remembered the submachine gun on the ground.

He tried to squat once and almost tumbled over. He widened his stance and lowered himself again. His thigh muscles screamed, but he was able to snatch up the weapon in his right hand. Then he took off down the tracks.

As he got used to the weight, he moved faster. A hundred meters down the tracks he spotted a small signalman's shack. He veered left across the rails to get to it and then lowered Sage to the ground on the other side, in the moonlight.

Sage was barely conscious. The man was sweating profusely and every breath was a groan. "My chest," Sage managed to say.

Sage's sweater was drenched with blood. Wardell raised it and saw a gaping hole. He could hear the

230

sucking sound of air leaking from a lung.

Sage coughed and blood dribbled down his chin. Then he gasped to Wardell, "Get out of here. I'm through."

"I'll carry you. We'll get you a doctor."

Sage coughed crimson again. "Get going," he said through clenched teeth. "You . . . you have to tell them."

Wardell's mind was racing. He'd seen enough of war to know that Sage was probably a dead man. But he couldn't abide the thought of leaving him.

Wardell was distracted by the sound of men at the fence behind him. He had seconds to move before they'd be after him.

He looked back at Sage, then started in surprise. The agent had another Russian grenade in his hands. With great effort, Sage pulled the hand out, stretching the spring.

"I'm letting it go," Sage managed to gasp. "Go."

The spring snapped shut. Wardell dashed down the tracks as fast as he could go. He got to a ditch near the far fence and dove to the ground as the grenade detonated.

He waited only until the rain of gravel stopped. Then he took off, running as hard as he could. His own chest ached as if he'd been shot and his legs felt as if fifty-pound weights had been strapped to his ankles. But he forced his mind off the pain. He was Davy Crockett, chasing Indians across the mountains. He was a hero. He couldn't give up. He couldn't give up.

Up ahead, on either side of the track, he could see lights. That must be the British zone. The sight gave him strength.

Then a soldier stepped, seemingly, out of nowhere and pointed a weapon at him. The soldier barked a command in Russian.

Wardell was moving fast, and with safety so near, he never considered stopping. To the soldier's surprise, Wardell barreled into him, sending him flying with the entire force of his two hundred forty pounds. The impact knocked Wardell off balance and he stumbled three steps before falling. He rolled over once and cracked his elbow on a rail.

As he was pulling himself together and starting to scramble to his feet, the weight of a body fell on him, knocking him into the gravel. An arm was locked around his neck, pressing against his Adam's apple. He felt himself choking and tried to throw the weight off, but the man was very strong. Wardell hit the ground face first, then managed to get to his knees again.

The pressure on his throat was increasing, and his lungs began to ache. He could feel the hot breath of his attacker on the top of his head as the man applied pressure.

A thought struck him. Somehow, he managed to twist enough to grab the butt of his pistol with his right hand and pull it out of his holster.

He wasn't sure how many of the seven rounds in the clip he fired. His only hope was to take one life. He tried to take a breath; then in one motion he pointed the pistol over his left shoulder and pulled the trigger.

The gun fired, hitting the Russian in the upper chest. The man's grip loosened as he screamed in pain. Wardell broke free, spun around, and pulled the trigger again. The pistol was empty.

The Russian dove at Wardell again. Wardell hit him

in the face with the pistol in his right hand. He heard the sound of bone splintering. Wardell clubbed him again, then a third time. The Russian collapsed.

Wardell felt totally exhausted and his mind was a haze. Later, he couldn't remember how he'd managed to get to his feet and continue running down the tracks. What he did remember was that when he finally couldn't move any longer and collapsed to the ground, he heard voices in English. Then he blacked out.

TWENTY-ONE

Dolan waited for Wardell in the office of an assistant press secretary. When they'd arrived at the White House from Andrews Air Force Base a little after seven P.M., most of the staff had been working. Now it was nearly ten, and only one officer and a skeleton communications staff in the next section were on duty.

Dolan had ordered a pot of coffee from the White House mess after waiting an hour, and he was now on his second. He paced back and forth, working off his edginess and the stiffness from the cross-Atlantic flight.

He was glad for the relative peace of the press office for a couple reasons. One, it left him to his thoughts— primarily of the awesome amount of work that might have to be done in the next few days. And secondly, it meant that no word of the shoot-out in Berlin had leaked to the press, or, rather, that it had not been taken seriously by the press. Word had come from Berlin while they were in the air; the Russian press had announced that General Penkovsky had been killed by

American agents. But that kind of announcement was often made to cover their handling of an internal problem, and the Western press hadn't bothered to pay attention; even though in this case, it was true.

Dolan was interrupted by the phone ringing. He hesitated, then picked it up. The White House operator told him that she'd been unable to locate Mrs. Wardell. Messages had been left at home and at her office.

Dolan thanked her. As he was hanging up the phone, David Wardell walked into the office.

"Who was that?" Wardell asked.

"Nobody," Dolan said impatiently. "What did the president say?"

Wardell smiled ironically. "He told me if I was going to fight, to pick on somebody my own size. I think he's right."

Wardell gingerly lowered himself into a chair. He'd torn a flexor tendon in his right arm, which was in a sling. His rib cage had been badly bruised, he had a black eye, his throat was marked and swollen, and his body was a mass of abrasions and sore muscles.

The doctors in Berlin had patched him up quickly and then given him a strong sedative. He'd awakened over the Atlantic. Dolan had hustled him on a plane to get him out of Berlin, in case the incident provoked the Russians to do something foolish.

Dolan saw that Wardell was in pain. He asked, "Coffee? Or something stronger?"

"Something stronger," Wardell said.

Dolan requested bourbon from the White House mess. Then he said to Wardell, "Do you feel like talking?"

"No," Wardell said. "But I'll fill you in briefly." He

sighed. "Truman really wore me out."

"Was anyone else there?"

"Forrestal came in after a while. Then Tom Clark."

"Clark? Why'd they want the attorney general?"

Wardell said, "You might consider Scalpel an act of war. Last time I read the Constitution, Congress had to declare war. In this case, obviously, Congress can't be consulted. The president wanted to see if that was legal."

"And?"

"There're a lot of options under discussion, Mack. You know that."

Dolan grimaced. "But we have proof that the Soviets will test their bomb in less than two weeks."

"Correction," Wardell said. "We had proof, which was blown up with Sage. Hell, I don't know, maybe he was lying to me. I can't read Russian. That cable could have said anything."

Dolan looked at him sharply. "Do you really mean that?" he asked.

"No," Wardell admitted. "I believed him at the time. He had no reason to lie, when we thought we were going to get back to the British zone without a problem." He paused for a moment to yawn, then added, "I believe that the report about the Russians and the bomb is true. I also believe they're planning some sort of military action in Berlin now that the election is over. That's what I told the president."

"And what was his reaction?"

"I think he's convinced the Russians mean business in Berlin. The news about the bomb was more surprising, but he's been told the Russians have had the knowledge for some time. He's very, very concerned."

236

A knock on the door silenced them. A steward brought in brandy. Dolan began pouring.

"Not much for me, Mack," Wardell said. "A drink is going to knock me on my ass. I feel like I could sleep for a week."

Dolan handed him a snifter. He raised his own. "To your rather miraculous escape."

Wardell nodded, then took a sip. "Miraculous it was." He took a sip, then added, "Something occurred to me a little while ago. Did you ever tell me what happened to Lieutenant Richie?"

"I did," Dolan said. "But you were already going under from that shot the doctors gave you. Richie was killed. He gave himself up to give you and Sage the earliest possible warning."

"Damn," Wardell said.

They drank in silence for a moment. Then Dolan asked, "I know you're exhausted. I've got a car outside to take you home. But can you tell me where we stand now? What's the bottom line?"

"The bottom line is that Truman is seriously considering Scalpel. But the kind of political, military, and moral consequences that would raise are complex. He wants to take time to fully explore other options—and to spend some time with himself to see if he can live with the decision. I understand that."

"I do, too," Mack said. "But time is short."

"Better we lose a day than make a catastrophic decision. I need to sleep on it, too."

"You mean you're still not sure?"

Wardell said, "No, I'm not. Truman asked me, of course. I told him that I'd see him again tomorrow. Before then, you and I should get together. I've got some questions to ask you, when I'm not so tired I can't remember the answers."

"Come on," Dolan said. "I'll get you home. I'll come for breakfast tomorrow."

Wardell slowly got to his feet, feeling like an eighty-year-old man. "Let's make that a late breakfast," he said.

Wardell let himself in the house. The downstairs was dark. He turned on the hall light, glanced briefly through a stack of mail, and went into the kitchen to get himself a glass of milk before going upstairs.

"David?"

"He turned. Laura, in a dressing gown, was standing in the doorway of the kitchen.

Her mouth dropped open when she saw his face. "What happened to you?" she asked.

"It's a long story," he said.

"I'll bet it is," she said. She stood, biting her lower lip for a second. Then she asked, "Did she throw you out? Is that how it happened?"

Wardell was puzzled. "She? Who are you talking about?"

"Susan Gordon."

He stood, paralyzed, not believing what she uttered.

"I see it on your face," she said. "That's all the confirmation I need."

"Confirmation of what?"

"Confirmation that you've been cheating on me. All that talk about the life we're going to build together, the children we're going to have. I suppose that will all happen in between trips to Europe to see your little blond friend. No wonder you want to retire two years before I do. More playtime."

Her words stung him, as if he'd been wounded again. "No, Laura, you've got it all wrong."

"What have I got wrong?" she demanded. "I've seen pictures of you two billing and cooing all over Paris. I suppose that's an optical illusion?"

"What pictures are you talking about?"

"A journalist friend of mine came into possession of some photos taken by a free-lancer in Paris. The photographer was trying to peddle them to a U.S. magazine. Fortunately, my friend got his hands on them and stopped the sale—for my sake, not yours."

"Who's this friend?"

She glared at him. "I'm the one who should be asking the questions, David."

He sighed, closing his eyes. Then he looked at her again and said, "You've taken me by surprise. And after a nightmarish two days. I want to talk this out with you fully when I'm better able to think. I have no intention of trying to convince you that there was nothing between Susan and me. But I will tell you, truthfully, that I have no intention of ever seeing her again. And Susan had nothing to do with this trip to Berlin. I wish to hell she had, even if it meant coming home to confront you."

She looked at him intently. Once again, her eyes inspected his injuries. "What did happen? Is that arm broken?"

"The arm is a torn tendon. I may have a broken rib or two."

"From what?"

He debated for a moment. Then he said, "I shouldn't

239

say anything. But if we're going to establish some communication, I think you've got to know what I've been involved in. Briefly, I was called to Berlin to meet with a very high-level Russian intelligence officer who's recently been passing along to us vital information about Soviet military preparations. Unfortunately, his friends found out about our rendezvous. The Russian was killed, as were the two agents who went into the Soviet zone with me. I barely managed to get out of the trap and get back to the Western zone."

She looked at him with amazement. "That sounds more like a spy movie than real life. What did a U.S. senator have to meet a foreign agent for?"

"I had to personally verify information that had to go directly to Truman. I went directly from the air base to the White House. I was with the president for three hours tonight, and I have to go back tomorrow."

A jolt of concern went through her. "What is this information about? It sounds very serious."

"It is," he said. "But that's all I can say. For now, anyway."

She stiffened. "I see," she said.

He moved forward, putting his left hand on her shoulder. "Laura, I know how upsetting this must be for you. I'm sick about the hurt I've caused. I'll make it up to you, I promise. If you'll promise me you'll listen."

She took a step back. His arm fell to his side. "I've always been willing to listen, David," she said. "It's you who hasn't listened. You promised me two nights ago before you went away that you'd take the time to hear me out, to discuss everything with me so we can be true partners. Now, I don't know what to think. You've gotten so good at that game you play—the calm, patient compromiser. I can't help but think that you just sit here listening and nodding your head; then you go out and do whatever the hell you want anyway. I don't call that listening."

His face showed how upset he was. "I don't think that's fair, Laura."

"Fair or not, it's how I feel. You'll have to convince me otherwise."

"I'm going to try," he said. "But not now. I can barely stand. And tomorrow morning Mack Dolan is coming for breakfast before I go back to the White House."

"Dolan," she said. "A nice choice of confidant. I suppose this business of yours is so important we'll have to postpone our more trivial conversation about our marriage. Shall I telephone Rachel in your office for an appointment?"

"Laura, it's not trivial. But the situation at hand is of monumental importance to our country. I can't tell you now. But soon you'll understand. Believe me."

"Believe you," she said. "I only wish I could."

She turned and walked out of the room.

Wardell stared after her for a moment. Then he looked down and saw the half-finished glass of milk on the table. Suddenly, his stomach felt tight as a drum. He emptied the milk into the sink and slowly climbed up the stairs to bed.

TWENTY-TWO

Laura couldn't sleep all night. Her mind was a welter of violent emotions, and she was so tense that the slightest noise set her on edge. She couldn't even turn the light off, for the dark thoughts she had made the night seem terrifying.

The anger that had been building in her since the meeting with Carl Waldman hadn't gone away. She didn't know if she'd ever trust David again. Did she want to? That question could only be answered over time.

And what about this mysterious trip to Berlin? As morning drew near, that troubled her more and more. David had told her several times that he expected the crisis to come to a head after the elections. Obviously, Berlin was the reason for the trip and the meetings at the White House.

But what was behind the meetings? She paced back and forth as the first faint rays of dawn streaked the gray-black sky outside her window. For a long time she fought against the thought that tried to wedge itself into her mind.

Then she confronted it. No one could ignore the heavy-handed way the government had brandished the threat of the atomic bomb since Hiroshima. Was this an acceleration of that threat? Were they going to move atomic weapons to Germany, closer to the Soviet Union? Were they going to give atomic weapons to Britain and France to increase the pressure on the Russians to back down?

Any further risk of nuclear war was anathema to Laura. She couldn't believe that anyone who'd seen Hiroshima could entertain any thought of another atomic explosion.

That included David. She had thought he was such a sensitive, rational, humane man. She had seen him deeply moved by the cataclysmic destruction in Japan.

Or had she? Had that been an act, too? Was the David Wardell she thought she knew just a façade, the face put forward by a skillful Machiavelli?

She didn't want to believe that. But she had to find out. Someway, somehow. And as quickly as possible.

Mack Dolan spread a map on the desk in David's study. He pointed a thick finger at a spot marked in red.

"That's Kazanov. Coordinates fifty degrees and zero minutes east, fifty-seven degrees and thirty minutes north. The target is just north of the city of Kirov. The planes will take off for the final time from Trondheim, Norway. They'll pass over Barentsovo More, the Barents Sea, Cheshskaya Guba, the Archangels, the open corridor south between Tsengora and Barkovskaya, then finally they'll swing west and south over the Kotlas Mountains, with the Luza River to the southeast as a visual guide."

"What happens when they reach the target?" Wardell asked.

"The planes will orient themselves from a diamond-shaped lake at Kasanov. They'll make their approach on a line from the southwest to the northeast corners of the diamond. The nuclear research facilities are eighteen miles ahead on that line. The paratroopers will be dropped, each with their assigned targets. When communications are cut with Moscow, then the planes will begin to land at the airstrip. The scientists staffing the center will be evacuated, along with important documents and other materials we find."

"And then?" Wardell asked.

Dolan looked him directly in the eye. "The planes clear the airspace. The atomic bomb is armed and dropped dead center over the research facilities."

Wardell took one sharp breath. Then he asked, "Estimated casualties?"

"Our intelligence isn't good enough to pinpoint exactly the number of support personnel in the area. Certainly, a significant number of Russian soldiers will be killed in the attack. The town of Kazanov has a population of approximately five thousand, and perhaps there are another five thousand scattered about the blast area."

"So you're saying ten thousand people will die?"

Dolan said, "Give or take a few thousand. Fortunately, the prevailing winds will blow the radioactive material out over a largely unpopulated area. Secondary radiation sickness or death should be minimal."

Wardell sat back, eyes closed. The images from his postwar tour of Japan flooded into his mind. He felt a cold chill go through him.

Then he sat forward again. "Mack, what happens next? What do we want Stalin to do?"

Dolan replied, "That's up to you politicians. I would certainly think that a Soviet troop pull-out of most of Eastern Europe is the primary goal. They took those countries as buffer states, and we want them back."

"I was at Potsdam," Wardell said. "I had a lot of chances to see Stalin in action. I don't think he's the kind of man you can blackmail."

"Maybe not," Dolan said. "He's a madman, and like Hitler he may be bent on self-destruction. But I'm not sure the other Soviet leaders are."

"You mean—"

"I mean not even Stalin might survive. I don't think his associates—with all their power, their fancy dachas, all gained through untold years of surviving purges and working laboriously upward through the system—are going to be thrilled with being incinerated. I think if Stalin acts up, he'll disappear."

"How can we be sure they have a sufficient sense of the threat? After all, we'll already have dropped the bomb."

"There will be other bombers, with live bombs, waiting on the ground, ready to fly," Dolan said. "And other targets. Major targets. We don't want to give the Russians a chance to pull themselves together psychologically. They'll have maybe twenty-four hours."

Wardell thought for a moment. Then he asked, "What if they launch a ground or air attack in Germany?"

"Some of our boys will die. But the people who gave the orders won't be around for long to enjoy it."

"That's a hell of a risk," Wardell commented.

"It's better than being on the other end of a blackmail threat six months or a year from now. What would you do if you were sitting in Truman's chair with a Russian bomber somewhere in the air near New York or Washington?"

Wardell scowled. "That's the worst-case scenario."

Dolan didn't reply.

Wardell sat for a long time, drawing intricate geometric designs with a pencil on a note pad.

Dolan finally asked, "Well, what are you going to recommend to the president? Bottom-line time, David."

Wardell grunted, as if enjoying a private joke. "I was thinking about going hunting, Mack. Typing out a short letter of resignation on that Underwood over there, having Rachel deliver it to the president pro tem of the Senate, and being on the first plane to Arizona before Truman gets word of it."

"But you're not going to do that?" Dolan asked.

"No," Wardell said. He got to his feet. "I'm going to the meeting at the White House. And I guess I'm going to tell the president that we have to do what has to be done."

"Including Scalpel?"

"Whatever has to be done to make this world safe for a while. Long enough for me to spend my days as a gentleman rancher. Somehow my appetite for Washington has been permanently spoiled."

Laura wasn't aware that David and Mack Dolan had

left the house. She'd been in a state of profound shock since she'd heard the general so matter-of-factly discuss the dropping of an atomic bomb on the Soviet Union.

She'd almost resisted the urge to eavesdrop on the conversation. To do so went against her code of behavior. But her intense interest in the crisis that was involving David so completely overrode her inherent distaste.

In the old colonial-style house, sound carried through the vents of the hot-air heating system. Laura's bathroom was directly above David's study, and many times she'd been preparing for bed when she'd heard him gently snoring because he'd fallen asleep listening to the late news on the radio. So she had listened to David and Dolan.

Now, she wished she hadn't been able to hear the awful plan for this Operation Scalpel. Scalpel. The word itself carried cruel, cold connotations, but at the same time, for the people involved in making this decision, it had a comforting connection to surgeons—those who heal by deftly cutting away poisonous tissue or tumor. A clean, antiseptic effect.

Only dropping an atomic bomb was far from antiseptic. It took her breath away to hear Dolan talk about ten thousand people killed as she remembered the horror of Hiroshima. And there could be a second bomb, and a third . . . as millions perished.

Laura turned and faced the sink. She ran cold water and splashed it over her face, which felt flushed. Then she walked out into her bedroom and sat down at her small desk.

What should she do or, rather, what could she do? Her primary hope was that the president was sane enough to reject this madness. She wished she knew the man from Missouri better. In many ways, he was an enigma. When he'd been nominated, he'd been dismissed as a party hack perfectly qualified to fill a meaningless government position. But when Roosevelt had died, Truman had suddenly been faced with the momentous decisions of completing the war effort and structuring the postwar world. He'd taken command with a self-confidence that had surprised Laura and many other people. She'd been further surprised by the very effective and personal election campaign he'd waged to overcome Dewey's seemingly insurmountable lead.

But what was he like personally? How fundamentally moral a man was he? This decision would tell.

And what if the decision to go ahead with Scalpel was made?

Her only alternative was to stimulate some sort of public outcry. But who would believe her? She'd been speaking out vehemently against atomic warfare for over a year. It would be easy for the White House to dismiss her warnings as "crying wolf."

The truth was that there was no alternative. She'd been a failure as a public leader and, worse, a failure at home. She'd had absolutely no effect on David at all, which stung and wounded her as little else had in her life.

The phone began to ring. At first she ignored it, too preoccupied to talk. Then her innate sense of responsibility dragged her to her feet and across the room. It was probably her office calling, wondering why she hadn't called in.

But the voice on the other end of the line was male.

"Laura? How are you?"

She took a deep breath and then said in a light voice, "Is this Carl? How did you know I was home?"

"You weren't at the office." There was a pause, then he asked, "You sound troubled; are you all right?"

She didn't know what to say. "I . . . I'm fine."

"Something is wrong," he said. "I know you, Laura. You're upset. Is it something with David? Something we've talked about in the past? You can confide in me."

"No," she said. Tears were coming to her eyes, and she had trouble speaking. "No."

"Please tell me. I can come over."

"No," she said firmly.

"Laura. We have to work together. What we stand for is so important that—"

She hung up the phone, cutting him off. Then she collapsed on the bed, sobbing.

Carl Waldman held the phone in his hand for a couple of minutes, thinking. Then he depressed the button and dialed a number. He let the phone ring once, then hung up.

The clock read a little after 10:30. Time to walk. He grabbed his camera, put on his overcoat, and headed down the three flights of stairs from his small office to the street.

He reached the Mall twenty minutes later. The expanse of grass had lost the rich lushness of early autumn, and its dullness was further emphasized by the grayness of the day. Early November wasn't a heavy tourist time; the next rush would come around the Thanksgiving holiday. Only a handful of people were in sight as he neared the Washington Monument and began taking pictures.

He deliberately restrained himself from looking around. He heard the click of a camera shutter before he was aware the other man had approached. He turned and smiled.

"Looks like a nice camera you have there," Waldman said.

The other man's face was somber. He was in his mid-forties, with dark hair and a gray flannel suit.

"Don't bother with that nonsense," the man said. "There's no one in hearing distance. Why have you called me out here on such short notice?"

"It's Wardell's wife. I just phoned her, and she was so upset she couldn't talk. I know Wardell went straight to the White House from the airport last night, and he and Dolan returned to the White House this morning. Something is up. I have a suspicion Laura knows what it is."

"Well," the man said impatiently, "find out what it is. That's the whole purpose of your assignment. You know how important that intelligence is."

"I know," Waldman said. "But she's been difficult lately. I thought after I slept with her in Bimini, I could control her. But she's retreated since then. I'll try, but—"

"But you might need further means of persuasion." The man looked away from Waldman, gazing out over the Mall as he continued. "We have to be very careful with the wife of a man like Wardell. However, this is a crucial time for us, comrade. A very crucial time."

"So?" Waldman asked. "What am I to do?"

"Return to your office. I have some consultations to

250

make. You will be contacted."

"By whom?"

"You will know," the man said. "And I have a warning for you. You must cooperate fully and immediately. The consequences will be very serious if you don't."

"And if I do?"

"You may get that reward, comrade. And at least you will live."

TWENTY-THREE

Secretary of Defense James Forrestal sat at the head of the conference table. David Wardell sat to his right, Stuart Symington, Secretary of the Air Force, and Kenneth Royall, Secretary of the Army, to his left. Farther down the table were two assistant secretaries of defense and nine men in uniform, including Mack Dolan.

Forrestal took a sip of water and began. "Gentlemen, the president has made his decision. The debate is over, and I'm not about to waste time continuing arguments that have been made before. Although I'm sure it's not necessary, I want to caution you on the extreme seriousness of the missions ahead and on the need for absolute secrecy. You're not to talk to yourself out loud about this operation, much less to anyone else who is not on the need-to-know list. I trust that's clear."

He looked around to see heads nodding.

"All right," Forrestal said. "To bring up to date those of you who weren't in the Oval Office this morning, the president has authorized the mobilization of the Scalpel attack force. Because of the extreme nature of Scalpel, however, the United States Government will make every attempt to achieve resolution of the Berlin crisis through other means.

"Two days from now, a representative of our government will deliver a document to Marshal Sokolovsky, the Soviet governor of Berlin, demanding the reopening of the land route to Berlin. A copy of that document will be delivered to the Kremlin by Ambassador Bedell-Smith."

"Who's going to Berlin?" asked Admiral Hillenkoetter, director of the Central Intelligence Agency.

"David Wardell," Forrestal said. "Having a member of Congress deliver an ultimatum is a sign that the American people are united in seeking a resolution of this conflict. The Russians are very sensitive on such matters."

Wardell added, "General Clay will accompany me. Any other military presence might be taken as a direct threat."

"But is it a threat?" Secretary Symington asked.

"Of course," Forrestal said. "If the land route is not reopened voluntarily within twenty-four hours—and I don't believe it will be—an armed U.S. convoy will start to move across the demarcation line."

"Considering the strength of the Soviet ground forces, they'd be chewed up if the Russians decided to fight," Mack Dolan said.

"The president took that into consideration," Forrestal said. "I'm sure everyone in this room joins me in hoping and praying that the Russians act like a responsible, civilized power by allowing the convoy free passage and reopening the land route."

253

"And if they don't?" asked a voice from the other end of the table.

"The Scalpel force will be in the air within the hour."

The meeting lasted until nearly four o'clock. Wardell spent another three hours with Rachel Lang, his administrative assistant, on correspondence and other unavoidable problems that had arisen during his frequent and recent absences. He didn't leave his office until nearly eight, and he waited outside in the late autumn chill for twenty minutes before the taxi arrived.

When the cab pulled into the driveway of his Georgetown home, he was almost relieved to see that the house was dark. The thought of having to spend hours with Laura going over his relationship with Susan Gordon was intolerable now that he was totally absorbed in the brinksmanship over Berlin. All he wanted to do was pack a bag and get a good night's sleep—maybe his last night's sleep for days.

That wasn't fair to Laura, he admitted to himself as he walked toward the front door. His marriage had been a failure to date, and he'd been largely to blame. He knew the guilt would linger with him for a long time. But he couldn't have it brought to the fore now.

He paused outside to fumble in his pockets for his keys. He was startled when the door opened.

"Laura! I didn't think you were home."

"I fell asleep in the living room. The lights of the taxi woke me." She looked at him a moment, then said, "Are you still coming in?"

He felt foolish for his awkwardness. "Of course."

He hung up his coat in the hall closet while Laura went into the living room to turn on the lights. When he followed her, he went to the bar to fix himself a drink.

Then he sat down opposite Laura, who was on the sofa, and thought, I've never seen her like this. She was very pale and drawn; there was a fragility about her that was shocking.

He took a deep breath; then he started. "I know how this revelation about another woman must have—"

"I don't care about her," Laura interrupted. Her voice was heavy with emotion. "Not now. What I do care about is your incredible plan to drop atomic bombs on the Russians. I don't know how a man I once loved could even talk about that."

David stared at her intensely. "How did you know about that?"

"I was listening. Upstairs, I've told you how sound carries. I couldn't help it, but I'm not ashamed of myself. Someone has to talk you and Dolan out of this madness."

Wardell looked down at his drink, at the swirling patterns in the amber liquid. He said, "I can't talk to you about this, Laura. You have to understand."

"Goddamn it, David," she yelled. "I'm your wife. I'm not some damn underling or newspaper reporter. You go off to Europe screwing an actress and you talk to me about trust."

"Laura, I—"

"You must hate me," she said. "You must think I'm an idiot, the way you treat me."

"No," he said. "I don't hate you. I love you. And I respect your intellect and judgment. I know I haven't acted as though I do in the past. But these years of our

255

marriage have been difficult."

"Not as difficult as what we face now," she said. "David, I beg of you. I'm sure you went to great lengths to get the advice of everyone in the government about this plan. Can't you take a moment to talk about it with me? Is it possible there is something you've overlooked?"

"Of course it's possible," he said. "But Truman has made the decision."

"Oh, no," she said. She buried her head in her hands. He crossed to her, putting his arms around her.

She pulled away. "Don't touch me," she sobbed.

He sat there, feeling totally helpless. His heart went out to her.

He waited until she regained control of herself. Then he said, "Laura, you are my wife. And as a sign of my trust, I'm going to tell you exactly what's happened and what's going to happen. Then you can make up your mind as to exactly how irresponsible we've been. Will you hear me through?"

"I've always been willing to hear you through," she said.

"Okay," he said.

The narrative took thirty minutes. David reviewed the contact with Penkovsky, the information he'd passed on, the events in Berlin, and the sequence of the attempts to resolve the Berlin crisis before resorting to Scalpel.

He waited what seemed like a long time before she spoke. "I can allow you one thing," she said. "I believe you believe you're doing the right thing."

"And you don't?"

"I think this argument is even worse than the justification for dropping the bombs on Hiroshima and Nagasaki. At that time, we knew the limits of the deaths that would result, and even I admit American lives were saved. But in this case the horrors could be continuing and open ended. So what if we delay the Russian atomic research program a year or two years or ten years? In the long run, every nation will have the bomb, and by our unilateral action we'll have made the use of those weapons an acceptable means of conducting foreign affairs. And in the next decade or two our civilization will be back to the Stone Age, a few bewildered survivors foraging in the rubble."

"I see how you can think that," David said. "But your opinion relies on the giant supposition that our forsaking the use of the bomb will restrain Stalin. Thirty million people died in World War II because we thought we could restrain another madman. We can't make that same mistake again. No matter how terrible the cost may seem."

Laura looked at him with intense sadness. "No matter how terrible the cost," she repeated. "I can't believe that I'm hearing you talk. The mouth, the voice are familiar. The words are those of a stranger."

Wardell sighed, shaking his head. "I don't know how we came to this, Laura. But I think we could stay here and talk for months and not get any closer. The decision is made, and I'm off to Berlin in the morning. I'm afraid you're going to have to come with me."

She stiffened. "I'm what?"

"I shouldn't have told you what I did tonight. Of course I trust you, but you realize that I can't take any chances. An inadvertent slip could expose the plan—and you—to danger. The alternative is providing security for you here. I'm sure you wouldn't find that pleasant."

"I find the whole idea repulsive," Laura said angrily. "How dare you imply that I'm some sort of traitor?"

"I'm not implying anything," David said. "You're overreacting. We don't have to stay together in the hotel overseas, we don't have to talk to each other. But maybe we'll decide to talk. Especially if our prayers are realized and this situation can be resolved without bloodshed."

"No," she said with determination. "I'm not going to Berlin with you. The thought of being involved in such a plan is abhorrent to me."

David rose. "In that case, I'll have to make arrangements to have someone stay with you. I'm sure Mack Dolan can find a Women's Army Corps officer. It's for your own protection."

She sat glaring at him, without responding.

He walked into his study to place a phone call. The Pentagon switchboard was looking for General Dolan when he heard the sound of the garage door being lifted. He dropped the phone and dashed for the front door. He got outside just as Laura backed the Chrysler down the driveway. He screamed at her, but the red lights disappeared into the night.

Wardell was sitting in the living room when the phone rang shortly after ten. He was expecting to hear Laura on the other end of the line. But instead a gruff male voice said, "David, you were paging me?"

"Mack," David said. "Yes, I did."

"Well," Dolan said. "Do I have to guess what it's

258

about or are you going to tell me?"

David hadn't decided what the right thing to do was. He trusted Laura and he didn't want to turn a domestic argument into a major issue. On the other hand, he couldn't compromise Scalpel in any way—any additional way.

"David, are you still there?"

"Sorry. Listen, Mack, could you come over? Now?"

There was silence for a moment. Then Dolan said, "I'll be there in twenty minutes."

Wardell took half an hour to fill Dolan in completely. Then Dolan got up and paced as he thought.

"I'm sorry to hear this," Dolan said. "I thought you and Laura were a perfect couple."

"We could have been. We should have been," Wardell said.

"You still could be," Dolan said. "Unfortunately, there're other things to think of right now. It's really too bad that she overheard our conversation."

"She's obsessed with the subject," Wardell said. "I've never seen her get that emotional over anything else. I'm sure it's partly because of the problems between us. The issue is where she will channel her feelings."

"Whatever," Dolan said, "we've got to find her. Do you have any ideas?"

"While I was waiting for you I made a few calls. Laura didn't have that many close friends in Washington. She worked so hard at her job that she didn't have much time for a social life."

"Could she have gone back to Iowa?"

"That's a possibility. Either tonight or, more likely,

in the morning. We could see if the car's at the airport."

"We're not going to have time for that, David," Dolan said. "You forget that we're leaving for Berlin first thing tomorrow morning. We're going to need help."

"What kind of help?" Wardell asked.

"I think you ought to give Hoover a call."

"Bring in the FBI? Isn't that overreacting? I mean, Laura isn't dangerous."

Dolan sat down next to Wardell. "You just told me you've never seen her so emotional. That means there's the chance, no matter how slight, that she might do something foolish that could seriously jeopardize Scalpel."

Wardell reflected glumly on the situation. Dolan was right, of course. He had to ignore the personal embarrassment this situation would cause him.

"You know Hoover well enough to make the call?" Dolan asked. "We could have the president talk to him."

"No," Wardell said. "Hoover sits in on most of my intelligence briefings, and I suppose we get along as cordially as Hoover gets along with anyone. I know the FBI is better prepared to handle a situation like this than Army Intelligence. But I can't help thinking how furious Laura is going to be when she finds G-men at the door."

"That can't be a consideration," Dolan said.

"No," Wardell said. He got to his feet. "I'll call Hoover now. And I'll see you at the airport in the morning."

TWENTY-FOUR

The door on the third floor of the small office building in Alexandria, Virginia, just across the Potomac from Washington, read "Reliable Domestics, Inc." The door was locked, and Carl Waldman knocked.

There was no reply immediately. Waldman nervously looked over his shoulder toward the stairs. He strained, but heard no footsteps. Then the door opened.

"Come in," said a short, balding man in his late thirties.

Waldman stepped inside. "I've come to inquire about the position as a valet," Waldman said.

"I wish you had," the man said dryly. Then he added, "We can forget all that code-phrase nonsense. I know who you are, Waldman."

Waldman was startled. "But I don't know you?"

"The name Volkert will do. That's what all the charwomen and the other lovelies I send out call me. Now, come with me."

Volkert escorted him through a cramped waiting room into a larger inner office. At one end was a large desk piled high with stacks of papers. At the other, a large overstuffed sofa was flanked by two armchairs.

Volkert sat behind the desk. He pointed to the other end of the room. "My casting couch," he said. "It is truly incredible the number of young things who are more than willing to use their bodies for the privilege of waiting on other pampered human beings hand and foot. I think most of them entertain cinematic fancies of marrying the handsome young heir, so they're getting themselves ready. The Scandinavians, however, do seem to have a true passion for sex. I spend more than a little time hoping my next assignment is in Scandinavia."

Waldman sat staring at the man who busied himself filling and packing a pipe. He was beginning to wonder if this was some sort of joke. His control at the Russian embassy was a stern, formal Russian. He'd been led to believe that the man he was sent here to see was a higher-ranking KGB agent.

The man lit his pipe, puffed, and emitted large clouds of smoke. Then he leaned back in his chair and said, "Now, my friend Waldman, let us get into this matter of Mrs. Wardell. Run through the entire situation from the beginning."

"The time is urgent," Waldman protested. "I've told the embassy everything that's happened to date. The FBI is already on her trail."

Volkert leaned forward. He said in a voice with a steel-hard edge, "Waldman, I know the importance of the situation. If I didn't you would never have been accorded the rare privilege of seeing my face. You weren't brought here to ask questions but to answer them. Talk."

The message got through. Waldman concisely repeated the course of his relationship with Laura, ending with the phone call last night. Then he finished by saying, "I drove out to the house this morning. I parked two blocks away, waiting until I saw the senator go by in a taxicab. But when I rang the doorbell, a man answered. I'm sure he was an FBI agent. I made sure I wasn't followed."

Volkert sat back without speaking, tamping his pipe and puffing. Finally, he said, "Listen to these instructions carefully. You are to go directly back to your office and prepare a news story. The focus of the story will be on the mysterious disappearance of a congresswoman, the presence of the FBI on the case, and the sudden trip of the husband, the well-known senator, to Europe. You can also include the name of this actress in the story. It should make quite the sensational piece."

Waldman was puzzled. "Laura, missing? I thought the agents were there to protect her?"

"You made an erroneous assumption. We are engaged in a race with the FBI to locate this woman. Hoover's people are very good at this sort of search, and they're devoting considerable resources to it. I've been following their progress quite closely."

"How do you know what the FBI's doing?"

Volkert flashed him an angry look. "Again, I remind you you're here to answer questions. I will not warn you again. Your job is to write that story."

Waldman thought for a moment. "I certainly could see it. But it will call attention to myself. The FBI took my name this morning, they might be watching me."

"I certainly hope they do," Volkert said. "Remember, you are a journalist. In this country, with its rather quaint attachment to freedom of the press, journalists are expected to poke around and create uproars. I want you to devote yourself openly to finding Laura Jameson."

"The story might cause her to contact me. Or she could go to the authorities and announce she's not missing."

"We have to take that chance," Volkert said. He leaned forward again. "You have performed well today, my friend Waldman. But it is absolutely vital that we obtain the opportunity to question the woman at length. You must trust me when I tell you that the goal is worth taking risks, the greatest of risks. I can assure you that if we succeed through your efforts, you will be more than adequately rewarded for your services to our cause."

Waldman took in a deep breath. Then he said, "I'll do it. Anything else?"

"When you return to your offices, you will find that you have acquired a secretary. She will be quite useful to you. In addition, she will know how to reach me at any time."

Waldman nodded.

"You may go now," Volkert said. "I assume you can find your way out."

Waldman left the room. Volkert heard the outer door shut. Then he got up and verified that the outer office was empty. He said in a conversational voice, "He's gone."

The bookcase on the left wall swung open. A

distinguished looking gray-haired man in his fifties came out. He crossed to the desk, took a cigarette from a silver box, and lit it. Then he said to Volkert, "What do you think of Waldman?"

"I despise people like him. His commitment to our cause is a titillating little secret game, like masturbation. He's a charming, manipulating bully with people he thinks he can control, and a spineless toady when confronted with anyone with real authority."

The gray-haired man said, "He has been useful. And we need all the help we can get now."

A distasteful expression appeared on Volkert's face. "Yes, I admit he could be useful. But we must be careful not to let him go too far. If the FBI puts any pressure on him, he'll crack immediately."

"That's why you assigned Anna to him?"

"Yes," Volkert said. "I didn't want to waste her, but I didn't have anyone else."

"She'll be useful if the woman contacts Waldman."

"If we find her at all," Volkert said. "And if Waldman gets into the slightest bit of trouble, she'll dispose of him immediately."

David Wardell was called to the phone in the VIP lounge in the hangar at the Andrews Air Force Base.

"Special Agent Frank Coffey," the man on the phone identified himself. "I was instructed to bring you up to date before your plane took off, Senator."

"I appreciate that."

"We've located your wife's car. Parking lot B at National Airport. The parking ticket was in the glove compartment. She got to the airport at 9:47 last night."

"Have you checked with the airlines?" Wardell asked.

"Not many flights go out at that time of night," Coffey replied. "We should have all the manifests by early afternoon. Your wife could have used another name, however. That might slow us down."

Wardell grimaced. The idea of Laura using subterfuge was so strange. But he supposed she could, considering her reaction to his request that she be assigned protection.

"Suppose she didn't get on a flight?" Wardell asked.

"We've got her address books, home and office. And the list of friends you gave us, Senator. An agent is interviewing Molly Braun, her secretary, right now."

"Molly's worked with her for nearly ten years," Wardell said. "If she can't tell you where Laura might have gone, nobody can."

"One final question, Senator. Do you know where your wife banked? We'd like to establish surveillance in case she needs money."

"The bank books and records are in the safe in my study. The combination is twelve–four–twenty-two–thirty-four."

"We'll check it out."

Wardell felt a tap on his shoulder. Mack Dolan told him it was time to board.

"I've got to go," Wardell said. "If you find her, contact General Dolan's office at the Pentagon. They'll get a radio message through to me."

Laura awakened with a start from some unremembered but troubling dream. She sat up in the oversoft bed and looked around, unsure for a moment where she was.

Then, as she surveyed the pink walls covered with the mementos of girlhood, she remembered.

The spur-of-the-moment decision to fly to New York. The cab ride from Idlewild Airport to Grand Central Station. Endless cups of coffee while waiting for the early morning train to Rhinebeck, New York, the small town on the Hudson where Molly's sister lived.

Molly's sister was just like her: calm, sympathetic, and efficient. She hadn't asked any questions about Laura's unusual visit. She'd chatted away about her two kids, both of whom were off at college, while she'd fixed Laura a big breakfast. Then she'd changed the linen in her daughter's old bedroom so Laura could get some sleep.

Now, at four o'clock on the afternoon after her flight, Laura lay languidly in bed, asking herself why she had fled. It seemed so melodramatic, playacting some half-remembered old movie she'd seen on TV. She was a member of Congress, not a damsel in distress.

Or was she? If certain people knew the secret she had been told, she'd be the object of an intense search. An atomic bomb could be dropped on another country in forty-eight hours, thus starting the darkest hour in world history.

Did she have the power to stop it? At first she'd thought she didn't. She couldn't think of a way to make use of the information that wasn't true treason. She wasn't naïve enough to believe that informing the Russian government would do any good. Stalin was

267

even more of a barbarian than Truman or the others involved in making the hideous decision. Unlike many of the left-wing antiatomic weapons people she came in contact with, she had nothing but repugnance for Soviet-style communism and their brutal repression of personal freedom.

Still, informing the Russians might make them back off when David delivered the ultimatum in Berlin. It might make them less willing to confront the armed convoy that would be sent to open the land route to Berlin. Then the Scalpel operation wouldn't be needed.

Or would it? If Stalin knew that the U.S. had planned to use the bomb on him, would he back off temporarily until he had his own weapon, then use it in the way David's information said he would? Would that create even more of a likelihood of total atomic war?

The weight on Laura felt immense. She wished she hadn't been so curious, she wished she'd never listened in on that conversation.

But she had, and she wasn't one to shirk her responsibilities. She knew she couldn't hide like a fugitive for long. She'd committed no crime. All she needed was a little time to rest and think.

The sound of pots and pans clinking in the kitchen below told her Carla was starting to prepare dinner. Her husband wouldn't be home for a couple of hours. Laura sighed, then decided to take refuge in a few more hours' sleep.

TWENTY-FIVE

Wardell, despite the weight on his mind, found that he was able to sleep during most of the long transatlantic trip on the C-54 which had been converted to an executive airplane. He awoke just after the last refueling stop, washed and shaved, and settled down to read the latest dispatches as the air transport made its final approach to Rhine Main in darkness of early morning.

Mack Dolan was still sleeping when the plane touched down. Wardell sent a steward to wake him, then deplaned. General Lucius Clay was waiting for him.

"I've just come in from Frankfort. I inspected the preparations for Steel Probe."

"That's the code name for the convoy?" Wardell asked.

"Affirmative."

"Were you satisfied?"

Clay replied, "I'd like four times the numbers. The

fifty tanks are the new T26E3 Pershings, which can really move and carry a lot of wallop. But the Russians must have a thousand tanks in the area. For support, there're just three companies of infantry and a company of combat engineers with temporary bridging materials to get over the rivers."

"It's not a token force," Wardell commented.

"Not unless we have to fight," Clay said sourly. "Then it might as well have been five tanks."

"Fighting's not the purpose," Wardell said. "We just need enough equipment to make the Russians think we're serious."

"We have that," Clay said.

"Then let's keep our fingers crossed."

General Dolan joined them, and they had breakfast in the officers' mess. After their C-47 received clearance, they made the short ride into Tempelhof airfield in Berlin.

Clay and Dolan went to American headquarters, Wardell to a hotel. It was after midnight in the States, so Wardell couldn't call for a progress report on the search for Laura. He'd received absolutely no word in flight. He was worried, but there was nothing he could do.

He showered and changed clothes. Then the desk called to say a command car was waiting for him. He made the twenty-minute ride to headquarters as the first streaks of dawn tinged the gray-black sky of the cold November morning. When the command car halted at the gate to the headquarters complex, Wardell noticed the clouds of white condensation coming from the nose and mouth of the guard as he checked the papers.

It was another reminder of the arrival of winter, the true challenge for the airlift. The Berlin crisis had to be settled, now.

Clay was sitting behind the desk in his office. He said to Wardell, "I woke Sokolovsky up. I'll tell you, the bastard has his wits about him, despite the hour. He informed me in the most polite way that he was unaware of any reason for us to meet, and that consequently he saw no reason to cross into West Berlin."

"You told him, of course, that we have an urgent communication from the president?"

Clay nodded. "And he condescended to meet us at his headquarters in two hours. That's nine hundred hours."

Dolan said to Wardell, "I cabled Washington. They'll instruct Bedell-Smith to go to the Kremlin with the message for Stalin at the same time."

The motorcade passed through the Brandenberg Gate traffic rotunda, then into East Berlin. To Wardell the Soviet sector seemed much more desolate than West Berlin. The roads were lined with ruined buildings. At major intersections concertina-wire barricades were manned by solitary guards in ancient sentry boxes. Wardell saw few pedestrians and fewer civilian vehicles.

At 0855 hours, the motorcade stopped at the curb outside a building with a huge Soviet flag draped against its front. The recessed building entrance was flanked by four uniformed guards carrying submachine guns.

"Friendly looking," Wardell commented.

"Wait until you see the friendly reception our message gets," Clay said.

The American driver opened the door. As Wardell and Clay climbed out, they were met by a young Soviet officer, who introduced himself in heavily accented English as Major Amirov. The Major escorted them into a large reception hall where three men in uniforms waited.

Marshal Sokolovsky was the man in the center, standing at his ease with his hands clasped behind him. He was in full dress uniform. Hanging from a ribbon circling his collar was the Order of Lenin, the Soviet Union's highest decoration. The two other officers wore the chevrons of full colonels.

The hall in which they stood was vast and dreary. The only decorations were large gilt-framed portraits of Stalin and Lenin, and another Soviet flag.

Major Amirov snapped to attention in front of the Marshal. "General Clay and Senator Wardell to see you, Marshal."

Marshal Sokolovsky nodded. Amirov turned to the Americans and said, "Let me introduce Marshal Sokolovsky, Colonel Stashinsky, and Colonel Makarov."

The Soviet officers nodded as their names were pronounced. Wardell almost stepped forward to shake hands, but he noticed Marshal Sokolovsky did not bring his hands from behind his back.

General Clay said, in English, "My respects, gentlemen. I wish to thank you, Marshal Sokolovsky, for agreeing to meet with us on such short notice."

The Marshal nodded to Clay, then to Wardell. His eyes were cold and appraising, his face expressionless.

"I understand this is a matter of some urgency," Sokolovsky said in slow, but clear English that surprised Wardell. In his briefing, he hadn't been told Sokolovsky spoke the language.

Wardell said, "It is a matter of urgency. As a senior member of the American Congress, I represent the American people in bringing you a communication from President Truman."

"And what is that communication, Senator?"

Wardell took a sealed envelope from his briefcase. The seal was that of the president of the United States.

"This is a copy of a document," Wardell explained, "which is at this moment being delivered to the office of Marshal Stalin in Moscow. It declares the intention of the United States government to reopen the autobahn to Berlin. The Soviet Union has now had more than four months to effect the repairs deemed necessary on the Elbe bridge at Magdeburg. In view of the difficulty your government seems to be having, American engineers will now construct a temporary bridge. A convoy of lorries and a unit of engineers will approach Magdeburg in twenty-two hours in order to erect this bridge. Under the terms of the Potsdam agreement, your government is requested to allow the convoy free access."

Wardell extended the document. Marshal Sokolovsky looked down at his hand, but made no gesture to accept the envelope. He glanced briefly to his side, and one of the colonels stepped forward to accept the written communication from Wardell.

Sokolovsky spoke in a harsher tone. "Your request will not be granted," he said.

"Our request is a courtesy. Our right to move a convoy forward from Helmstedt is guaranteed by international agreement. We intend to exercise this right."

"There have been no proper discussions," Sokolovsky said. "This document is an ultimatum and is completely unacceptable. If your American convoy attempts to cross the Soviet frontier, such an act will be considered an invasion. That will not be tolerated."

Wardell looked into the Marshal's eyes and said in a flat, even voice, "Any attempt to turn back the convoy by force will be considered by my government an unfriendly act."

Sokolovsky said nothing. He stood glaring at Wardell, his lips compressed.

Wardell said, "You have the document. Now I wish you a good morning. I hope we can meet again in less strained circumstances."

Sokolovsky gave him an almost imperceptible nod.

Wardell turned and walked with General Clay out of the reception hall. Major Amirov hurried after them and escorted them to their automobile.

Wardell waited until the command car was moving before he asked General Clay, "What do you think? You know Sokolovsky well."

Clay said, "I don't think he was surprised. The Russians had to be expecting something like this before winter really set in. But Sokolovsky was only going through the motions. He knows the decision isn't his.

It'll be made by the man in the Kremlin Bedell-Smith is seeing right now."

Wardell's face was grim. "That's not a very comforting thought," he said.

"Not to the boys who will be riding on that convoy," Clay said.

TWENTY-SIX

The main portion of the Soviet embassy in Washington was used by the ambassador and his diplomatic and personal staff. The rear wing, formerly the kitchen and servants' quarters when the large building had been a private home, was protected by iron bars and steel shutters across the windows, and it was closed off from the rest of the embassy by double, steel doors.

Jason Volkert, dressed in the white uniform of a milk deliveryman, pressed a bell concealed under the main staircase of the embassy, which stood quiet and dark in the predawn hours. The doorkeeper inside peered through the eyehole, then swung the doors open.

Georgei Partarov was waiting for him. Partarov was listed on the embassy roster as assistant to the first secretary. In reality, he was the KGB station chief. In terms of real authority, he was more powerful than the ambassador.

Partarov didn't intimidate Volkert. The heavyset man marched up and said angrily, "Do you know the risk you're taking with this ridiculous charade?"

Partarov said, "I didn't order you here. I received the highest-priority cable from Moscow. The highest-priority cable."

Volkert's eyebrows rose. "What was this cable about?"

"A little more than an hour ago, an American document was delivered to the Kremlin and to Marshal Sokolovsky in Berlin. It contained an ultimatum—an armed convoy will move to reopen the land route to Berlin in twenty-four hours."

"Hmmm," Volkert said.

"Obviously, the Americans are aware of our military superiority in Europe. Therefore, their demand is either a bluff, a foolish miscalculation, or—"

Volkert finished the sentence. "Or they have alternative plans."

Partarov said, "The document in Berlin was delivered by Senator Wardell. Whatever plans the Americans have formulated must have needed Congressional approval. That means more than a bluff to me."

Volkert took a pipe from his side pocket and began filling it. "To me it means it's more urgent than ever to locate the senator's wife."

"Those are the orders from Moscow," Partarov said. "The most extreme measures and risks are authorized. I have received word that Marshal Stalin is in a rage. Part of his wrath has been directed at our failure to provide warning that such an ultimatum was being considered. Should we fail to provide warning of the Americans' plans, I think we should have little need to worry about being exposed."

Volkert grimaced. Then he lit the tobacco and puffed clouds of smoke. "The FBI has had little success. She

277

evidently flew to New York, but they haven't succeeded in tracing her from there."

"I find it unusual that the news stories about her mysterious disappearance haven't caused her to surface to quell the rumors. After all, she's not a fugitive."

Volkert replied, "She may be on her way back to Washington right now. Waldman's story only appeared on the wire services last night. Or she could have decided to ignore it. The American papers are full of such gossip items."

"We can't afford to place all our hopes on her reappearance," Partarov said. "And we can't match the FBI in their thoroughness. We have to take alternative measures."

"Such as?" Volkert asked.

"I have great difficulty believing that a woman who flees her own residence under extreme emotional distress in the middle of the night flees without contacting anyone. According to my source in the FBI, she was carrying little money. The homes of even casual friends are being watched. She must have had help."

"I agree," Volkert said. He thought for a moment, then said, "The most logical place to start would be the person closest to her—her assistant, the Braun woman."

"I want her interrogated," Partarov ordered. "Immediately."

Volkert responded, "I don't think we can do that now. It's nearly six in the morning. That gives us little time to make adequate arrangements before she leaves for work. Even then, should she fail to appear in the Congressional office at eight A.M., there would be

immediate concern that could cause grave consequences for us."

"What do you suggest? Time is short."

"I suggest we use Waldman to make contact early
this evening. He should be able to use some pretext to
lure her to a convenient spot. Anna will be with him,
and she's more than capable of doing everything that
needs to be done."

Partarov pondered for a moment. Then he said,
"Very well. But I want to warn you, and Anna, of the
consequences of failure."

Laura stopped in the tiny Catskill village of Pine Hill
for groceries. Then she followed the hand-drawn map
Molly's sister had provided, down the narrow, winding
country roads to the turn-off onto the steep dirt road.

Only a light dusting of snow covered the ground, and
the unpaved surface was bare. She had no trouble
navigating the Studebaker the half-mile to the cabin
nestled in a tall stand of pine trees at the foot of a
gnarled mountain that towered above them.

Carla and her husband had been very kind, but
Laura had decided after a few hours that she wanted,
she needed, to be totally alone. Carla offered Laura the
use of their cabin in the mountains, and Laura quickly
accepted. She'd been warned it was likely to be cold
and lonely. But that wasn't the major concern on her
mind.

Laura grabbed her suitcase full of borrowed winter
clothing and picked up the bag of groceries. The door
to the cabin was unlocked, and she walked in.

The large single room was inviting and very neat.

There was even wood stacked in the potbellied stove in the center, waiting to be lit. Laura touched a match to the yellowed paper underneath. By the time she had the groceries put away, heat was already cutting the November chill.

She pulled a chair near the stove and sat basking in the warmth. She felt like a little girl again, perching in her grandmother's kitchen and watching the preparations for the huge meals that were a family holiday custom.

One of the best of those holidays was Thanksgiving, which was coming up in a little more than a week. When she'd been a girl she'd looked forward to that holiday for months, not only because of the dinner itself, but because it signaled the start of the magical Christmas season.

She'd had so many dreams when she was that age. Dreams of marrying a dark handsome man who would father her own brood of children that would flock around her as she cooked holiday meals. And there would be grandchildren some day, and a fairy tale retirement as a beloved matriarch.

She wasn't a little girl anymore. And instead of the large family, she was a thirty-seven-year-old woman who was totally alone. Her parents were both dead, her mother from cancer, her father from a stroke four years ago. She had no children, no farmhouse kitchen full of warmth and cheer. And now, no husband.

Effectively, no husband, she thought. The rift with David seemed as broad as the ocean that separated them now.

David must be in Berlin, she thought. He must have

delivered the message to the Russians and set the awful plan in motion. She wondered what he was thinking as he waited. Was his mind centered on military and political tactics and contingencies? Or did other thoughts intrude, images of Thanksgivings that might never come in a world blighted by atomic war?

She hoped he had such thoughts. But the time for him to do anything to stop the course of events was past. The time for her to do anything was past.

She sighed, closing her eyes. The only comfort was the blessed heat. The only thing that seemed tolerable to her was sitting in that chair forever.

Wardell hung up the phone and sat behind the desk in the office he'd borrowed at General Clay's headquarters. He was still sitting silently when Mack Dolan walked in.

Dolan read his mood. "No word?"

Wardell was slow to respond. When he did look up, he said. "Worse than that. The story has hit the newspapers."

"What story?"

"Romantic triangle on Capitol Hill. Laura and I are supposedly separated after a violent argument over my romance with Susan Gordon. Laura has gone into seclusion, and I'm so worried that the FBI is looking for her."

Dolan sat in a chair. "How in the hell did that get out? Does the FBI know?"

"Coffey traced it pretty easily. And I'm surprised. A guy named Carl Waldman."

"Waldman? I've heard the name. Isn't he one of those leftwing types?"

"Yes. But I've always considered him a responsible man. I've given him three or four long interviews over the years, and I've thought his resulting stories were fair. This gossip stuff doesn't seem up his alley."

"He may have fallen on hard times," Dolan said. "I've never trusted reporters. They're all looking to serve up somebody's head on a platter."

"Maybe," Wardell said.

Dolan studied him a moment. Then he asked, "Are you afraid this story will do you some damage?" he asked.

"I don't give a damn about my reputation," Wardell said. "It's Laura I'm worried about. She's always been so concerned about keeping herself above suspicion— she won't take a dime from the lobbyists, won't charge for making speeches. I had to talk her into accepting complimentary magazine subscriptions. When she hears this story, I'm afraid she'll stay out of sight for a long time."

"Maybe that's best . . . in terms of Scalpel."

"Fuck Scalpel," Wardell said angrily. "In the last fourteen years I've given more than my share to my country. Why in hell did you have to drag me into this mess? It nearly got me killed playing spy, it's destroyed my marriage, my public reputation is gone. And I don't know how I'm going to live with my conscience for the next fourteen years if this decision is wrong."

Dolan looked sadly at his friend. "I'm sorry, David," he said. "If I'd only known about Laura, I would have—"

"You would have what?" Wardell interrupted. "Not come in here just now to talk to me? That's the only thing. You're a damned fine soldier, Mack. You needed me just like you needed those boys in France to climb up out of those ridges and charge those Hun machine guns. They had wives and kids and futures ahead of them, but your job was to win the war."

Dolan frowned.

Wardell spoke again, his voice calmer. "I don't blame you, Mack. It's fate. Along with mistakes on my part—nobody dragged me into bed with Susan. I accept that—even though I regret like hell how things have turned out."

They sat in silence for a few moments. Then Dolan said, "I came in to tell you that the Scalpel force has arrived at Lakenheath from the States. The C-97's are going through a final maintenance check, and they'll fly down there from Prestwick by evening. With the other aircraft, they'll be ready to move by twenty-two hundred hours tonight."

"Will they get the order?"

"The White House has authorized the transfer to the Norwegian staging area at Trondheim."

"And the convoy?"

"Poised and ready to go."

Wardell got to his feet. "I can't stay here in Berlin any longer, Mack. Besides, my job as errand boy is over—if Sokolovsky wants to do any jawing, he can talk to Lucius. I want you to arrange for me to fly to Frankfort, then get transportation to the convoy staging area."

"That could be close to action, David. I don't

know if—"

"I've been closer to action," Wardell said with determination. "I've played a pretty important role in the decision to send those boys down the road. I want to be there."

"Okay," Mack said. "I'll see what I can do."

TWENTY-SEVEN

Carl Waldman sat in the front seat of the Chevrolet parked in the motel parking lot, drumming nervously on the steering wheel.

The woman Volkert had sent sat next to him, calm and impassive. She was in her late twenties, blond and very attractive facially. She had nice breasts, but was a little wide at the hips. Waldman had a thing against broad-hipped women.

Still that wasn't what turned him off on this Anna. There was an icy hardness about her, more chilling in that she was a woman. She scared the hell out of him, and he wished to hell he'd never gotten involved with the Russians.

Up to now, he hadn't regretted his decision for a moment. The goddamn war had cost him his arm, and within two months after the war ended, the Army had threatened to court-martial him just because he'd had the guts to protest the Gestapo tactics the Allied occupation armies were using against the left-wing resistance groups that had fought so valiantly against the Nazis. To save himself from that court-martial, Waldman had been forced to take a dishonorable discharge.

Back in the states, he'd resumed his writing career, using his pen as his weapon. But the publications he wrote for had little public following, and people treated him with condescension at best. Frustration gnawed at him.

Then the Russians made their approach. He'd never hesitated. He was a damned good reporter, and now he had a source for his information that meant something. He still didn't get the public acclaim, but the private sense of power was worth it—had been worth it. He now felt that he was careening down a precipice totally out of control. He couldn't see a way to get out in which he wouldn't get hurt.

"A car," the woman said. Her voice was unaccented, but as cold and emotionless as her expression.

Waldman looked toward the entrance. An old black Ford sedan had turned off the highway. A woman was driving, and he thought he recognized Laura's assistant.

"That may be her," he said.

"Then you shall proceed," she said.

Waldman got out of the car. The Ford was in a parking spot about twenty-five feet away. The woman who had gotten out was locking the driver's door. When she turned, Carl knew it was, in fact, Molly Braun.

She didn't see him. She started walking toward the motel lounge. He intercepted her.

"Molly," he said. "I thought you'd gotten tied up."

She turned to face him. She was short, no more than

286

five feet two inches, with long, light brown hair and a fair complexion that looked too healthy for her to be a city girl.

"I couldn't decide whether to come. Those articles about Laura and David, they were—"

"They weren't my fault," Waldman said. He took Molly's arm in his right hand. "You've got to believe me. I was the one who prevented pictures of David and that actress from being published."

"Laura told me," Molly said. "That's why I finally decided to come here to hear you out. I owe that to Laura."

Waldman looked nervously around. "You weren't followed?"

"No. I used the private door from the office. That's another thing I don't understand. All this secrecy."

Waldman's face was somber. "There's something strange happening, Molly. Something potentially dangerous. I've got some documents that will shock you."

"Where are they?"

"I took a room. So we could look at them in private. Around this way."

The small motel was a long, low building with ten units facing the road, and ten units in the rear. Waldman steered Molly by the elbow around to the back. He took the key to room eighteen from his pocket and pushed the door open.

She stepped in first, saying, "I still don't like all this—"

Hands grabbed her from behind. One covered her mouth. The other arm circled her neck, the hand grabbing her hair. She struggled, waiting for Waldman to come to her assistance.

Instead, she saw that he bent down and grabbed her legs with his one arm. Molly was dragged over to the bed and thrown on top. Waldman rolled on top of her, keeping her from getting free with his weight while his hand replaced the other's in preventing her from shouting. Molly managed to sink her teeth into his skin, but he gritted his teeth and kept applying pressure.

Then she felt a pinprick line of pain in her left arm. Her mind started to swim and blackness descended.

Anna pulled the i.v. needle from Molly Braun's arm. The legislative assistant's head slumped on to her chest, her mouth open, her eyes half-closed.

Waldman's face was white and beaded with perspiration. He lit another cigarette from the butt of his last one. He watched Anna pack the i.v. stand, the bottle, tubing, and needles into an attaché case.

"What now?" he asked.

"First, I report in," Anna said. She crossed to the phone, then gave a number to the hotel operator.

"Isn't that risky?" Waldman asked. "They keep records of calls."

She gave him an impatient look. "There will be no one at the number five minutes after I hang up."

The call was completed. Anna repeated the information it had taken thirty minutes to coax from the groggy woman—the address of the sister, the general location of the cabin in the mountains. Anna listened while the information was read back to her; then she replaced the receiver.

"What now?" Waldman asked nervously.

"We have to dispose of her," Anna said.

A chill went through Waldman. "You mean—"

"Do you realize what the consequences are if she talks to the authorities? You will be tried for treason and executed."

Waldman's gaze went to the woman in the chair. She groaned and rolled her head to the other side. For an instant, he thought her glassy eyes fixed on him. His stomach tightened.

"Listen to me," Anna said. "I am going out to your car. I will drive it around to this door. You will carry her out and put her in the back seat."

"What if someone sees me?" he asked.

"It's dark. I will be out front in her automobile. If another car begins driving around to the rear, I will honk the horn."

Waldman took a deep breath. "Then what?"

"Ten miles down the road, there is a sharp curve with a steep drop off to a river below. We will put her in the driver's seat of her car and roll it off the road. It should be at least a day before an autopsy, which would reveal that she had been drugged." Anna picked up the attaché case and crossed to the door. "Wait until you hear my voice before opening the door again."

Waldman watched the door close. Then he sat down in the hard chair in the small room.

Suddenly, the thought struck him—he couldn't do it. He couldn't commit murder. True, he had killed in the war. But that had been another person entirely who had so eagerly enlisted in Infantry Officer Candidate

289

School. His later revulsion for war was deep and real. That he'd been a total fool in working for the Russians didn't mean he had to become a murderer, too.

He had, however, committed crimes. He had lured Molly here. But he didn't think a capital case of treason could be made. After all, the Russians had forced him to do so under pain of death. And he could make a deal in exchange for his considerable knowledge of Soviet espionage. He might get a prison term, but it would probably be a short one.

And he would save two lives, that of the semi-conscious woman in the chair and Laura's. It surprised him to find he really did care for her. He couldn't let the Soviets get her.

He lit a cigarette and paced as he thought. Instead of turning right on the highway, he'd go left. Anna, in Molly's old Ford, couldn't catch him if she tried. He'd drive straight to the FBI.

He heard his car pull up outside. The engine was shut off. He waited for Anna's call. But instead he heard what sounded like the trunk opening. A couple of minutes later he heard it slam shut; then she was at the door.

She gave him his keys. "Get her in the car as quickly as possible. You lead the way. I'll follow."

He nodded. She started walking around toward the front of the motel.

It took him a few minutes to untie her. When he lifted her, she felt light as a feather. He put her in the back seat, then climbed in the driver's side.

He lit another cigarette to steady his nerves. Then he depressed the clutch and turned the ignition. His hand started for the column shift, to put it into first.

His hand never got there. The package of plastic explosives detonated as current flowed through the ignition wire. Waldman's last fleeting sensation was a deafening explosion. The Chevrolet bucked, rising two feet off the ground. Then it crashed down to the pavement as it was totally engulfed in a huge wave of orange-black flames.

TWENTY-EIGHT

Shortly before dawn, a fine rain began to fall. The temperature had fallen, and the dampness produced a bone-deep chill in Wardell. The weather forecast included the possibility that the rain would turn to snow by nightfall.

The elements of Steel Probe had moved to their point of departure; they were assembled on a secondary road which issued onto the autobahn near the frontier of the Soviet Zone at Helmstedt.

Since his arrival shortly before midnight, Wardell had heard a steady symphony of aircraft engines above, the drone of the regular continuing airlift into Berlin, punctuated by the roar of Soviet jets and the hum of small Soviet aircraft on observation patrols.

Wardell was bone tired. But he knew if he lay down, he wouldn't sleep. In Berlin, the tension was intolerable. At least here, he was partially energized by the fresh air and the bustle of the men preparing for the departure of the convoy in two hours.

He finished his cigarette, and walked back into the

command tent, out of the rain. Lt. Col. Frank Russell, the armored officer in command of the Steel Probe force, was studying a detailed contour map of the area the autobahn crossed on its way to Berlin.

Russell nodded to Wardell.

Wardell asked, "This weather going to cause you any problems, Colonel?"

"No, sir," Russell replied. "It might help us, if the ceiling gets any lower. The Russians won't be able to track us from the air."

"Where do you expect problems, if the Soviets decide to fight?"

Russell grimaced. "Driving that road is like running a gauntlet. They could hit us anywhere."

"Like sitting ducks," Wardell commented.

Russell smiled. "Ducks with teeth. We'll give them a fight. But they've got the numbers."

"Let's hope they decide to back down."

Russell said, "They must know we're serious. A few hours ago Frankfort broadcast a red alert in a code we know the Soviets have broken. British units in Germany have gone to red alert, also."

Wardell didn't respond. He knew the red alert was not part of a bluff, but a preparation for the launch of Scalpel. If the atomic explosion didn't result in the Russians' backing down, there would indeed be war all over Europe.

Wardell looked at his watch. A little after 0700 hours. The Scalpel force would be on the ground in Norway now. The men would be eating and rechecking their chutes, weapons and other equipment. The planes would be refueled. And the atomic bomb would be inspected one last time.

Wardell shook the thought out of his mind. In the last few hours, he'd come around to the belief that the convoy would get through unchallenged. Even though Stalin would have atomic weapons soon, he didn't have them now. Attacking the convoy would be a high stakes—

"Senator?" a voice said behind him.

He turned. "Yes?"

"A call for you has been patched through from Steel Foundry."

A call patched through from headquarters in Frankfort, Wardell said to himself. It had to be either Berlin, or word from the States.

He followed the corporal to the signal tent. The corporal directed him to a radio receiver. "Put on the headphones, sir. Push that button to talk."

Wardell did as instructed. He told the radio operator in Frankfort he was ready. There was a short delay; then a voice came on the line that he recognized as that of Coffey, the FBI man.

"What is it?" Wardell asked.

"The Maryland State Police responded to the reports of an explosion at a motel fifteen miles outside the District. They found a bomb had been placed in the journalist Waldman's car. In the car were the badly burned bodies of a man and a woman."

Oh no, Wardell said to himself. A jolt of panic went through him. It was a moment before he could ask, "Is it . . . is it Laura?"

"No," Coffey said. "It took us awhile to establish identity, but not as long as it would have if we hadn't been keeping track of people close to your wife. We got dental records in a hurry. The man was Waldman. The woman was Molly Braun, your wife's legislative assistant."

"That's awful," Wardell said. He'd always liked the efficient, cheerful woman who was perhaps his wife's closest friend. "Why would anyone kill them? What were they doing at a motel?"

"We don't have all the answers. Waldman certainly had enemies, and they certainly could have gone to the motel for a liaison. But we don't think so. The motel owner reports a blond woman who doesn't match Braun's description rented the room this afternoon."

"I don't understand," Wardell said. "Are you talking about some sort of romantic triangle?"

"Molly Braun deliberately slipped away from the office to avoid being followed. We have to suspect it has something to do with your wife's disappearance. And we have to assume that someone other than the FBI is looking for her."

"Like who?" Wardell asked.

"Soviet intelligence would be my guess," Coffey said. "Our domestic espionage people have suspected Waldman for at least a year. We had nothing concrete, but when you place that suspicion in this context, the conclusion is obvious."

Soviet intelligence after Laura, Wardell repeated. A wave of fear mixed with guilt flooded over him. Why in heaven's name had he been so foolish as to tell her about Scalpel? And how did the Russians know she had that knowledge? Maybe they didn't know.

No. His presence in Berlin presenting the ultimatum was proof that he was intimately involved in the U.S. plans. Maybe they were going to kidnap Laura for blackmail purposes. Maybe they were fishing for information.

"Senator," Coffey asked, "are you still there?"

"Yes," Wardell said. Then he asked, "Do you have any additional leads?"

"Not yet. But we're intensifying our investigation of the Braun woman and her activities since your wife disappeared. We're also placing surveillance on all known Soviet agents."

"Does Mr. Hoover know about this?"

"Yes, sir. He's ordered additional manpower. We're doing everything we can."

"I'm sure you are," Wardell said. "And thank you for calling."

Coffey went off the line. Wardell sat with the headset on for a moment. Then he made a decision. He'd done his job in Europe. He was strictly an observer now. The most important thing he could do was return to the States as soon as possible to help in the search for his wife.

Wardell turned to the Signal Corps corporal. "Get General Dolan for me," he said.

Jason Volkert waited in the car a half-block from the home of Molly Braun's sister and brother-in-law. He felt himself unusually tense, and he knew the reason was the haste with which this operation had to be carried out. He was a very careful man and he had an abhorrence of unnecessary risks.

Very early in life, he had concluded that he had unusual personal attributes that could make him a very wealthy man. He had a quick and agile mind that operated equally well under intense pressure; he had an

296

extraordinary flair for languages; he had a natural ability to command others; and, most importantly, he had absolutely no trouble dismissing moral or ethical considerations from his mind when making a decision. This was demonstrated early in his career when it became necessary for him to kill a woman who had fallen in love with him, and of whom he was quite fond. That particular operation had brought him to the attention of other governments, and soon more lucrative work followed.

For the last four years, he had been working for the Soviets, and recently he had begun to think that had been a mistake. They paid very well, and the generally abysmal quality of their own intelligence agents made satisfying them relatively easy. For a man who didn't like risks, this Washington assignment in normal times was a plum, but the problem with the Russians was that under pressure they tended to panic.

Volkert now found himself more exposed than he had been in twenty years. Part of this, of course, was his own fault. The assignment had been so easy he'd become lax, failing to prepare for a rapid disappearance should that prove prudent.

Measuring the risk of fleeing now and having an army of Soviet agents seeking him against that of completing this dangerous search had led him to the conclusion that he should get the disagreeable task over as quickly as possible. Now he was waiting for one of his men to come back from scouting the house.

Even this break-in involved some risks he'd rather not take. He'd prefer that the telephone lines into the house be cut, but in the dark his man couldn't tell which wire was for the telephone and which carried electricity.

He also had no idea of the interior layout of the house, nor of the exact number of people sleeping inside. Finally, he felt exposed in this silent residential area, where the houses were so close together that a barking dog or a scream might wake neighbors.

Still, it was better to move with haste now. The authorities would eventually identify the body in the car, and relatives would be notified.

Anna, sitting next to him in the passenger seat, touched his arm and pointed. Volkert rolled down his window.

"The back door is open," the man said. "No sign of a pet. No lights on inside."

Volkert nodded. Without a word, he opened the car door and started for the house. Anna and the man followed.

As he approached the square two-story structure, he saw a car at the other end of the block—two of his men acting as sentries. Two more men remained in a car parked behind his in the other direction.

At the back of the house was a patio leading to a sliding glass door. Volkert drew his pistol, a Browning 9-mm automatic. Cautiously, he pulled the door open.

He entered what appeared to be some sort of recreation room. A large radio sat in one corner, a pool table dominated the other end of the room. He switched on a flashlight, looking for a telephone. He didn't spot one.

The recreation room door led to a kitchen. There was a phone on the counter. Volkert pointed with the flashlight beam, and his man cut the cord.

A quick reconnaissance of the ground floor showed

298

only an empty guest room. The family must be sleeping upstairs.

The stairs went upward from the center hall. Volkert was a third of the way up when the telephone rang in a bedroom on the second floor.

Despite his bulk he took the remaining steps two at a time. Anna and his man automatically took the two rooms to the left while he headed toward the telephone.

The bedroom door was closed. He tucked the flashlight under his arm, pushed the door open, then grabbed the light again and swept the room.

The beam caught a man in a nightshirt sitting up in bed and reaching for the phone.

"Freeze!" Volkert shouted.

A woman screamed. The man's hand stopped.

Volkert stepped forward. "Get out of bed. The woman first."

The man's hand reached for the phone. Volkert fired, hitting him in the shoulder. He knocked the phone to the floor.

Volkert hurried to grab it. He could hear a faint voice from the receiver saying, "Hello? Hello?" Then he yanked the cord from the wall.

Anna came into the room. She said in Russian, "The rest of the rooms are empty."

Volkert said, "Tell Boris to keep watch downstairs. You come back here with me." He turned to the bed. The woman was weeping as she stared at her husband's wound.

"That was foolish," he said in English. "You will obey me instantaneously. Now, out of bed."

They obeyed. They stood, the man's arm around his

wife's shoulders.

Anna returned to the room. Without instructions from Volkert, she took out a roll of electrical tape and bound the man's arms behind his back. He groaned with pain.

Anna turned. She grabbed the neckline of the woman's short nightgown and ripped it off her. Instinctively, the woman cringed, trying to cover herself.

Volkert said to the man, "You will give me exact directions to your cabin in the mountains."

"No," the woman cried. "Laura. I mean—"

"She's exactly right," Volkert said. "We want to have a chat with her sister's employer."

The man glared at him. "Why should I tell you? You'll kill us anyway."

"That is a possibility," Volkert said. "However, I would like you to consider the suffering your wife could go through before she dies. It will be substantial, I assure you."

"Don't tell him anything, Don!" the woman sobbed. "We can't let them kill another person, too. We'll be killing Laura!"

The man's eyes flashed from Volkert to his wife.

"Well?" Volkert said.

The man didn't reply.

Volkert turned to Anna and said, "Cut off her right breast, please."

The woman tried to run. Anna grabbed her and with surprising ease managed to bind her arms. She rolled Carla on her back and took a long knife from a sheath on her belt.

"Don't!" the man stammered.

"Don't!" Carla pleaded.

Anna made a slight incision with the knife, drawing blood.

The man poured out the directions, so quickly Volkert had to ask him to repeat them twice. All the while his wife became more hysterical.

Volkert was asking the man a final question when a voice called up from downstairs, "Sirens coming."

Volkert nodded to Anna. She stood away. He shot the man in the temple, then turned and shot the woman twice in the chest. Then they turned and retreated down the stairs.

By the time they got outside, they heard the clatter of automatic weapons fire from their right. Volkert broke into a run. When he reached the car, he shouted to the men in the car behind them. "Go help the others. You've got to give us time."

They obeyed, jumping in their vehicle and roaring past.

Fools, Volkert thought as he started his own vehicle. As much mind as Pavlov's dog, rushing toward their own deaths. But, he reflected as he put the car in gear and accelerated, dogs had their usefulness.

TWENTY-NINE

The jeep got Wardell to headquarters in Frankfort shortly after 8:30 A.M. Wardell impatiently passed through the four security checks necessary to reach the command center, where he found Mack Dolan barking orders into a telephone.

Dolan was only on a few minutes. He hung up and asked Wardell, "How do things look at the convoy staging area?"

"Fine," Wardell snapped. "But you know that. How soon does my plane get out of here?"

Dolan didn't reply for a moment. Then he said, "Come with me a moment, David."

"What's this all about?" Wardell asked suspiciously.

Dolan had already turned. Wardell had no choice but to follow him down the hall to a private office.

Dolan closed the door. Then he faced the senator and said, "I'm afraid you can't go back to the States now, David."

"What do you mean, I can't go back?"

"We know the Soviets are after Laura. And it's a

good bet they're looking for you. With Scalpel set to go, we can't take the chance of your being snatched."

"That's ridiculous," Wardell snapped. "I'll be on a military flight. And once I land in New York, I'll go directly to the FBI."

"Sorry," Dolan said. "I know how concerned you are about Laura. But I've been assured everything possible is being done. There's nothing you could do."

Wardell was tense with anger. "If my body is so bloody important, why did you risk sending me into East Berlin?"

Dolan said calmly, "There would have been little likelihood of Scalpel getting off the ground unless you did. The situation is different, now. It was even a risk bringing you here from the convoy staging area, but we're better able to provide security here."

"I see," Wardell said sarcastically. "I'm a member of the United States Senate, but to the Army I'm a commodity. Well, I'm not going to stand for this. I insist on being put through to the White House."

"Truman knows and concurs, David," Dolan said. "If you want to verify that, I'll be glad to arrange for you to talk to him. He can tell you himself how concerned he is about Laura. The president is receiving reports from the FBI every hour, and he's authorized use of military aircraft to transport agents if necessary."

Wardell sighed in frustration. He took in deep breaths, trying to calm himself.

Dolan put a hand on his shoulder. "I know how you feel, David. But you have to accept the situation."

"What am I supposed to do?" Wardell asked. "Are you going to lock me in a room somewhere?"

"Of course not," Dolan said. "You can stay here. I

can arrange a room for you to get some rest, or you can join me in the command center as the convoy moves out."

Wardell stood and faced him. "I'll come with you. If I'm by myself, I'll go crazy. But promise me one thing, Mack. The minute Scalpel is concluded, I'm on an airplane to the U.S. I mean, an aircraft is on stand-by. You owe me that."

"You've got it, David. The minute it's safe, you're a free man."

At 0855 hours, the armored convoy had moved from the cover of the dense stand of trees onto the secondary road. The point vehicles included the scout and out-rider Pershing tanks, and in the connecting file to the main force, the first of the three engineer units. Colonel Russell's command tank led the main body of the force.

The anticipated low-pressure system had veered north, and the temperature had held above freezing. For the moment the drizzle had stopped, and they had no snow to contend with.

Thank God for small favors, Colonel Russell said to himself. He glanced at his watch: 0858 hours.

He called down to his radio operator, "Sergeant, raise Steel Foundry."

He heard the metallic sounding exchange between communications personnel in his headset while waiting for his code call numbers to alert the headquarters officer who would be his conduit to the supreme commander.

A brief exchange opened the channel. His orders were confirmed.

Russell called down to the radioman, "Open us up to point."

Crackling static was followed by an acknowledgment.

"All right, Hobson," the Colonel said. "Move us out."

At precisely 0900 hours, the lead Pershing tank of the point formation crossed the frontier marking, sweeping the double strands of concertina wire aside and moving forward to the road barrier the Russians had established at the entrance to the small town of Helmstedt. The tank reached up to the edge of the wooden barrier, then stopped abruptly, dwarfing the Russian checkpoint.

A single light burned inside the small building adjacent to the road. But to Major Hobson's amazement, no one came out. He gave the signal and the Pershing rumbled forward, splintering the wooden barrier and grinding beneath its tread the weighted fuel drums that held the barrier in place. The tank opened a path to the access lane onto the autobahn.

The forward tank crested a small hill. The gunner in the open hatch spotted a small garrison bivouacked to their right. A small number of Russian soldiers stood in a silent group, watching. The gunner swung his fifty-caliber machine gun, but the Russians made no effort to approach.

Russell's urgent call for a report came through Hobson's headset.

"No resistance," he said.

Back in his command tank, Russell nodded to himself. His calculation was correct—no problem at the border.

His eye ran the length of the elevated ninety-millimeter gun barrel that emanated from the body of the tank, and with his left hand he slapped the metal side just below his hatch.

"Roll on, baby," he said to the tank. "Let's cover those miles fast."

"How long have they been rolling?" Dolan called out.

"Forty-seven minutes, sir," came the reply.

Dolan turned to Wardell with a scowl. "It seems like half a day." He asked over his shoulder, "Where are they?"

"About eight miles from the river Elbe, sir."

"Christ," Dolan swore. "That's not even a quarter of the way to Berlin. Those tanks must be crawling."

Wardell said, "They only move twenty miles an hour or so in that size convoy." He smiled, adding, "In the Great War, we used to consider a couple hundred yards a day a huge advance."

"You're right," Dolan admitted. "But at least we were right there in the middle of it. This sitting back and waiting for word is ten times worse. I've never been patient. When I was playing football at the Point one year, I pulled a hamstring muscle that kept me out for three games. After the first, the coach forbade me to sit on the bench. Watching drove me crazy."

Wardell looked at him with a somber expression on his face. "Then you know how I feel being here when they're looking for Laura."

Dolan nodded. "Yeah. I do."

He turned as a first lieutenant approached. "Report

306

from Intelligence, sir. They report an unusual volume of Soviet radio communication between Berlin and units along the autobahn. Code section is working to decipher, if possible."

"Report any success to me immediately," Dolan said.

The officer saluted and left.

"What does that mean?" Wardell asked.

"They're not arranging a battalion picnic," Dolan said. Then he turned to Wardell and added, "It could mean nothing more than they're keeping a close watch on our progress."

"Or?"

"Or they're issuing battle orders."

The rain started again about an hour after they crossed the frontier. Water dripped from Major Hobson's helmet and the high humidity consistently fogged his field glasses. Patiently, he rubbed the lenses dry, and continued to pan the murk in front of them.

"Situation report," came request from the command tank.

Hobson glanced at his watch: 1005 hours. Russell's request came every five minutes like clockwork.

He dropped the glasses for a moment, letting them hang from his chest. The point formation was climbing a medium rise through dreary farm country. Hobson frowned. Was this worth fighting so many wars over? He'd take his native Maine any day.

"Coffee, sir?"

The gunner was holding up a thermos. Hobson nodded, and the man poured some steaming liquid into

307

a metal cup.

Hobson cupped the container, warming his hands. Then he took a sip.

"Sir! Look!"

Hobson turned at the voice of the forward turret gunner. The tank had reached the top of the hill overlooking a shallow plain surrounding the village of Wächtersbach.

"Holy shit!" Hobson muttered. He threw the cup over the side and hurriedly put the binoculars to his eyes.

A fan-shaped formation of Soviet T-34 tanks straddled the autobahn ahead of them. To the left, half-concealed by the haze, were a reserve formation of tanks and self-propelled antitank guns. All together, Hobson estimated at least one hundred fifty armored vehicles.

He glanced at his watch. Then he barked into the microphone of his headset, "Ten-seventeen hours. Contact. Enemy defensive position ahead, approximately three hundred meters."

Russell's voice came over the headset. "Halt where you are."

Hobson gave the order. Then he gave Colonel Russell the estimate of the enemy's strength.

"Pull back behind the crest," Russell ordered. "I'll send a jeep forward with an officer to see what their intentions are."

"Roger, sir," Hobson said. He started to give the order to pull back. Then he heard the whistle of incoming artillery. He ducked as a shell exploded twenty meters to his right. Machine-gun fire from the tanks ahead raked the road in front.

"Taking fire!" Hobson shouted. "Estimate—"

A Russian shell exploded against the nearside track of the Pershing, blasting the tank over on its side. The turret hatch burst open and Hobson was flung half clear, flames blistering his skin. Through the agony of his pain, he heard the screams of his four-man crew trapped below.

He pushed on the steel hatch rim with his hands and slid forward until his face and shoulders touched the grassy earth. His fingers clawed the grass as he pulled himself clear. By rolling in the wet grass, he managed to extinguish the flames burning his clothes. Blood was trickling over his burns, intensifying the pain.

Death came slowly. He watched helplessly as his overturned tank burned. Dimly, as darkness descended in his mind, he saw two more Pershings erupt into flame.

When the point tank's transmission was cut off by a loud explosion coming through the headset, Russell gritted his teeth in anger. He saw from his position, four hundred meters behind the point formation, the numerous explosions from the increasingly intense artillery bombardment. He barked an order to pull the convoy back to a preset defensive position.

Then he said to his radioman, "Get me Steel Foundry."

The hour after Colonel Russell reported conflict flashed by for Dolan and Wardell. With the senator's help, the general monitored situation reports from the convoy as the tank battle raged. Those reports were passed on to the White House via another open line. On a third line, Dolan received updates on the readiness of the Scalpel force in Norway.

The pattern of the retrograde movement had been planned ahead of time, with unit commanders thoroughly briefed on a series of fall-back defensive positions. The planning, however, didn't allow for the size or the ferocity of the Russian force. Instead of merely repelling the convoy, they pursued the tank force all the way to the frontier.

Two hours after contact, the remnants of the units regrouped. Thirty-one tanks had been hit, and the infantry and engineer support units had suffered heavy casualties in the bloody, resounding defeat.

After it was over, Wardell sat in a chair to the side, lost in morose thoughts. Dolan came over to join him.

"Word from Washington?" Wardell asked.

Dolan shook his head. "Truman's meeting with his advisors now. They've been expecting some communication from the Kremlin, but the wires have been silent. I think Stalin intends to let action speak louder than words."

Wardell grimaced. Then a lieutenant called Dolan to the phone. Wardell saw him suddenly become animated. He got up and reached his side as he replaced the receiver. He turned to Wardell with a gleam in his eye.

"I've been waiting three years for this, David. Finally, we can let our actions speak louder than words."

Wardell couldn't say anything. He listened as Dolan spoke into the secure line to Norway: "The Eagle orders the birds to leave the nest."

Wardell reflected that he heard the simple sentence that would trigger one of the critical turning points in the history of modern society. Operation Scalpel was launched. In a few short hours, the United States would drop an atomic bomb on the Soviet Union.

THIRTY

Once again the phone rang once. A man said, "Hello."

Laura hung up without saying a word. She stood for a moment in the chilly phone booth outside the closed gas station, wondering.

She knew she had the right number this time—she had the operator place the call. So where was Molly? Laura knew her assistant dated men, it wasn't just that it was a man's voice. It was the tone of that voice—authoritative, obviously wide-awake—and the fact that the phone was answered the first time, practically before it had stopped ringing.

The only logical conclusion was that the people David had looking for her were serious enough to station a man in Molly's apartment twenty-four hours a day. She was evidently causing a great deal of trouble.

It was amazing how her attitude had changed. She'd awakened around midnight, after sleeping through most of the thirty-six hours she'd been at the cabin. Her sleep had been deep and dreamless, as if she'd been shedding years of exhaustion.

When she got up, she'd felt like a new woman. And almost magically, she'd had a new perspective. Especially about this running away. That had been foolish and immature.

That wasn't to say she regretted her strong stance about the horrible military operation David described to her. She still thought it abhorrent. But in her pique she was causing anguish for a great many others.

The primary victim, Laura was sure, had been Molly. By two o'clock in the morning, after a couple of hours of reflection, Laura had made up her mind to start back to Washington in the morning. Despite the hour, she had to call Molly. She'd dressed, then started up the Studebaker. It had taken her nearly twenty-five minutes on back roads to find a working telephone booth.

Now she couldn't reach Molly. She supposed she should have asked for Molly, maybe even talked to the man. But then they might send someone for her, and she didn't want that. She'd return on her own.

The wind picked up, howling down the cleft between the trees through which the two-lane road ran. Laura suddenly felt alone and vulnerable. She put a nickel in the telephone, then gave the operator Molly's sister Carla's number.

A busy signal came on the line. Laura asked the operator to investigate. After a few moments, she was informed the line was out of order.

Another oddity. The phone booth seemed even more deserted. She got back in the car and pulled out onto the road.

The thought of going back to that isolated cabin was

unpleasant. She almost decided to drive straight on to Carla's. Then she lectured herself again—her purse and most of her money was in the cabin, along with her clothes. She'd have to drive all the way back in the morning, unless she asked Carla to send the things to her. Carla had put up with enough on her account.

At the intersection, Laura took a left and retraced her path. She got back to the turnoff to the cabin faster than she thought. She was amazed the trip had actually tired her. At least she could kill the hours until morning by getting more sleep.

She walked around to the front door. She started up the steps, then stopped. Something was strange. She'd lit a new candle when she'd awakened and left it burning. Now the cabin was totally dark.

Again, she fought the urge to get back into the car. The cabin seemed tight, but every cabin had drafts. The candle had probably been blown out.

She opened the door and took two steps toward the table on which the candles sat. Then hands grabbed her. One contained some sort of damp foul-smelling cloth. She struggled, but her head began to swim dizzily. Her thrashing grew markedly more feeble. She blacked out.

"Frank."

Special Agent Frank Coffey looked up. He had a phone cradled under his right chin, and he was leafing through a thick file on the desk. "Just a minute," he said.

He listened to the voice come on the line. Then he said, "Get those footprints on the next plane to Washington. Make sure you pack the casts so they don't break."

He hung up. Then he said, "What is it, Bill?"

"Cliff James called from the Braun woman's apartment. Twice in a row somebody dialed the number, then hung up when they heard his voice. He thinks it was a woman."

"If she didn't say anything, how does he know?" Coffey asked in exasperation. "Christ, we've got enough leads to follow."

"This is a lead. The calls were placed by an operator, so the phone company traced them easily. They were made from a public phone in Halcott Center, New York. That's up in the Catskills."

Coffey leaned forward. "Where in the Catskills?"

"You get it, too," Bill said. "It's in the general vicinity of the area in which the neighbors of Braun's sister said they had a summer cabin."

"That cinches it," Coffey said. "We know Laura Jameson stayed in Rhinebeck for at least a night. It's natural she would have borrowed the cabin if she wanted to get away. And she borrowed the family's second car to go up there."

"What do we do? We still haven't found anybody to tell us exactly where this cabin is. They've only owned it a year."

"You get on the phone to the local law, if there is any. Send every available man up there. Tell the first team on the scene to hire a small plane as soon as it gets light. They can spot the car from the air."

Bill noticed Coffey putting on his jacket. "Where are you going?"

"I'm going to make use of the offer from the Air Force. I'm going up there. I've got a hunch we're close."

315

"They'll get her before you get there."

"I hope so," Coffey said. "But as far as I'm concerned, finding the congresswoman is the lesser half of the job."

"What's the other half?"

"Finding the Russian agents who've been pulling this shit. That's the big prize."

Her will to resist was a knot on the beamed ceiling. The knot was large, and unusually square, and it reminded her of her home state of Iowa.

Its shape changed as time crept by and more of the drug seeped through the intravenous needle into her bloodstream. The kerosene lantern flickered, and the knot seemed to expand and contract like a jellyfish.

A jellyfish. When the image came into her mind, she felt like laughing. Would the man asking the questions think that was funny? If he did, would he go away and leave her alone, to stare at her jellyfish?

Not jellyfish. A knot. And she was a woman. She wouldn't talk, she wouldn't answer their questions.

Then she blinked her eyes and it was gone. A surge of panic swept through her, and she summoned the energy to struggle. But she was tied securely to the table, and she couldn't move.

So she'd drown. The room floated around her, all swirling and hazy, like looking out from inside a fishbowl. She had to reach the surface, she told herself. She couldn't breathe.

Yes, she could breathe. How strange, underwater and taking in air. But how long would she breathe? How long before she died?

The voice answered those questions. The voice told her if she was a good girl she wouldn't die. Yes, she'd come up from underneath the water and she could go to bed and sleep until the bad dreams went away. All she had to do was answer the voice's questions. Simple little questions. What difference did it make to her now? Such stupid things. David would understand.

David. Who was David again? Was he just a word? No, the voice was asking about him. There was a David who was a naughty boy. And her mother always told her to tell on naughty boys.

It was dawn before Volkert had extracted the entire story. Sodium Pentothal was a clumsy method, and it didn't always work. Some people had the will to resist the sympathetic voice that offered a way out of the hallucinogenic nightmare the drug produced. It wasn't so much a truth serum as a way to open the door to the pathways of the mind, and it required patience and many openings of false doors before the information one sought could be obtained.

Still, Volkert preferred it to other more physical means of interrogation. The problem wasn't the very few people with the iron will to resist intense pain. Rather, the person being tortured would rapidly get to the point of saying anything to avoid the pain. Even the most experienced interrogator found it difficult to sort out the truth from what the person thought he wanted to hear.

This woman had been a rather easy subject. That she'd been alone in a cabin for a couple days made her even more susceptible to the drug's effects. Volkert had seen interrogations that lasted two days instead of three hours.

And the story she told was remarkable. Volkert never would have believed the American government would have the backbone for a plan as bold as Operation Scalpel. The boldness behind the plan would shock Stalin as much as the actual dropping of the bomb itself.

As Volkert listened, his mind raced. A radical change in the international power structure was about to take place. As a man who owed allegiance to no flag, it was his duty to himself to discover the best way to profit from this information.

"Comrade."

Volkert turned. Boris had come inside.

"Yes."

"I spotted a small plane overhead. It looked like it was making sweeps over the countryside."

"No doubt they are looking for this cabin," Volkert said. "Search this place one more time to be certain we leave no traces. I'll be back in a minute."

Volkert stepped outside the cabin. The air was still and cold, and a thick layer of frost covered the ground and the two automobiles parked outside. Above the sky was nearly white as the sun prepared to rise above the horizon.

Volkert walked down the road a few paces. Then he stopped, listening. He thought he heard a siren in the far distance, and the shouts of men.

He stood for a moment, thinking hard. Then he went back inside the cabin. He said to Anna, "No doubt they will find this place soon. This information must get to Moscow immediately."

318

Her face was intensely somber. "Yes, it must."

"You and Boris leave immediately in my car. I suggest heading north instead of south to the city. When you're an hour away, far enough to be clear, call control."

"We should call from the nearest phone," Anna said.

"No," Volkert replied. "They'll be likely to monitor the local phone exchanges. The call will never get through."

"I see," she said. Then she asked, "What will you do?"

"I'll take the woman's car. They'll be looking for it. I'll head south to lead them away."

"But—"

"No objections," Volkert said. "I'm the leader. It's my responsibility."

"And the woman?"

"I'll take care of her. Leave at once."

Anna nodded. Then she and Boris left the cabin.

Volkert listened to the sound of the engine starting. He heard the car turn around and speed down the dirt road.

He smiled. If his suspicions proved correct, they'd get no more than a mile or two. If they'd pinpointed the general location of the cabin well enough to be conducting an air search in the immediate vicinity, they certainly had all the roads blocked off. Anna and Boris would be stopped.

And, since they were well-trained Soviet agents, they wouldn't think of surrender. They'd try to shoot their way out and they'd be killed.

Volkert's gamble was that the FBI would believe there were only two agents. He was going to slip away through the woods.

He quickly gathered some supplies—a knapsack to strap on his back, matches, cans of food, an opener, a compass he found in a drawer.

Then he stopped to look at the woman. She was still asleep, bound to the table. It was a shame to have to kill such a beautiful woman. But he had no further use for her.

He splashed the kerosene from the five-gallon can all around the floor. He picked up the kerosene lantern and walked out the front door. Then he turned around and threw the lantern.

The inside of the cabin exploded in flame. He hurried toward the pine trees. In the distance, he thought he could hear the sounds of gunfire.

THIRTY-ONE

The thunder of massive engines echoed through the stillness of Trondheim Fjord. Rising to altitude and banking into formations, the flights of B-36s moved out over the water and turned north, toward the Arctic Circle. The sky reflected flashes of light, and, holding the point position of the lead formation, Col. Dale Cagney transferred flight control to his copilot and attempted a visual check of the near formations. He saw his wing flights to the left and right, exactly where they should be.

He checked the time, removed his gloves, then flipped the interpersonnel communications switch that opened the channel to his crew.

"This is Cagney," he said. "Time to settle the questions you've been having as to our mission. The reserve tanks probably gave you a clue. We are over the Barents Sea. We'll be turning south and within an hour we'll be penetrating the air space of the Soviet Union. Our supercargo is an officer from G-2, and he's along because he's fluent in Russian. If the Reds pick us up on radar further south, he will attempt to talk our way past the communications checks.

"But you will have to keep your eyes open. We are on a dual mission. The first is to fly escort and cover for some C-97s that are bringing a regiment of paratroopers in under us. We are going south to a point over the Kirov district. Our target is a manufacturing installation near a marker point called Kasanov. It is going to be occupied by our forces and evacuated, and we are then going to blow it away completely. The Russians are building atom bombs there. That's what this is all about."

"After the landing force is airborne," Colonel Cagney continued, "our formation will disperse. We are staying over Kasanov, and Yellow and Blue flights are going west toward Moscow. Green flight is heading for a place called Kuibyshev. We will hook up with escort formations and effect a holding pattern for further orders." He paused, then added, "For your information, we have an atomic bomb on board."

"Jesus H. Christ," a voice said over the intercom.

"Colonel?"

Cagney waited.

"Is it live?"

"Yes, Michaelson." Cagney recognized the voice of one of his gunners.

He'd assumed the men had guessed the nature of their cargo. During the stopover at Lakenheath in Britain, the crew had watched four men connect additional equipment into the aircraft's electrical system. Another control panel had been installed forward of the bomb bay, about thirty inches high and twenty wide. It contained switches, dials, and a row of colored indicator lights. Back of it, four cables trailed to the bomb bay and were ultimately plugged into the massive weapon that had been rolled out on its trolley and winched up into the front bomb bay.

This had been done several hours before the liftoff from Lakenheath. The same procedure, Cagney knew, had been executed on eleven more of the twenty-four B-36s comprising the full formation. The new control panel was designed to monitor the batteries inside the weapon, to maintain a constant check for any electrical shorts within its firing circuit, its radar set, and timing mechanisms; even to check for changes of barometric pressure in the bomb bay.

There was silence on the intercom for a moment. Then a voice asked, "Is it war, Colonel?"

"The Russians have attacked our ground forces in Germany," Cagney replied. "If our mission succeeds, we'll avoid war."

Cagney was signaled by his navigation officer.

"Course change, Colonel."

Cagney corrected the course per the flight plan.

"We're in the corridor to the White Sea now," the navigator called. "Russia straight ahead."

The crew settled down to silence, listening to the thundering pusher engines. The flashes of the aurora borealis had faded and all they had to contemplate from the scattered ports was the blackness of the sky.

Finally, after fifty-seven minutes, the navigator said, "Coast ahead."

It was not a visual sighting, but from habit Colonel Cagney looked out below.

Well, he thought to himself, here we go, sonny.

They passed over the coast. The intelligence people

had done their homework, Cagney thought. If the Russians had coastal radar, they'd have picked up signals by now.

"Lieutenant Forester," he said to the Intelligence officer.

"Yes, sir?"

"You tied into our communications?"

"Roger, Colonel."

"All right, crew," Cagney said. "Stay alert. We are in enemy territory. And keep a lid on any chatter. There doesn't seem to be any operative radar up here. But some Russian radio operator may just be making routine channel sweeps."

There was a brief silence. Then the navigator said, "Archangel northeast, Colonel."

They would be drifting slight east, Cagney thought, staying clear of the headwaters of the Volga and the population centers along its line. He checked the time again. They would be flying over the Vologda, west of the Kotlas range, and intelligence estimated it to be one of the least populated areas of European Russia, with no known military or air bases.

So far, so good. The C-97s should be crossing the North Cape about now. Cagney would have felt a hell of a lot better with some F-80 fighters riding wing. But there had been no aborts and no signs of interception— which was damn good, because they were now past the point of no return.

Wardell and Dolan had flown from Frankfort to Lakenheath, command center for Scalpel. They reached British soil shortly after the first aircraft should have reached Russian air space. Dolan immediately got on a security channel to Washington.

When he finished, he found Wardell having coffee in a small wardroom. Wardell looked up anxiously.

"Good news, I think, David. They think Laura is in a cabin in the Catskill Mountains. Air units are searching for the exact site and ground teams are in the area. They should find her shortly."

"Damn," Wardell said. "I want to be there."

"You'll be home within twelve hours. I guarantee that."

Wardell didn't reply. He sat, thinking of his wife.

Dolan poured himself a cup of coffee. Then he said, "You might be interested to know that Truman's received an ultimatum from Stalin."

"Really?"

"About what we expected. Immediate halt to the airlift. Seven days to evacuate Berlin completely. Thirty days to evacuate West Germany."

"Or?"

"Intelligence reports massive Soviet troop movements toward the border. With the shape of our defenses, it would be just like Hitler's blitzkreig—they could roll all the way to the channel."

"But they won't."

"No," Dolan said with satisfaction. "Not if Scalpel succeeds. Stalin's mustache is going to curl."

"Has Truman replied to the Russians?" Wardell asked.

"Not yet. They've been pushing for a reply, and to stimulate it they've been doing some heavy shelling at certain border points near the autobahn. We're losing some boys, but Truman's hanging on."

Hanging on, Wardell thought to himself. He found it hard to hang on himself, the minutes passing with excruciating slowness as he awaited word of his wife.

The sound of the explosion startled her to a half-consciousness. Her head pounded with an awful headache, and a wave of nausea swept through her. She turned her head to the side and vomited.

Then the flames were all around her, searing her skin. She cried out, twisting frantically against her bonds. The smoke was thickening rapidly, and she was racked with coughs at every breath.

The drug still confused her mind, but some basic survival instinct took over. She worked her shoulders and kicked out her legs tirelessly despite the increasing pain.

The fire was under her now. The cabin was a cacophony of noises: hissing wet wood, crackling furniture, and groaning timbers sagging as they burned.

Suddenly, her arms were free. The fire beneath the thick table had burned the ropes through. She sat up, then worked the rope from her legs.

She only got a step toward the open door before her clothes ignited. The hair on her arms sizzled, then the hair on her head caught. The pain was like a wall. But with one last burst she dove for the opening. She stumbled, then tripped. Her momentum tumbled her down the stairs, cracking her head.

She wasn't conscious when the FBI man dove on her to smother the flames. The ambulance attendants reached her a moment later. They carefully put her on a stretcher, then sped down the dirt road to a Cessna on the highway waiting to fly her to a hospital.

THIRTY-TWO

The formations of C-97s, relayed through Trondheim for their final refueling, had tracked the identical course as the preceding B-36s, flying west of Archangel, south over the Vologda, then banking east over the broad range of valleys that the charts indicated were dotted with agricultural communities for a thousand miles east to the Urals, and were bounded on the south by the industrial complex around Gorky, to the east by Kirov.

The combined formations assembled at thirty thousand feet above this plane. As the final group commander led his unit into place, Colonel Cagney launched the primary action.

A small assault force of signal experts with combat escort would be dropped first. On Cagney's signal, five giant C-97s banked to the south in a rapid circular descent, coming in from south of Kirov only five hundred feet above the ground. Their ground marker was a rail line between Kirov and the smaller city of Novoviatsk. Kasanov was a recognizable complex of industrial buildings twenty-two kilometers northeast, beyond a small diamond-shaped body of water.

Cagney watched the transports peel off. Then he said to his radio operator, "Make a signal to Lakenheath."

This would be the first time radio silence was broken since the lift-off from Trondheim.

Cagney checked the time. Then he said into his microphone, "This hour, Scalpel phase one launched."

He knew the broadcast of the six-word message would alert a thousand radio monitors across the Soviet Union. Yet with Kirov so close, their avoidance of radar had run its course.

"Lieutenant Forester," Cagney said.

"Yes, sir?"

"Open communications with the nearest Russian tower. And dammit, do your stuff right. We're on the money if we don't fuck it up."

Wardell was listening to a briefing on the continuing fighting in Germany when a lieutenant came up to him.

"Sir, Washington on the line for you."

Wardell hurriedly followed the lieutenant. He picked up the headset and put it on.

"Wardell here," he said.

"Just a moment, Senator."

He drummed his fingers impatiently while he waited. Then a voice came on the other end. Even with the distortions of the radio transmission, he recognized the distinctive accent.

"Mr. President," he said. "This is a surprise."

"David, I wanted to pass along the news to you personally. Hoover called to tell me that his people got to the cabin where Laura was staying. Unfortunately, the Russian agents arrived there first."

Wardell took a sharp breath. His stomach knotted. "Then she's . . . she's dead."

"No," Truman said. "Evidently they planned to kill her by setting the cabin on fire. Somehow, that very brave woman managed to get outside. However, she's suffered serious burns and other injuries. I can assure you she's getting the finest medical care."

Wardell couldn't believe it. He'd had the strongest premonition Laura was not alive.

"What is her condition?" he asked. "Is she going to make it?"

"The doctors are still evaluating her condition. I've issued orders that the finest specialists are to be flown in on military aircraft."

"I appreciate that," Wardell said.

"David, you and General Dolan might be interested to know that both of the Russian agents were killed trying to get away. We're positive they didn't have the chance to pass along anything they learned from Laura."

"That's good, Mr. President."

"I want you to know, David, that I find it hard to tell you how much your counsel and your extraordinary personal sacrifices have meant to your country. If the next few hours bring us fortune, you've helped create a world of peace for generations to come."

"I hope that's true. But what I have in mind now is getting to Laura's side as quickly as possible."

"As far as I'm concerned, you can leave Lakenheath immediately. I've made arrangements to have a plane waiting for you in London. You'll be flown to New

York. Another military plane will take you from New York to the hospital upstate."

"Thank you, sir."

"Thank you, David. The prayers of Bess and I are with you and Laura now."

Wardell took off the headset.

"Congratulations, David."

He turned to see Mack Dolan behind him.

"I don't know what to think," Wardell said. "I don't know Laura's condition."

"She's alive. For now, that's what's important."

Wardell nodded. Then he said, "I've got to get to London."

"There's a plane waiting for you. And before you go, another piece of information. Scalpel phase one has been launched. So far everything has gone perfectly."

"How long will phase one take?"

"It should be no more than thirty minutes—a very critical thirty minutes. If no Russian fighters scramble during that time, the rest of the mission will succeed."

"And if they do?"

Dolan frowned. "We'll have a hell of a fight on our hands."

Wardell said, "Keep me informed. You can reach me on the ground in London."

Volkert followed a stream that cut through a winding valley. After an hour's trek, he came upon another cabin, this one unoccupied. He broke in. In a bureau, he found thick wool shirts, denim pants, and hiking boots. The clothes fit well, and he put on four pairs of socks to avoid sliding inside the too large footwear.

He also found a razor. He shaved off his mustache and found a knit hat to cover his baldness. Then he resumed following the stream.

It was late morning when he came to a paved road. A sign indicated two miles to a small village.

Volkert still hadn't decided what he was going to do. He assumed the Scalpel mission had been launched or was in the process of being launched. A phone call could get the urgent message to the Kremlin in a quarter of an hour. That was what he was paid to do.

But while the information might reach the Russians in time for them to shoot down the Scalpel aircraft, he knew the situation was still an intelligence disaster. Stalin was not a patient or forgiving man. Volkert's reward might consist of escaping with his life.

Should that happen, the messy handling of this case would hurt Volkert's reputation. During his career he had only worked for major governments whose espionage requirements were sophisticated enough to spare him too much dirty work. He could always find employment with some of the new African nations or with a dictatorship in South America. But the work would be highly unpleasant, the company repulsive, and the danger far too great for the money.

These considerations led him to the conclusion that he had to do something dramatic—not something to insure the failure of the Scalpel mission, because it was too late for that to be profitable. Rather, he had to come up with a plan to counter its success.

He rounded a bend and saw the tall sign of an Esso station ahead. He collected his wits for the time being, to get to New York. Then he would concentrate on the critical days ahead.

THIRTY-THREE

The eighty parachutes ballooned out beneath the low-flying aircraft, and Capt. Michael Lander hugged a .45-caliber submachine gun against his chest as he watched the ground come up. He had retained an impression, gained from a greater height, of three roads and a radio tower at the edge of the building complex. They had planned the action without prior aerial photographs, and only a hypothetical estimate of the exact location of their targets.

Four units, he thought as the ground rose swiftly toward him. Madison and his strike force with the main unit to the radio tower. Lander hoped to hell he'd seen it.

He readied for the touchdown now, slackening his body, preparing to roll with the impact, his hand set over the parachute release clasp. As he struck the ground, the jarring threw him to his side, and he felt the parachute begin to drag him. The wind was stronger at ground level, and the chute billowed noisily. He struggled for a moment, then managed to strike the release. He fell heavily to his left, scraping his left arm on the hard soil.

The soil of Russia, he reminded himself. He quickly located the submachine gun he'd dropped, then moved to the center of the clearing. He saw a dozen more parachutes, and his men were gathering.

Sergeant Harrison was at his side. "You take the linemen with Madison's commandos," he ordered. "Blow the shit out of that radio station fast."

Harrison went off. The other men were gathering into four groups. It was taking longer than Lander would have liked to get started. He couldn't help glancing upward to see if any Russian fighters were in the distance.

The sky was bare. He ran through his final briefing. His assignment was to destroy all outside communications lines, including the radio unit and telephone wires. He also had been told that there would likely be a major electrical supply facility. If it was self-supporting, he was to blow it. If it wasn't, he was to cut the power transmission cable.

The communications had priority, however. That's why he was on the ground first. The success of the entire operation depended on it.

Lander looked around. He saw some parachutes snarled in a stand of spruce trees a hundred meters to his left. Some men were trying to help their trapped buddies.

Lander issued an order for them to form up and move out. He'd received orders about that eventuality: anybody snarled up or injured would receive help only after the objectives were realized.

He issued orders, then took command of a squad

himself. The four units took off in four directions, north, south, east, and west. Their instructions were to look for roads, since the telephone wires would run along them.

The first road was within a quarter-mile of the drop site. One of the linemen strapped on metal cleats to climb the wooden pole.

"Tap into the line before you cut it," Lander ordered.

"What am I listening for?"

"Any transmission. Especially if the voices sound excited."

The lineman nodded. He was at the top in a minute or two. He detached a handset from his belt and raised a double wire clamp to splice into the first of the suspended lines.

He listened for a moment, then called down, "Line dead."

"Cut it," Lander ordered.

The line fell to the ground. The lineman started to tap into the second line. An instant later an explosion shattered the top of the pole. The crosstree toppled, sending the lineman crashing to the ground.

Lander instinctively dropped, his submachine gun raised and ready. It took him a moment to realize what must have happened—the lineman must have tapped into a power line.

Lander joined two men kneeling by the fallen soldier. One looked up and said, "He's dead, Captain."

Captain Lander looked down at the young, blondish boy. He couldn't be more than nineteen. He'd come all those thousands of miles to be the first American to die on Russian soil.

And he wouldn't be the last if they didn't complete their mission. Lander ordered another lineman to cut the remaining wires. Then he led the squad across an open field in the direction of the high fence surrounding the Soviet atomic research facility.

Colonel Cagney brought his B-36 into a long shallow bank, coming about at one hundred eighty degrees. He could see out the side port that the radio tower was lying on its side, torn loose from the foundation. Directly ahead was the expanse of Kasanov aerodrome.

Looking up, he saw the lead flight of C-97s approaching at a height of three thousand feet. He nosed down, ordering his gunners to strafe the field as they crossed over it. As they approached the runway, he could see pilots running toward six MIG-9s parked off to the side of a hangar. The guns of the bomber raked the tarmac. Cagney caught glimpses of bodies spinning, and one of the MIGs exploded in flame.

Then the field was behind him, and he pulled back on the stick. The rest of his flight was raking the field, and he doubted any of the MIGs would get into the air.

He banked the bomber again. Parachutes were now floating down over the airfield, a seemingly endless flow of blurred ribbons coming out of the transports. The assault force assigned to seize the airfield had been dropped.

Below them, Cagney could see sporadic flashes as ground antiaircraft guns opened up. He grimaced. The B-36s couldn't make another pass at the field. They would have to fly directly into the descending parachutes. So the assault force would take casualties in the air. But he believed their numbers were sufficient to carry the day.

He pulled back on the stick to gain altitude. To his

right, he saw higher formations of C-97s dropping parachutists. The assault on the research center was under way.

"Colonel?"

"Yes."

"Fifty-nine minutes of fuel left."

"Thank you, Sergeant."

Cagney's thoughts went back to the assault on the airfield. They'd better secure it soon so that the C-97 tankers could land and the rest of the formations refuel.

Running out of fuel with an armed atomic bomb aboard over enemy territory was not a pleasant prospect. And still there was the ever-present danger of Russian fighters on the horizon.

Cagney couldn't figure out why they'd had no air opposition. Lieutenant Forester had been able to maintain the charade with the Russian air control tower for almost fifteen minutes, but then they'd switched to another frequency and begun sending coded messages obviously intended for high headquarters. So why hadn't fighters arrived?

Cagney couldn't spend too much time speculating. He was grateful for every free moment. He concentrated on keeping his plane level as he saw field guns and quarter-ton trucks dropping on parachutes toward the research facility. And inside the fence, he saw units drawing automatic weapons fire.

He glanced at his watch. Then he ordered his signal operator to raise Lakenheath for his latest report.

Wardell's plane landed outside of London just as a few drops of rain were starting to fall. Then the ceiling descended and the shower turned into a downpour. Wardell was told his plane was unlikely to be able to take off for at least two hours.

The VIP lounge had been reserved for his use. He poured himself a Jack Daniels and sat down to read a cable from Mack Dolan. The reports were encouraging: the Kasanov aerodrome had been seized with light to moderate casualties; the perimeter of the nuclear research facility was under control, though fighting still raged inside; a high silolike building had been destroyed, the heavy-water storage. Wardell smiled at this last information. No heavy water alone would mean another year or two of delay. Scalpel was already a success in that regard.

He put the cable in his briefcase and picked up a two-day-old copy of the *New York Times*. After the last few days, reading the newspaper was a special pleasure.

He looked up from the paper a few moments later when the door opened. A young man in a gray, striped suit introduced himself as a courier from the American Embassy.

"We have some envelopes for you, Senator," the man said. "The one on top is from the ambassador."

Wardell thanked him. He read the note from his former colleague who now represented the United States at the Court of St. James. He appreciated the warm sympathies in the note.

Other envelopes contained packets of material forwarded from Washington by his assistant. He put those in his briefcase to read later. He almost missed a small blue envelope stuck in between the larger manilla ones.

He glanced at the handwriting on the front, and a ripple of emotion went through him. He tore it open.

337

David,

I don't know what to say, except I'm sorry. For a second time, I've caused you pain, when all I ever wanted to do was love you.

That is forever impossible now, I know. I don't expect to ever see you again, and I wouldn't try. I'm in London for a few months, and I found out through a friend you might be coming through. I took the chance that this note would reach you.

I profoundly hope from the bottom of my heart that you and your wife are able to resolve your differences and resume your marriage. I know how much you love her. You never told me, but I could tell. That I continued to pursue you was selfishness on my part.

I consider myself in your debt. All I hope is that in the future I may have a chance to repay that debt.

Susan

The letter moved Wardell deeply. He supposed some people would be appalled if they knew he were thinking of another woman while Laura hung between life and death.

But in his mind and in his heart, he'd put Susan Gordon behind him. He had loved her, however. In different circumstances, they could have had a life together.

Laura and his feeling for her were the different circumstances. Susan was right: Wardell did love her. And now he prayed he would have the chance to show it.

THIRTY-FOUR

One of the B-36 gunship escorts was the first aircraft to put down on the Kasanov northern strip runway. From aloft, that runway had appeared to be the longest, and it proved just adequate for the massive aircraft.

The C-97 tankers followed. An air control unit established a command post in the tower and deployed a preselected refueling system along one of the other runways.

Colonel Cagney, still circling the area, could see the long fueling lines extended from the fifteen C-97 tankers. His own aircraft had twenty-two minutes' fuel remaining. If all went well, he'd be on the ground in eight minutes.

If all went well. The C-97 transports that had been fueled were stacked in a preparatory flight line on the third runway. They'd be sitting ducks for attacks from the air, especially when the B-36s landed.

The sky, however, was still clear of Russian aircraft. Widening the perimeter of his patrol flight, Cagney saw the convoy of small vehicles moving along the narrow road that ran four kilometers from the aerodrome to the complex of buildings housing the Soviet nuclear development facilities.

Captain Madison had just accepted the surrender of the remaining scattered elements of the small Soviet garrison within the compound. The convoy arrived, with Major Owen Barsky in the point vehicle.

Barsky carried a clipboard with a lengthy list of names. The names were spelled phonetically with English letters, though Barsky himself spoke fluent Russian.

Madison saluted. Barsky returned the salute, then asked, "Have you rounded the scientists up?"

"I think we have everybody who's here."

"Igor Kurchatov?"

Madison smiled. "We've got the big fish."

"Gurevich? Shibayev?"

"I think we have all on the list but three, who are in Moscow."

Barsky nodded. "I'll verify the names myself. Your interpreter has told them they're boarding those airplanes?"

"They refuse to leave."

"We'll see about that."

Barsky moved down the corridor to the room where the scientific personnel were being held. Captain Madison stepped out onto the grounds of the compound and lit a cigarette.

Near the fence, he saw forty or fifty Russian troops sitting on the ground, hands clasped behind their necks. To their right, a squad was collecting the bodies of dead Americans for evacuation.

The fighting had been short, but intense. Most of the

U.S. casualties had resulted from implanted mines and other fixed defensive weapons. An artillery bombardment or strafing runs by fighter planes would have cut the deaths by fifty percent. The thought sickened Madison, who was very attached to his men.

He knew, however, that the mission was so important that lives had to be sacrificed. Still, this knowledge didn't make writing letters home to the dead men's families any easier.

"Madison."

He threw his cigarette to the ground and turned. "Yes, sir."

"I understand the complex has been searched. Manuals, files, and other documents have been loaded?"

"Yes, sir."

"Then we're just about set to go. I'll take the scientists with me. You disarm the prisoners and let them go. Tell them to get the hell out of the area. Then get to the airfield as fast as you can."

"What about our dead, sir?"

Barsky's face was somber. "We've had more wounded than we expected. The medics need space on the transports. We're going to have to leave them here."

"That's not right, sir. Their families—"

"That's an order, Captain. Make sure you've got their dog tags for shipping to Graves Registration. That's all we can do."

Barsky walked toward the jeep to make a report via his SCR-300 radio to Colonel Cagney, whose B-36 should be on the ground being refueled.

Madison watched him walk away. "Dammit!" he spat. Then he walked off toward the prisoners and their guards.

*   *   *

The mood at Lakenheath gradually changed from high tension to a growing elation as every stage of the Scalpel operation went off exactly as planned.

Mack Dolan scanned a cable and handed it to General Lucius Clay, who had flown in from Germany.

Clay said, "C-97s are in the air with the troops. I can't believe this entire operation was conducted without harassment by Soviet fighters."

"I think we have the German front to thank for that. I know your boys have been taking quite a beating, Lucius. But we've had reports of a huge movement of Soviet fighters to German and Eastern European bases. Stalin thought he was on the attack."

"I realize that," Clay said. "But they must have a few fighters left somewhere."

"I think confusion helped, too. The Russians have been so obsessed with Europe that they've neglected construction of northern radar facilities. We didn't get picked up until we were at the target. Then we cut the communications right away. With all the attention on Germany, I doubt if anybody in Moscow believed the scattered reports coming in."

"They'll believe them in a few minutes when that bomb is dropped," Clay said.

"Let's hope so," Dolan said. "If Stalin decides to retaliate against Frankfort, it would be a blood bath."

When all the aircraft were airborne again, Colonel Cagney released the C-97s for their flight north. The U.S. carrier *Enterprise* had slipped into the Barents Sea and a flight of fifty brand new McDonnell F-2

Banshee all-weather fighter bombers was lined up on deck. The Banshees would launch shortly and meet the C-97s near Archangel to escort them back to Trondheim in Norway.

When the C-97s were on their way, Cagney gave the signal to the 24 B-36s to disperse. Each had a specific target in Russia, though only eleven carried atomic weapons. It would be up to the Russians to try to guess which ones.

The B-36s peeled off into the sky. Cagney leveled off at thirty-one thousand feet and circled over Kasanov. He ordered the final signal to be sent to Lakenheath and relayed to the Condition Room at the White House for the final decision.

Secretary of Defense James Forrestal turned in his chair to face the desk. "Mr. President?" he asked.

Truman's face was as calm as it had been during the entire operation. "I'd like you to send this message to Moscow when you give the final go signal to Scalpel:

"As of this hour, your research facility at Kasanov has been destroyed by an atomic blast. Cease all military activity immediately, or destruction of your major cities will begin."

"Is that it?" Forrestal asked.

"That's enough," Truman said with satisfaction. "That'll knock the smug look off that bastard's face."

Colonel Cagney acknowledged receipt of the signal. Then he ordered the checklist to begin.

An engineering sergeant manned the console while the checklist was read.

"Green plugs installed."

"Check," the bombardier said.

"Remove rear plate."

"Check."

"Insert breech wrench in breech plug."

"Check."

"Unscrew breech plug, place on rubber pad."

The reply was affirmative. The officer continued through the entire list: insert charge, four sections, red ends in breech; insert breech and tighten; connect firing pin; install armor plate; install rear plate.

Finally, the officer said to the bombardier, "Come up out of there. The last thing is to secure the catwalk and get the tools out of the bay."

"All right, sir."

"You sure you tightened the breech with sixteen turns?"

"Yes, sir."

The officer spoke into the microphone. "Colonel, we'll be ready for the run in two minutes."

Cagney acknowledged the message. The officer reached down and replaced the green plugs in the console with red plugs. Then he sat down at the console.

"Coming up on Initial Point," Cagney said. "Mark . . . mark . . . mark . . . okay, now, son, it's your airplane."

The navigator turned a switch and the bomb-bay door dropped open. He hesitated an instant for a final scan of the panel lights, then turned the next switch. The weapon fell clear of the restraining hooks. It pulled itself clear of the monitoring cables and the signals on

344

the console went dead.

"Away," the navigator called.

Cagney had already sensed the lightening of the aircraft as the heavy bomb dropped. He advanced the throttles and turned the B-36 to the right.

Inside the falling bomb, a timer triggered the first switch on the firing circuit. Seconds later, the barometric switch tripped at two thousand feet above the ground. The bomb made a screaming sound like an artillery shell as it dropped at near the speed of sound.

Then it reached one thousand feet. In the cockpit, Colonel Cagney watched through a special viewer. He was overwhelmed. It was as if the morning light had become night, and a new, immensely greater brilliance had pulled the sun to earth.

The shock wave came up toward them like an expanding bubble. Cagney warned the men to brace themselves an instant before the giant aircraft was thrown upward, and the roar of its engines was drowned in a deafening roar. Then a second shock wave buffeted the plane, almost taking Cagney by surprise.

Finally, he regained control of the aircraft. He took a moment to calm himself, then turned the plane northward. Looking to his left, he saw the fast-rising column of smoke, red and deep blue at its core, shooting up with incredible speed. Below, the mushroom cloud spread so wide the target was totally obscured.

Colonel Cagney thought of a phrase he had heard years before, knowing he never really understood its meaning until now. In the words of his long-departed father, he'd finally had his "peek into the furnace." It was a peek he never wanted to take again.

IV

LAKENHEATH

THIRTY-FIVE

David sat in a chair by the bed, holding Laura's fingers in his. She'd drifted off to sleep in the middle of their conversation. It had happened often in the last two days, because she was being sedated to help her cope with the considerable pain of her burns.

But that didn't matter. She was alive and she was going to live. The doctors called her escape miraculous. Another few seconds and her first- and second-degree burns would have been third-degree burns. Another few breaths and her lungs would have been burned, the resulting lack of oxygen causing brain damage.

None of that had happened. Her burns would cause her considerable pain, there would be some scarring, and the risk of infection would be present for a few weeks. In addition she'd broken her left arm in the fall and there had been some internal bleeding. But she was off the critical list and on the way back to health.

Wardell hadn't known that, the night before last when he'd rushed to the hospital. A nurse escorted him into her room. He'd stood in the doorway and his emotional reaction had almost made him lose his balance.

The memory that sprang into his mind was over-whelming, the image of his first wife spread out on a Stryker frame, staring at him with those dark eyes moments before her death. Now his second wife had also been burned. He felt like the hero in some Greek tragedy, cursed by the gods to relive the same agonies as punishment for some unknown offense.

Then Laura had opened her eyes and said, "David. Thank God you're here."

And he knew. Before the doctors briefed him, he knew she was going to live.

He felt pressure on his fingers. He looked over and saw that Laura had awakened.

"How long did I nap?" she asked.

"About an hour."

"A short one," she said. She hesitated, then said, "You don't have to sit there while I'm sleeping, you know."

"I like to," Wardell said. "It gives me time to think."

"About what?"

"About you. About us. About our life together."

She smiled. "That's a nice thought. But what about the Senate?"

"I'm submitting my resignation. I've given enough. It's someone else's turn now."

She turned her head, looking at the ceiling for a moment. When her gaze again met his, she said, "David, I've been wondering. What do you think about what's happened, now that it's over? Do you really think it was right? Was it moral?"

"Are you sure you want to talk about it?" Wardell asked.

"I won't get emotional," Laura said. "I'm beyond that now. But I want to know."

Wardell thought for a moment. Then he said, "I don't think I'll ever be able to answer that question. There are some questions of morality that are unanswerable. You may think it's totally immoral to steal, but if your children were starving and stealing was the only way to get them food, is that immoral? You may think killing is immoral, but if you had had the chance to shoot Hitler in 1942, would that have been immoral?"

Laura said, "But this situation wasn't that clear. It's more like having to make the decision to shoot Hitler in 1936. We dropped that bomb not because of what the Russians were doing, but because of what we thought they might do in the future."

"I see your point," Wardell said. "I guess history will be the judge, as it is in most cases. But if things continue to work out as well as they have, we may indeed have insured a new era in world affairs."

"What has happened?"

"In concrete terms, relatively little. The land route to Berlin has been reopened, and the Soviet divisions have begun to retreat from the border. The Kremlin has agreed to send a negotiating team to meet with us in Vienna starting next week."

"Is that all?"

"There are other signs. Mack Dolan and the others are elated. There has been absolutely no direct word from Stalin since the Scalpel operation has been launched. All communications from the Kremlin have been unsigned, and Bedell-Smith can't see anyone. The concensus is that Stalin has been killed or imprisoned. At the very least, there's some sort of power struggle going on."

"And there will be bloodshed among the leadership. Maybe more purges, and more tens of thousands of people sent to labor camps in Siberia." Laura shook her head. Her voice was more sad than emotional. "World politics isn't my area of expertise, David. But I feel one thing very strongly. Scalpel is going to backfire on us. I believe that there is a higher moral law—or maybe even physical law—no permanent good can come out of anything that's totally wrong. I feel that dropping that bomb was wrong."

"Laura . . ."

She squeezed his hand. "David, this is the last I'm going to mention this. It will never come between us again, I promise. I just want you to know the way I feel."

He leaned over and kissed her. "I want to know. I want to spend the rest of my life listening to you."

They sat in silence for a few minutes. Then a nurse came in to bring Laura to a treatment room. Twice a day she was put into a whirlpool bath to wash the dead skin off her burned areas. The treatment was painful, but absolutely necessary to recovery.

"I don't know how you can go to that room so cheerfully," Wardell said.

She smiled. "Because it's making me better. And because I know I'll see you later."

The nurse told Wardell, "We'll be giving her a

stronger shot after the treatment. I expect her to sleep for a few hours afterward."

He kissed his wife. "I'm going back to the motel. I'll see you this afternoon."

That evening, Wardell flew to Washington. As much as he hated to leave Laura, there was some business he had to take care of, not the least of which was her transfer to Bethesda Naval Hospital.

He went to Capitol Hill early the next morning. Shortly after ten, he returned to his office after breakfast with Arthur Vandenberg, President Pro Tem of the Senate.

Rachel Lang, his assistant, was waiting for him. There were tears in her eyes.

Wardell embraced her, then said with a gentle smile, "It's over, Rachel. But it's been a good career."

She shook her head. "It's not going to be the same, David. After all these years."

"You'll have to break the new man in. I hope he's easier to tame than I was."

She smiled. "You came tame. I had to liven you up."

"That you did," he said. Then he asked, "What's up? I'm still a senator for the rest of the day."

"A man in your office to see you. From the FBI."

Wardell had asked Agent Frank Coffey to stop by. He wanted to thank him personally for saving Laura.

They chatted for a few minutes about the search. Coffey said, "It's a remarkable change in the last few

353

days. We've been on the defensive since the war—for every agent we caught, a dozen new ones started operation. Now they're running for the hills. The embassy is chaos."

"You've made a lot of arrests?"

"We've rounded up everyone we've had under surveillance. The more we find out, the better bargain we can drive in Vienna. And the sense of panic is driving people to talk that we couldn't have broken any way before. I think we've effectively crippled Soviet intelligence for years. Maybe permanently."

"You sound like the people in the Pentagon," Wardell said. "I've never heard such optimism."

"It's been a long time since we've been able to be optimistic," Coffey said. He got up to leave. As he was shaking hands with Wardell, he said, "One last bit of information you may be interested in, Senator. I know you took a personal interest in the Fuchs case."

"Karl Fuchs? The scientist we suspected of spying for the Russians? I thought he was in Britain."

"The British picked him up for us. We'd been hoping he'd lead to other atomic spies, but now that doesn't matter. We were arranging extradition. Then yesterday an armed gang broke into the jail where he was being held, evidently to free some black marketeers awaiting trial. Fuchs escaped with them."

"I doubt he'll get far," Wardell said.

"I hope not," Coffey responded. "There's a bunch of people who want to chip in to buy him a thank-you present."

"For what?"

"For passing the information along to the Russians.

354

If they hadn't developed the bomb so quickly, Scalpel never would have taken place. And we'd still be beating our heads against the wall."

Wardell planned to spend the day saying goodbye to colleagues on the hill. But he found the prevailing mood of optimism irritated him. The atmosphere was like V-J Day, the triumphant end of a war.

Maybe he was affected by Laura's gloomy prediction. But he also felt that nothing had really been worked out with the Soviets yet. All Scalpel had produced was a delay in the Russian atomic arms program and a breakoff in the conflict in Germany. The Soviet Union was still a powerful nation and all the grave issues had yet to be resolved.

Instead of making his rounds, he had lunch with Rachel Lang at an out-of-the-way place in Georgetown, then drove home. He was due at the White House for cocktails that evening, so he planned an afternoon nap.

He got a shock when he walked into his house. Susan Gordon was waiting for him in the living room.

He stood in the doorway and stared. She looked much thinner, and very tired. She was holding a coffee cup, and Wardell could see it trembling.

"Your housekeeper was very kind," Susan said. "She let me wash up and fixed me a bite to eat."

He didn't speak for a moment. Then he said, "I appreciated the note you sent me in London."

"I meant it, David," she said. "I really didn't intend ever to see you again. But I was also very serious about repaying my debt to you. That's why I flew from London to make this dramatic appearance." She smiled, then added, "The critics always say my entrances are the best part of my performances."

"Susan, you don't owe me anything," Wardell said. "What happened was as much my fault—"

"Can we talk now, please," Susan interrupted. "I've come a very long way, and I'm exhausted."

Wardell got more coffee for Susan. Then they went into his study.

"You know I've put Hong Kong behind me," she began. "That was a very different person who led that life."

"I know," he said.

She smiled. "Thank you." She paused, then continued. "There were some good things about the war, some good times despite everything, some good people I miss. And Paris being the center of international life it is, some of those people from Hong Kong appear every so often. About a year ago, a man named Sam Gannett was reassigned to Europe by your CIA. Sam had gotten me out of trouble more than a few times when he was stationed in Hong Kong. I liked him, and when he was in Paris we'd have dinner."

Wardell didn't say anything. He just sat, looking at her.

She continued, "I guess you want to know the point of all this?"

Wardell nodded.

Susan took a deep breath. Then she said, "Two days ago I walked into my hotel room in London after a rehearsal. Sam was waiting for me. But it wasn't a social call. Sam looked as though he hadn't slept in days, and he was very somber. Before I even had a chance to say hello, he asked me if I remembered a man named Jason Volkert. Unfortunately, I did."

She paused, tightening her lips as if she were swallowing something bitter. "Volkert was supposedly an Austrian. He ran an import-export business in Hong Kong, but that was just a front for a wide range of black market and other activities."

Wardell looked at her. "Why do you say supposedly an Austrian?"

"As an actress, I'm very sensitive to language. Volkert spoke several languages very fluently. But none of those languages, including German, seemed to be *his* language, as English is ours. It was just an impression, obviously, but I'm convinced of it."

"What difference does it make?"

"None," Susan said. "Except as further evidence of how dangerous a man Volkert was. With his wealth, his contacts, and his total ruthlessness, he made himself useful to many different sides during the war—at first primarily to the Japanese, then later, as it became clear the Japanese were losing, to the Americans, the British, the Russians. I think he ended up working for the Russians. There was a very strong rumor that he was responsible for the murder of dozens of anticommunist Chinese who were preparing to go back to the mainland."

"Very interesting," Wardell said. "But what does this have to do with the present?"

"You probably know that after the war, many of the French Resistance units secretly stockpiled huge supplies of weapons. Sam Gannett found out that Volkert had hired thirty highly trained, highly armed men from a secret Communist cell. The men and arms had gone to Britain. Just a few hours before Sam came to see me, Volkert's men had attacked a British prison and rescued a Soviet spy."

Wardell sat forward. The name Karl Fuchs leaped into his mind. "Are you sure of that?"

"Sam was sure," she said. "He was very close to the situation—too close. He left my hotel on foot. A car roared by and he was cut down by an automatic weapon."

"I can verify that," Wardell cautioned.

She looked at him with fire in her eyes. "Do you think I flew across the Atlantic to lie to you?"

He touched her arm. "No. I'm sorry, of course not." He paused for a moment, then added, "I still don't understand. Why did Sam tell you this? And why are you here?"

"Sam asked me to help him."

"How?"

"By contacting Volkert." She looked down, avoiding his eyes. "I . . . I had some dealings with him in Hong Kong. Dealings I'm very, very ashamed of. But I was a different person then. I've told you . . ."

He put his hand on hers to stop her. "You don't have to say more. I know that."

She squeezed his hand. Then she looked at him and said, "I was to contact Volkert. He'd always been very attracted to me. Sam thought . . . thought I could find out what he was up to."

Wardell was puzzled. "Isn't breaking a spy out of prison enough? The men were probably back in France hours later."

358

She shook her head. "No. That's what worried Sam. Besides, he said Volkert only used a half-dozen men in the prison attack. He's not the type of man who would pay thirty when he needed six. Sam thought it was a prelude to some other action—something that would have a grave effect on some sort of negotiations."

My God, Wardell thought to himself. The negotiations in Vienna.

No information about the Scalpel attack had been given to the press. The fighting in Germany had been reported, of course, and the subsequent pull back. But Truman had believed that the Soviets would be much less willing to give concessions if it were publicly known they had a gun to their heads. Plus, antiatomic bomb demonstrations in the States might give them hope that Truman might be forced to back down.

Susan's information opened up another horrible possibility—some sort of armed action, like taking hostages or capturing a symbolic British government building. That would force the issue into the press, and it could conceivably ruin all that Scalpel accomplished.

Wardell looked back at Susan. "Why have you come to me? Why didn't you tell American intelligence in London?"

"I tried to. But they looked at me as if I were crazy." She took a deep breath, then met his eyes. "David, I'm willing to take the risk of meeting Volkert. I'll do it because I want to; I have to pay back my debt to you, and to my country. But I'll only do it with your support, with you in London providing support."

"Why me?" David asked. "I'm not an intelligence professional."

Her face was somber. "That's why I have to have you there. You forget I've worked for the Americans before. They'll use me as if I were a piece of meat, even if they believe me in the first place." She was silent for a moment. Then she asked, "Do you believe me, David?"

He took a long time to answer. "I don't know for sure," he said. "But . . . but I think so."

THIRTY-SIX

The engines of the C-54 growled as it climbed into the black sky over Newfoundland. Wardell sat back in the seat, staring into nothingness, until the plane leveled off and banked eastward to continue its flight to England.

Susan hadn't awakened during the refueling stop. She was still sleeping in the compartment fitted for use by the Joint Chiefs and cabinet members.

Wardell couldn't sleep. He replayed over and over in his mind the conversations that had kept him on the telephone for hours after he'd heard Susan's story.

The only fact that he'd been able to verify was that Sam Gannett had indeed been killed. But the CIA told him that Gannett had been trying to infiltrate an Eastern European spy ring and that was the likely reason for his death. They placed little credence in Susan's story.

The same was true at the Pentagon. The success of the Scalpel operation seemed to have filled everyone in the government with the absolute conviction that one decisive stroke had ended the battle permanently. Wardell had been uncomfortable when FBI agent Coffey had demonstrated that attitude during his last briefing. As he'd been increasingly exposed to it during the afternoon, he'd become more and more disturbed.

Maybe it had to do with Laura. Her somber prediction that no good could come out of an "immoral" act like Scalpel had originally sounded to him like a speech from the witches in *Macbeth*. But throughout the afternoon, her words echoed in his mind until, against all reason, he was convinced grave danger lay ahead.

His conviction led to a late-evening telephone call to Arthur Vandenburg. To the amazement of the President Pro Tem of the Senate, Wardell withdrew his resignation. Vandenburg objected, but finally admitted that there was no reason Wardell couldn't decide to do so. So he was still a senator, still Chairman of the Senate Armed Services Committee, and still CIA liaison.

With that settled, Wardell called the White House. Truman hadn't asked for an explanation when Wardell requested an airplane be made available to fly him to Britain.

Then came the last phone call. To Laura. Strangely, she wasn't surprised by what he told her. Maybe it had been the medication, but . . .

"David?"

Wardell turned. Susan came to sit next to him. She was wearing a silk robe. The top buttons were open, exposing her creamy white skin.

"What are you thinking about?" she asked.

Wardell didn't reply for a moment. Then he said, "I

don't know if I want to answer."

She looked at him somberly. "I want to tell you something," she said. "I've been lying awake for hours, thinking about you. I want you so badly I'm shaking. But that would be wrong. That would be . . ."

Wardell reached out and pulled her to him. She resisted for a moment, then yielded. Her mouth opened, her tongue sought his. His hand caressed her neck, then cupped the breast that arched to meet it.

"David," she panted. "Oh, David."

Jason Volkert held on tightly to the gunwale as the fishing boat pitched in the deep swell two hundred yards from shore. He turned to the man next to him and asked in French, "We're behind schedule? Are you sure your men know what to do?"

Paul Marais, the grizzled ex-Resistance leader, just stared at him contemptuously for a moment. Then he turned and made his way across the deck to the wheelhouse.

Volkert took in a deep breath, cautioning himself to control his impatience. Marais's men had been highly professional so far. Besides, there was little Volkert could do now to replace them if they weren't. It was too late to turn back.

The idea that had come to him as he'd fled from the Catskill Mountains to New York had been the most brilliant of his life. This mission would be the crowning point of his career. And not only for the millions that the Russians would pay him for his success—although that would make a lavish retirement. But even more important, he, Jason Volkert, would have a profound effect on history. With success, he would buy himself immortality.

He'd never before realized the desire he had to be famous. He'd worked all his life in the shadows, taking pride in not being known. But now that wasn't enough. The most powerful men on earth would know his name.

That was worth the risk—any risk.

He turned back to stare toward the shoreline, from which a beacon swept the thick gray clouds. And below, he could make out the lights of the control tower of Lakenheath Air Force Base.

He checked his watch. Nearly one A.M., a half hour behind schedule. The changing of the perimeter guards was at two, so they were running out of . . .

Then he saw the signal. A red lantern flashing one long and two short. He turned toward the wheelhouse as Marais came toward him.

"Get the men ready," he told Marais. "We're going ashore."

Wardell was awakened by Susan's caress. They made love again, this time with far less urgency. Their bodies seemed to pick up the vibrations of the plane, and every touch brought rippling electric sensations that built to intense heights of pleasure.

Then it was over. Susan's head rested on Wardell's chest as they recovered their breath.

Finally, she said to him, "That was wonderful, David. But I don't understand—"

He touched her lips with his fingers, quieting her. "There are some things that don't have rational

364

explanations," he said. "I've finally learned that, after far too many years of placing my entire faith in reason and logic."

"I don't understand," she said.

He kissed her gently. "All I understand is that our making love was right. For this time, for this place, for whatever lies ahead." He was silent, thinking. Then he said, "I think this will truly be the last time. I think Laura sensed that, and she wasn't afraid to let me go. She knows she'll never lose me."

"No," Susan said. "I've always known that."

They didn't speak for a long time. Then Susan said, "I was terribly frightened. I still am, but not in the same way."

"That's why it's right we made love," Wardell said. "It's all I can give you now."

"I know," she said. "And that's enough, whatever lies ahead."

Volkert ignored the sprawled body of the dead American soldier. He crouched in the low grass ten meters from the fence, scanning the expanse of the air base through field glasses.

He lowered the glasses when Paul Marais came up to him.

"I can't understand," Marais said. "This fence is the only line of defense?"

Volkert said, "You did not believe me. Overconfidence is an American trait, like arrogance to the Germans. Why else do you think the Japanese were able to destroy the entire American fleet at Pearl Harbor? You would have thought they would have learned a lesson from that, but their subsequent victory has made them even worse."

"They will pay for that," Marais said.

"Yes," Volkert replied. "But that doesn't mean we can get careless. Your men are in place?"

Marais nodded.

Volkert gripped his arm. "You can't forget your most important responsibility. Fuchs has to get to that bunker alive and unhurt."

"He'll get there," Marais said.

"Then give the signal," Volkert ordered.

Marais moved a few yards to his right and whispered to a short, muscular man. That man and eight others picked up bales of rubber shreds they'd brought ashore. They carried them three hundred meters along the fence line. On the other side of the barrier a flight of B-36s was parked on a runway.

The men stacked the shredded rubber against the fence. One man splashed a couple of jerry cans of gasoline on the piles while the others moved fifty meters to the right. Four men set up two German MG-34 machine guns on their bipod mounts. Fifty cartridge belts were fastened together and two spare barrels were laid out for each weapon. Next to the machine gunners, another Frenchman unstrapped an American bazooka and unloaded a dozen rockets from his backpack.

When the weapons were ready, one of the Frenchmen whistled. A match was lit and the gasoline ignited with a roar.

A jolt of excitement went through Volkert when he saw the flames leaping into the sky. The control tower must have spotted the fire almost immediately, for he heard sirens at the same time the first whiffs of the thick, black smoke from the burning rubber reached him.

The first vehicles roaring across the runway were a jeep and two deuce-and-a-halfs carrying troops. Fire-fighting vehicles followed. As Volkert watched the headlights, Marais's men were moving past him through a hole they'd cut in the perimeter fence.

Volkert lost sight of the trucks as they neared the fire. He heard the screech of tires and a lot of shouting.

The machine guns opened fire, and the clatter of automatic weapons was punctuated by screams of agony. Volkert heard a whooshing noise, then a deaf-ening explosion as a rocket from the bazooka slammed into a parked B-36.

Antiaircraft sirens joined the cacophony as the base went on full alert. Volkert waited until he saw a convoy of additional reinforcements rushing toward the blazing perimeter to his right.

Finally, he gave the signal. With twenty heavily armed men, he moved to the left, toward Bomb Bunker Number Three.

Wardell was looking out the window at the lights of the Irish coast when he was called forward. When he stepped into the cockpit, a white-faced radio operator handed him a decoded handwritten message.

He read the message three times, the knot in his stomach becoming tighter and tighter.

Finally, he looked at the young radioman. "You confirm this, son?"

He nodded.

Wardell turned to the pilot. "You know what this message says, Major."

"Yes, sir."

"We're changing course. We're going to land at Lakenheath."

"I don't know if we can get in there, sir. The field has probably been closed."

"I don't give a shit," Wardell said. "Radio General Dolan. If he should have any objections, come back and get me. I'll talk to the President directly."

The pilot turned to him. "Anything you say, Senator."

Wardell started to leave. Then a thought struck him. He turned and said to the crew, "I realize how you all must feel flying into a base where foreign agents have seized an arsenal of atomic bombs. I'm sorry for the risks involved. But all you have to do is get me on the ground. Then you can get on your way and into London."

After a short silence, the pilot spoke. "We appreciate that, Senator. But I understand there's quite a pile of those bombs at Lakenheath. I wonder if London is safe?"

The question didn't have an answer. Wardell turned and went back to Susan.

THIRTY-SEVEN

The C-54 screeched to a halt at the end of the runway. Out the window, Wardell could see the shells of bombers burning out of control on a far runway. The air was foul with smoke, and as he walked from the pressurized cabin, Wardell's eyes immediately began to tear and he coughed.

A command car was waiting for him. The driver shot a glance at Susan, but Wardell took her arm and helped her inside.

More than anything else, the air base reminded Wardell of London during the blitz. The air was filled with the sound of sirens and the flashing of lights. The command car halted at a hangar near the captured bunker. Airplanes had been taxied out to free space for a makeshift field hospital. Wardell felt Susan trembling as they made their way through the rows of groaning, wounded soldiers waiting, on stretchers, for the overwhelmed medical staff.

Mack Dolan had taken over a squadron commander's office. He was on the phone, listening, as

Wardell walked in.

Finally, he said, "Thank you, doctor." He hung up the phone, then turned to Wardell. His face was red and grim.

"You picked a hell of a time to visit," Dolan said. Then he noticed Susan. "What is she doing here?" he demanded.

"She's the reason I'm here," Wardell said. "And if she'd gotten to me a day earlier, this might never have happened."

"What do you mean?" Dolan asked.

Wardell told him the story about Jason Volkert.

When he'd finished, Dolan said, "That fucker certainly got himself good people. They shot the shit out of the base guards. We have at least seventy-five dead and twice that wounded."

"What does he want? Has he given you an idea?"

"Yeah," Dolan said sarcastically. "We've got his Christmas shopping list. It's real short. All he wants us to do is step aside and let him fly out of here with one atomic bomb."

Volkert watched with growing impatience as a tall, thin man with disheveled hair, a high forehead, and thick black-rimmed glasses worked on the huge gleaming metal cylinder. Finally the man stood and turned.

"Is it armed?" Volkert said.

"It was not constructed to be detonated in this manner," the man said in German-accented English.

"Fuchs, I didn't ask that," Volkert said. "Will it go off?"

The man swallowed. Then he said, "Yes, it will."

"And the others?"

"Sympathetic detonation. Quite like one grenade going off in an armory."

"Good," Volkert said. He started to turn away. Karl Fuchs grabbed his arm.

"You can't mean that," Fuchs said. "You can't be serious about actually detonating that weapon. We'd all be—"

"I know what would happen," Volkert interrupted. "So do they out there. You spend your time hoping they're as appalled by the idea as you are."

"And if they are?"

Volkert smiled. "If they are, we're wealthy men. And we'll probably walk around Moscow wearing the Order of Lenin."

"I don't care about medals," Fuchs said.

"Then try to care about having something left to pin it to," Volkert replied. "I do, and I'm getting back on the radio right now."

When the transmission was over, Wardell turned to Susan and asked, "Is that his voice?"

"Yes," she said. "Even though the radio distorts it, the phrasing is his."

"Good," Dolan said. "I'm glad it's the guy you described. Sounds like he's more interested in money than getting his ass blown to kingdom come."

"I wouldn't underestimate him," Susan said.

"Who's underestimating him?" Dolan said. "I'm saying most people wouldn't be crazy enough to push the button when the time came." He turned and said to an aide, "Jenkins, get on the horn. Tell Captain Palmer to have his men ready to attack in five minutes."

Wardell moved forward. "Wait a miute, Mack," he said. "You're not planning to assault that bunker, are you?"

Dolan gave him a hard look. "What I'm planning is none of your business, David."

"What orders have you received from Washington? What did the president tell you?"

"Fuck Washington," Dolan said angrily. "If they'd listened to me three years ago, we wouldn't be in this fix. Three long years you politicians screw around while Russians push the world around. And now that Scalpel has finally been carried through, some madman makes a few threats and the politicians are looking to back down."

"It's not just a madman," Wardell said. "He's got fifteen nuclear warheads under his control."

"What difference does that make in the long run?" Dolan asked. "We've got more atomic bombs at Trondheim, and back in the States. We've got the Russians on the ropes and I'm not going to let them off. All those brave boys who died in the Scalpel raid would have died in vain if we give in."

"What about the hundreds of thousands of British civilians who'll die if those bombs go off? We're only sixty miles from London. The city could become a ghost town, another Hiroshima."

"Hiroshima!" Dolan spat contemptuously. "I'm tired of Hiroshima being thrown up in my face. Maybe the people who thought dropping the bomb was so horrible should have been in the first wave storming the beaches of Japan. Then they would have seen what was truly horrible."

"That has nothing to do with this situation," Wardell said.

Dolan looked at him. "So what do you think we should do?" he asked.

"I don't know. Stall for time, as long as we can. And hope in the meantime we can talk sense to the Soviets."

"The Soviets are delighted," Dolan said. "They can't lose. They've disavowed all connection with the guys in that bunker—after all, they're Frenchmen. But if they get away with the bomb, the Russians have saved their asses."

"You're simplifying this situation," Wardell said. "This is a time for collective thought. I want to talk to the president myself."

Wardell started for the radio.

"Stop, David!" Dolan said. "I'm not letting you do that."

Wardell whirled, angry now. "You can't stop me. I'm a United States Senator. I think you've gone off the wall, Mack."

Dolan glared at Wardell. Their eyes locked for a moment. Then Wardell started for the radio.

Dolan turned to a pair of military policemen. "Arrest him," he ordered.

"But sir, the—"

"Do you want to be court-martialed?" Dolan bellowed. "Arrest both of them."

Wardell stood still for a moment, unable to believe his ears. Then he dashed for the door. A third MP appeared in front of him, blocking the way, and hands grabbed him from behind. He struggled briefly, but it was no use.

Dolan moved over to face him. He said, "I'm sorry I

have to do this, David. But I can't let all I've accomplished be ruined."

Wardell didn't say a word.

Dolan said to the MPs, "Tie them up and lock them in the next room. One of you stay on guard outside the door."

The door slammed shut, leaving Wardell and Susan in darkness.

"I can't believe what's happened," Wardell said. "He's gone mad."

"Volkert will set that bomb off if he's attacked," Susan said. "He'd die anyway. He has nothing to lose."

"Dolan doesn't realize that," Wardell said. "Scalpel has been his obsession since the war. He should have been transferred back to the States. But who dreamed this would happen?"

Except Laura, he added to himself. The immense corruptibility of human beings again demonstrated. Once exploding one nuclear weapon becomes acceptable, it's far easier to think of a second or a third. The incredible destruction that would be caused by the explosion of those bombs in the bunker a few hundred yards away meant nothing to Dolan—no more than sending out a patrol during the First World War. The awful had become real—atomic bombs were a tactical weapon.

That's why Dolan has to be stopped, Wardell realized. Laura was right all the time. The world would be paralyzed with fear in the escalating development and threat of atomic warfare.

"David!" Susan called out in a low, excited voice.

"What is it?"

"The metal leg of this desk has a rough edge. I think I may be able to saw through the rope."

"How long?"

Susan didn't answer for a moment. Wardell could hear her panting with exertion.

Then she said, "I don't know. I feel it working."

"Can I help?"

"Not now," she said. "Concentrate on planning what we can do if we do get free."

"Sir?"

Dolan turned. "Yes, Captain?"

"A convoy of British soldiers is at the gate. Their general demands to be let in."

"Permission denied."

"There must be a thousand troops, sir."

"Palmer is almost in position to move out. You only have to stall them for a few minutes. Do you think you can do that?"

The captain stiffened. "We'll do it, sir."

Dolan watched him leave the room. He dispatched another messenger to tell Captain Palmer to wait for him before he began the assault. Then he sat at a desk and scribbled a few lines on a note pad.

He got up and handed the notepaper to the radio man. "Send this message to Washington. Make sure they understand it's to be sent to my wife."

"Yes, sir."

Dolan walked over to the desk. He picked up his pistol belt and strapped it on. He unholstered his .45, made sure a full clip was in place, and put it back. Then he put on his helmet.

He took a moment to collect himself before going out to lead the storming of the bunker. He knew the woman with Wardell was right—that madman in the bunker was likely to set off the atomic bomb. He knew that in all likelihood he was going to die.

But that was a soldier's duty, to die for his country. And few sacrifices would pay greater rewards than the one he was going to make. What were a few thousand or even hundreds of thousands of lives if a lasting peace could be insured?

The task ahead of him was grim. His reward, Dolan felt, would be a permanent place of honor in military history.

Volkert remained in the heart of the bunker with the stockpiled atomic weapons. He kept a close eye on Karl Fuchs, who was pacing furiously.

Paul Marais appeared in the doorway. He said in French, "It is getting light outside. I can American troops getting into assault position."

Volkert replied, "The moment the first shot is fired, you signal me."

Marais left. Fuchs came up to Volkert and asked in English, "What did he say?"

"Our American friends have apparently been watching too many Western movies. They appear to be preparing to attack."

"No," Fuchs said. He paused for a moment, then asked, "What are we going to do?"

"You know what we are going to do," Volkert said. "We're going to explode that bomb."

Fuchs' thin face turned even whiter. "You can't. We'll all be killed. We'll—"

Volkert slapped him. "Get yourself together. What do you think will happen if we don't explode the bomb when they storm us? We'll die anyway."

"But you promised they would back down? You told me that they wouldn't risk an atomic blast."

Volkert looked at him calmly. "I may have been wrong."

Fuchs stared at him in disbelief. "I can't be a mass murderer. I won't have a part in this."

He turned and ran for the armed warhead.

Volkert shot him in the back. Fuchs pitched forward onto his face. He struggled for a moment, reaching out futilely with his right hand for the fuse wires a few short feet away.

Volkert walked over and shot him again, in the back of the neck.

Marais and two men ran into the room, submachine guns cocked and ready. "What happened?"

"Nothing," Volkert said. "Go back to your stations."

The MP opened the door when Susan cried out. Wardell brought the chair leg down on the back of his neck. The guard pitched to the floor.

Wardell grabbed the MP's submachine gun. Susan pulled the .45 from his holster and followed the senator down the hall.

Only the radio operator was in the command room. He gaped in astonishment as Wardell burst in.

"Where's Dolan?" Wardell shouted.

"He's . . . he's out there."

Wardell turned.

The soldier lunged for him. Wardell heard the movement and spun back, swinging the butt of his weapon. He caught the soldier in the jaw.

"Let's go," he called to Susan.

They sprinted through the door into the hangar. Medical personnel and patients turned to stare as they zigzagged through the cots and stretchers. Wardell reached the door to the runway, opened it, then dashed out.

The sky had turned a light gray as the sun neared the horizon. Wardell saw Mack Dolan walking with an aide twenty-five meters ahead. He shouted at the general to stop.

Dolan turned. He watched Wardell and Susan approach. His aide brought his weapon up toward Wardell. Dolan reached out and pushed the weapon down.

"Don't interfere, David," Dolan said. "This isn't your affair."

"It is now," Wardell said. "I can't let you storm that bunker."

Dolan looked at him with piercing eyes. "You can't let me. That means you're prepared to stop me. So do it. Shoot."

Wardell for the first time was conscious of the weapon in his hands. He stared down at it for a moment, then back at Dolan.

A surge of emotions went through him. Dolan had been his close friend for thirty years. They'd fought together, planned together. Now it came down to this.

"Come on, David," Dolan said. "If you're going to do it, do it now. Or I'm going to my men and kick that

378

son of a bitch out of the bunker."

Wardell's finger tightened on the trigger. But his mind wouldn't give the command to fire.

"I thought so," Dolan said. He started to turn away.

A surge of anger went through Wardell. He pressed the trigger. But the safety was on. He reached to flick off the safety with his thumb.

Then he heard the loud report of a weapon next to him. Dolan cried out as the shot hit him in the chest. He spun around as he was hit again.

Wardell turned to see Susan, five yards to his right, squeeze off a third shot from the .45. "Susan," he cried. He took one step.

Then Dolan's aide triggered a burst from his weapon. A crimson line was stitched across the front of Susan's dress.

"No!" Wardell cried. In a rage he spun and fired off half a clip in a sweeping arc. The aide screamed as shells tore into his groin. He fell to the ground beside the general.

Wardell threw the weapon away and knelt by Susan. Her chest was covered with blood.

"Susan," he said. "Please."

She opened her eyes to look at him. Her lips moved, as if she was trying to say something.

"Don't talk," he said.

"David, I . . . I . . ."

Her eyes closed. He pulled her to him, tears in his eyes. He didn't hear the sound of trucks roaring toward him, nor the shouts of voices as Dolan's men came running up to their fallen leader.

* * *

Marais appeared in the doorway. "I heard shots," he told Volkert.

"Are they attacking?" Volkert asked.

"I don't see anyone. But I hear a lot of activity."

"Post a messenger," Volkert said. "At the first sign of a charge, send him to me."

Volkert moved next to the huge cylinder. It was hard to believe that something like this could wipe out hundreds of square miles. Too bad he wouldn't be alive to see the destruction he'd caused.

He stood still, hand near the fuse, listening.

Two minutes passed, then three. Then came a sound from an unexpected source—the radio.

The voice was cool and unmistakably British. "Mr. Volkert," said the voice. "I think it is about time we resolved this unfortunate situation, don't you think."

Volkert's hand dropped away from the fuse.

EPILOGUE

Arizona, August 30, 1949 — The sun lingered just above the horizon, an orange-red ball that seemed to have set on fire the vast expanse of desert.

Wardell sat on the porch of his ranch house, staring without seeing the splendor before him.

He didn't move as the door opened. Laura came out with two drinks in her hands. She saw the newspaper on her husband's lap and asked, "You saw the report?"

He turned to her. "The president called me last night while you were out."

Laura handed him the drink. Then she asked, "Why didn't you tell me?"

"What difference does it make? We knew that the Russians would explode an atomic bomb sooner or later."

Laura sat and looked at her husband. "What did the president have to say?"

"We talked about a lot of things. I think Truman appreciates the opportunity to talk to somebody who's not involved in the day-to-day grind anymore."

Laura was quiet for a moment. Then she said, "I hope you don't mind me bringing this up. But . . . do you still think it was the right thing to do? Giving in to the Russians at Lakenheath?"

Wardell turned to look at his wife. He saw the worried expression in her eyes. Then he smiled and reached out for her hand. "Yes, I do. I mean that."

Laura caught something in his expression. "But . . . ?"

"You caught me," Wardell said. "I was thinking about Mack Dolan. And Scalpel. If it had only worked, the world would have been spared so much trouble."

"Would it? Do you really believe that no other country would have developed atomic weapons if we had them? And the British and maybe the Canadians."

"You're probably right," Wardell said.

"The only hope is to banish nuclear weapons from the face of the earth," Laura said with vehemence.

Wardell leaned over and kissed her on the cheek. "Now who's the dreamer," he said.

THE BLACK EAGLES
by Jon Lansing

#1: HANOI HELLGROUND (1249, $2.95)

They're the best jungle fighters the United States has to offer, and no matter where Charlie is hiding, they'll find him. They're the greatest unsung heroes of the dirtiest, most challenging war of all time. They're THE BLACK EAGLES.

#2: MEKONG MASSACRE (1294, $2.50)

Falconi and his Black Eagle combat team are about to stake a claim on Colonel Nguyen Chi Roi—and give the Commie his due. But American intelligence wants the colonel alive, making this the Black Eagles' toughest assignment ever!

#3: NIGHTMARE IN LAOS (1341, $2.50)

There's a hot rumor that the Russians are secretly building a nuclear reactor in Laos. And the Black Eagles are going to have to move fast—to prevent the nuclear fallout from hitting the fan!